WANDERING MAGIC

WANDERING MAGIC

MAGIC, LOVE, AND MISCHIEF BOOK 4

4 Horsemen
Publications, Inc.

KAIT DISNEY-LEUGERS

Wandering Magic
Copyright © 2025 Kait DIsney-Leugers. All rights reserved.

4 Horsemen
Publications, Inc.

Published By: 4 Horsemen Publications, Inc.

4 Horsemen Publications, Inc.
PO Box 417
Sylva, NC 28779
4horsemenpublications.com
info@4horsemenpublications.com

Cover & Typesetting by Autumn Skye
Edited by Jen Paquette

All rights to the work within are reserved to the author and publisher. No part of this publication may be reproduced, stored in a retrieval system, or transmitted in any form or by any means, electronic, mechanical, photocopying, recording, scanning, or otherwise, except as permitted under Section 107 or 108 of the 1976 International Copyright Act, without prior written permission except in brief quotations embodied in critical articles and reviews. Please contact either the Publisher or Author to gain permission.

All characters, organizations, and events portrayed in this novel are either products of the author's imagination or are used fictitiously. No generative artificial intelligence was used in the creation of this book or its cover.

All brands, quotes, and cited work respectfully belongs to the original rights holders and bear no affiliation to the authors or publisher.

Library of Congress Control Number: 2024950689

Paperback ISBN-13: 979-8-8232-0759-1
Hardcover ISBN-13: 979-8-8232-0760-7
Audiobook ISBN-13: 979-8-8232-0762-1
Ebook ISBN-13: 979-8-8232-0761-4

For Dad, who helped me flesh out the story even though I only asked for travel logistics. All the good ideas in this are his. Sorry, Dad, there is no drowning dwarf in this one.

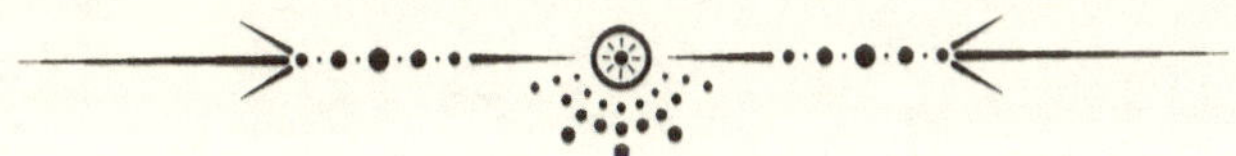

Acknowledgements

I would be lying if I said this book wasn't a total headache to write. I didn't know what I was doing, especially when it came to writing a heist. I've watched every episode of *Leverage*, so that helped. So many people have listened to me complain about this book. First and foremost, Elle Stewart, who keeps asking for Aron's book, and one day I might write it for her. Leslie Sommers, you have listened to me whine at all hours of the day over calls, texts, and lunches. Your help was absolutely invaluable, and I would have rage quit on this one without you. Also, Amanda at the Last Word, who indulges my rants with laughter and is trying to turn me onto K-Pop.

Special thanks also goes out to the Writer's Block girlies, including Leslie, Heidi Nickerson, and A.K. Ramirez. Ladies, you kept me on track and hyped me so much.

To the ladies of Wondertwins Events, Chelsea and Danielle, and all the authors at the Pop-Up BookShoppe for creating an awesome community where we get to get our books out there and get the full convention experience, I've made some wonderful friends in all of you. (I will not apologize for the sliding scale of cocks from that panel.)

It wouldn't be one of my books without huge thanks going to the Reylo Authors discord. You all are such a wonderful and supportive group and creative as hell. I love putting your books on my shelves!

Finally, thanks to my family. To my mom who keeps telling me how proud she is but also tries to convince me to write less smut. Dad, who helped more than he knows with this book. Storm, for appreciating my red carpet PowerPoints that were clearly an excuse to not write. And, of course, my husband and goblin babes. You all make it extremely difficult to write, but still I persist!

TABLE OF CONTENTS

ACKNOWLEDGEMENTS VII
CHAPTER 1 1
CHAPTER 2 12
CHAPTER 3 24
CHAPTER 4 38
CHAPTER 5 47
CHAPTER 6 56
CHAPTER 7 71
CHAPTER 8 79
CHAPTER 9 88
CHAPTER 10 108
CHAPTER 11 115
CHAPTER 12 119
CHAPTER 13 136
CHAPTER 14 150
CHAPTER 15 159
CHAPTER 16 167
CHAPTER 17 180
CHAPTER 18 201
CHAPTER 19 215
CHAPTER 20 222
CHAPTER 21 233
CHAPTER 22 242
CHAPTER 23 248
CHAPTER 24 256
CHAPTER 25 265
CHAPTER 26 275

CHAPTER 27 288
CHAPTER 28 300
CHAPTER 29 309
EPILOGUE. 317
BOOK CLUB QUESTIONS .327
AUTHOR BIO 329

CHAPTER 1

atherine Fry sat in a Thailand jail for the third straight day staring at the blank stone wall as she contemplated how she ended up there. She hadn't realized the warrant for her arrest was still valid, considering it was nearly one hundred and fifty years old and issued by the kingdom of Siam, but that was the thing about immortal creatures; they tended to hold onto things. Not that she had done anything illegal per se, other than run out on one of her husbands in a time when women were still considered property. The fact that she also took all of his money was of little consequence, at least to her.

Chakri was not a forgiving man, or naga, as he was in actuality. A demigod with several snakes protruding from his back, he clearly had not forgiven Catherine for her indiscretions. She should have stayed out of Bangkok altogether. There were too many memories, too much personal turmoil, and it should have been a place she never stepped foot in again.

But Catherine had found herself nostalgic as of late. Ridding herself of immortality had made her capitulate to her past, and it urged her to reconnect with her lost history and make up for past sins before her time was up. Death was a welcome friend after over five hundred years of living, yet she would make the most out of her last years before finally passing into the next life.

In order to continue her pilgrimage through her past, though, she first needed to get out of the jail cell. With no magic to speak of and certainly no time to waste, Catherine had only her own wit to rely on. Not that her wit was as sharp as it used to be, or at least it felt that way. Only a few short years of mortality had started to make her feel like she was aging that more rapidly, like the status of her body for over five hundred years was finally coming due all at once, even if that was not really the case.

Dr. Catherine Fry, the history professor, would not be able to escape a Thai prison. But she was Miriam Kokush, master thief, or had been in another life, and no iron bars would hold her. Thicker walls had held her before, yet she always managed to find a way out. This prison cell would be no different. Even with Chakri hanging about somewhere. She had escaped him once, and she would do it again.

Somehow.

They brought her food two times a day, though it left much to be desired. A thin soup with a bit of old rice and a cup of water that was lukewarm by the time it made it to her; hardly appetizing, but she choked it down nonetheless. Starving herself wouldn't help her situation.

For probably the hundredth time since she was imprisoned, she wondered when Chakri would finally show up. Naturally, he would let her linger for a while, no doubt hoping that would wear her down or break her entirely. But Chakri had never really understood her nature, and if he sincerely thought a few days or a week in a five-by-five barred room would do the trick, then he was sorely mistaken.

The small mat on the floor was not particularly comfortable, but it was far better than lying on the dirty cement floor while she stared up at the ceiling, formulating a plan of escape. She had places to be after all, including a trip back to New Britain to see her young mentee Brie St. James, a bright girl with now a longer future ahead of her—in part due to the fact that Catherine had given her immortality to the young woman. It was for the best. Catherine was tired of living forever, and Brie had an immortal husband she was eager to spend eternity with.

Not that Catharine had spent anywhere near an eternity with any partner. Throughout her long years, she had gone through perhaps hundreds of partners, several husbands, and a few wives. She had even been a part of a harem or two. She wasn't looking for love anymore or even lust. Catherine merely wanted to bring closure to her life, and if she ran into a few ex-lovers, well, that was part of the journey. Though, at the moment, she was reconsidering that last part.

Sleep came over her quicker than she would have liked. Lately, Catherine had been more tired than usual, but that was likely due to her body feeling older now. Not that she appeared it. Despite the streaks of gray, she still appeared as a woman in perhaps her early forties, though she had been much younger when she was cursed with immortality. Each century of life had aged her a few years or so, a little something special given as part of her curse. Eventually, she would have looked like an old crone, but that would have been centuries away. Now, she would only have a few decades. There was still a lot of traveling to be done before that time came.

While she rested, Catherine dreamed of a time long ago when she was still a girl in Crimea in a tiny Jewish village. The world was smaller then, contained within her crowded house with her mother, father, siblings, and maternal grandparents. They were all dust now, forgotten in time, much like her village and so many Jews who had lived in Eastern Europe in her youth.

A happy youth had led to a restless adolescence and eventually to chaotic adulthood until she had to face the consequences of her actions. That is when her sleep grew less peaceful. Memories of that fateful event that would lead to her becoming cursed disturbed her mind and pained her physically. The curse had left her immortal and chasing after a fallen angel acting out against his mother.

But Ezra was happy now with his wife Brie, who had basically taken over as his immortal watcher, and he had reconciled with his mother. Catherine wasn't needed anymore. She was free to adventure for what remained of her life, but look where that had gotten her.

It could have been days of her dozing but was likely only a handful of hours before she was awoken by the cell door opening on rusty hinges. The squeal of the metal grating was enough to set her head pounding.

Standing in the doorway, a dim light illuminating him from behind, Chakri the naga looked very much the same as he did the last time she saw him. The black hair he used to wear in a top knot was gone, though, shorn close to his scalp. His lightly tan skin had a slight golden undertone to it, his face all sharp angles from his cheekbones to his nose. A lithe form, though his shoulders were broad, and his torso gradually tapered down to his narrow waist. He wore no shirt, but several strands of gold chain crisscrossed his body. Below that, though, he was no longer a man. Instead, he was all snake, greenish skin shining even in the dim light. The second half of him was all muscle, thick and dangerous, as Catherine easily recalled.

Behind his head, three snakes sprang from his back, dark green, each lolling heavily on their own. Three pairs of black eyes in serpentine faces fixed on her. On more than one occasion, Catherine had seen Chakri's own dark eyes gleam with cruel delight as he choked the life from one of his enemies.

Now those dark eyes were narrowed on her, and there was nothing but loathing behind that look.

"Miriam," he said in an accented hiss. There was a time his sultry voice sent pleasurable shivers down her spine. Knowing he had something unpleasant planned for her now, she accepted that the shivers had less to do with pleasure, and everything to do with genuine fear. Despite the centuries that had passed, Catherine had still escaped with a large amount of his wealth and his favorite mistress, though Catherine had only kept her as lover until they reached the outer reaches of the kingdom when the woman left to return to her family. Chakri likely didn't know that part. Nor would he care.

"Chakri. It has been a long time," Catherine said, sitting up slowly on the mat.

"Not long enough, it seems, since you seemed to think you would come into my country again without repercussions. How arrogant of you, Miriam." His words hissed on every "ess," his eyes never changing from their hard glare. The look alone tried to strip her soul bare, but Catherine had several lifetimes to build up layers to her innermost person, and nothing Chakri could do to her would even begin to scratch the surface in breaking her.

"And here I thought you would have forgotten by now. It was a passing inconvenience, after all. Seems juvenile for you to hold a grudge this long." Catherine kept her tone bored. She wouldn't let fear of unknown pain keep her from taunting her ex.

Chakri studied her features, marking the new grays in her hair, the deepening lines adorning her face. It wasn't like he didn't know every inch of her body, or at least, how her immortal body had been. Only a few years had aged her body so far. She hadn't changed all that much since their last meeting.

Three tongues slipped out of the snakes, tasting the air. A wicked smile spread across Chakri's face, one that Catherine knew from experience to fear. "I no longer taste your immortality, Miriam. Something quite dreadful has happened to you."

Catherine rolled her shoulders, still determined to feign indifference against her former paramour. "I wouldn't call it dreadful seeing as I willingly gave it away. Immortality can get so boring; I don't know how you can stand it." It wasn't all bravado. She had only lived five hundred years, and there was little else for her to experience that held any excitement. Chakri was much older, had seen countless empires rise and fall, yet still he lived on because he liked the power and praise that came with being a revered naga.

Catherine had been a nobody mortal and became a nobody immortal. The only power she had ever possessed was her mind. So far, it had been enough. Sitting in front of Chakri now, she wasn't so sure. Not that she would let him see her fear. Chakri would draw the whole ordeal out even longer if he sensed she was afraid, and those snakes of his could taste fear in the air.

"Oh Miriam, to think you were once so exceptional, and now here you rot in a stone cell. A fitting end for you after everything you put me through." Chakri's grin was betrayed by the icy tone of his voice, and it took everything within Catherine not to cringe at the sound.

Her eyes roamed over Chakri's body and the space between him and the still open cell door. The naga was huge, blocking most of the exit. No chance of escaping around him, even if she were faster than he was.

She wasn't.

Catherine's mind reeled through possible methods of escape. She accepted that her prospects were bleak. In a former life, she might have tried to seduce him into letting down his guard. That had worked many times in her favor. But that tactic wouldn't work on someone she had royally screwed over a few centuries ago. It also did not help that she didn't feel particularly seductive when her back was constantly aching.

Somehow, she was going to have to find a way to talk herself out of this one. Or at the very least, find a way to get Chakri to lead her out of the cell. Without those four walls and iron bars surrounding her, she might have a better chance of escape.

"I was hardly the first one to rob you blind, Chakri. And I highly doubt I was the last." Was it dangerous to goad him on? Absolutely. But Catherine had little options, and any reaction was better than none at that point.

Blotchy red patches formed on the naga's lightly tanned skin, and his eyes bulged with anger. He looked very much on the verge of screaming, but after only a few seconds, he took a few deep breaths, and the ugly red on his face faded. So he had managed to find a way to manage his anger.

Good for him for working on himself, Catherine thought, though it forced her to rethink the one tactic she had.

She was pulled from her scrambling mind by Chakri's calm, collected voice. "A rat's death won't suit you, Miriam. And yes, death is coming for you. But I want it to be as humiliating as possible. Perhaps I'll strip you naked, let all behold your body, and then hang you? I'm sure I can get more creative if you like, but I do like the old ways, it's less mess."

And that right there was all Catherine needed for a plan to start forming in earnest.

She smiled up at Chakri, bitter and with more teeth. "Sounds like a good time, darling."

After another night in the cell without much sleep and no further visits from the naga, Catherine stood in an open patch of dirt waiting for her execution. There was no reading of the charges, no reading of anything she had done, not even a religious leader to issue last rights. Only the simple quiet. There were only a handful of soldiers standing around, and in the front of them stood Chakri holding a torch. His eyes glittered with triumph, and the snakes behind his head undulated with excitement. Catherine kept her face placid, letting no emotion come through her mask.

It seemed that Chakri planned to ignore Thailand's modern form of execution via lethal injection, opting instead for a more traditional route under the Law of the Three Seals. It didn't matter that Siam was no longer a kingdom; there was still room in Chakri's mind for an execution by fire. Which was how Catherine found herself wrapped in an oil-soaked cloth waiting to be set ablaze.

Not her finest moment.

In the middle of the night, a plan of escape had formed, and now she had mere minutes to execute it before the fires consumed her.

The thing about being an immortal for so long and having no magical powers of her own was that Catherine had to rely upon certain tricks. She had completely forgotten about the one on her person that had been hidden away so no one could find it ages ago. The magic had been expensive, only to be used in a dire situation. Well, things didn't get more dire than literal minutes away from execution.

In the early hours of the morning, Catherine had loosened the false tooth that replaced a long-lost molar. The magic was potent and hopefully still powerful enough to get her out of the mess she found herself. The magic and hope were all she had.

As she stood awaiting her death, Catherine cursed herself one last time for asking her goddess friend to not intervene in her life. It was the same goddess who had cursed her and charged Catherine with watching her son for centuries, but over time, they had become friends. And when Catherine had decided on her little walk-about, she didn't want any divine intervention.

Curse my own stupidity. I have five PhDs for nothing.

"Miriam Anurak, this is the end," Chakri said with a toothy grin, holding the torch aloft. The snakes behind him writhed in excitement. Despite her predicament, Catherine could only roll her eyes. She hadn't been Miriam Anurak for centuries, nor had she agreed to take Chakri's surname and had never used it herself. Typical naga male.

Her hands were bound and under the cloth, leaving Catherine little choice on how she made her exit. Using her tongue, she pushed the tooth from its resting position and moved it to her cheek. "You are right, Chakri. This is the end."

With no grace at all, she spit the tooth on the ground in front of her, enveloping her entire person in a cloud of reddish smoke. She felt the magic pulse around her skin, and for a moment, it felt like she was weightless, floating through space without a tether.

Just as suddenly as it started, she felt her feet slam into the ground, and she pitched over onto what appeared to be a roof. The early morning breeze left goosebumps on her skin—her completely naked skin since the magic didn't transport inorganic material. Couldn't be helped, but at least she was rid of the oiled cloth.

In the distance, she could hear shouting, but she didn't dare move from where she now lay on the roof. It was a flat enough surface with a ledge to keep her hidden from view on the ground. She was out of certain doom, absolutely, but that didn't mean she was out of danger. For one, she had nothing, not even a stitch of clothing. Secondly, she was still stuck in Bangkok with Chakri and his men definitely after her and no money to get herself out of the country the legal way.

This was where old skills came into use, and her next step was to find some clothing and, much like her last time in Bangkok, rob somebody blind for the funds to get away.

Some things never changed.

CHAPTER 2

The small café in London wasn't the best. It served mediocre sandwiches and pastries that always tasted a day old, and it really was a gamble on whether she actually got a decent pot of tea. But Catherine had been frequenting this particular café since it was built around the early 1700s, though it wouldn't be found on any of the café walking tours. Calling it a hole-in-the-wall was a generous overstatement.

"Can I getcha anything else, love? Or are you going to nurse that pot all day?" the proprietor of the café asked, her tone a bit short. She was not a tall woman, rounded and creased with age. Wispy gray strands of hair fell from her tied bun. Her apron was crisp and clean, unlike the rest of the café, which seemed to have a permanent layer of grime.

"No, thank you. I think I'll continue to nurse the pot for a while more," Catherine said with equal shortness. Catherine had long ago decided when it was appropriate to be nice and when to give back what she got.

The woman gave Catherine a hard glare before turning and stomping away, muttering something about "entitled Americans." Catherine smiled. Technically, yes, she was American. There were documents that certainly said she was born there. But then again, there were plenty of documents saying she was born in many different places, and she claimed citizenship in over a dozen countries.

Having spent the past hundred years in the States, she had quickly adopted an American accent to fit in. Assimilating was one of the ways to avoid suspicion because suspicion alone was enough for people to try to kill her. Catherine was whomever she needed to be at any given time, and with her gift for languages and a wide knowledge base, she could reinvent herself quickly.

In London, she was Dr. Catherine Fry, tenured professor of history. She had been this version of herself for decades now, and Catherine thought it would be the last incarnation of Miriam Kokush. Her last legacy would be as a student of history and a shaper of young minds. There was no greater impression to leave behind in Catherine's opinion. A better legacy than Miriam the thief.

"You're still a bit of an arsehole, Mir," a husky feminine voice said from behind Catherine's chair. Before Catherine could turn, the owner of the voice came around and plopped down in the seat opposite Catherine at the table. The woman was tall, curvy in a sensuous black dress that ended just above the knee, and an ox blood leather bag was slung over her shoulder, which she dropped unceremoniously next to her on the floor. A thick dark braid was thrown over one shoulder, and when Catherine met the woman's gaze, she was transfixed by the most beautiful pair of cerulean eyes she had ever seen.

Just as she had been the first time she met the woman centuries ago, Catherine was struck dumb by the majestic beauty of the woman before her. "Lovely to see you again, Titania. It's been too long," Catherine said when her voice finally returned. She wanted to sound more annoyed. Meetings with Titania were always a delight and an absolute headache.

Titania's lips ticked slightly upward. "It's been too long because you insisted on staying in the Colonies at that charming university rather than come see me." It was true that Catherine had not returned to England in some time, and every time she did and met up with Titania, she always left with fading memories of countless nights of pleasure and a broken heart. But such was her lot when she had an affair of convenience with the queen of the fairies.

"That life is behind me. I'm mortal now. My days are numbered." Catherine sounded matter-of-fact, disjointed from the reality. As much as she looked forward to a final rest, part of her wasn't quite ready to let herself age and die. She had simply lived too long. But she wasn't going to let Titania see her conflict.

Titiana made a thoughtful noise as she motioned for her own tea to be brought. "So I have heard. How unfortunate that such a life as yours shall be cut short. It pains me dearly, my sweet Miriam." Flowery words, though Catherine could feel the intent behind them. Even the queen of the fairies couldn't lie. Bend the truth perhaps, but not outright lie.

Though they had never been truly committed to each other, Catherine and Titania still cared for each other deeply. Neither of them wanted anything more than the casual arrangement they carried on for centuries. But Titania had been more than a lover—she had been a dear friend.

"All things must die eventually, Titania. Even you will one day pass through the Veil," Catherine said, thinking what a dimmer world it would be when the mighty fairy before her ceased to exist.

Titania made a face of disgust, though it did little to mar her beautiful features. "Let's not talk about dying anymore. It's making me depressed. Besides, from what little I know of mortal life, you still have at least a few decades to go, short though that is."

She was right, of course. It wasn't like Catherine was on death's door just waiting to shed her mortal coil. By outward appearance, she was barely middle-aged and could still live well into an advanced mortal age. But it seemed so short after the life she had already lived.

"Then what would you rather discuss while you are here?" Catherine asked, taking a small sip of tea. She didn't rightly care if the tea had gotten cold. She was still determined to nurse the pot for as long as possible out of spite.

A grin spread across Titania's face, tantalizing and wicked as only a fae could manage. "Well, now that you mention it, besides wanting to see your lovely face again, I have some news." Of course, Titania would start with a cloying smile and a tease. She would draw out the anticipation before getting to the point for as long as possible. Drama was what she thrived on.

"Well, less news, and more of a favor—which you owe me after that debacle in Avalon," Titania continued. Catherine cringed internally. She would rather not think about what happened in Avalon, but it was only a matter of time before the queen of the fairies called in that favor. Owing anyone anything was something Catherine tried to avoid, though she had a few of her own favors to collect upon in what remained of her time. It seemed fitting that her own debts would be dredged up.

With a lifted finger, Catherine motioned to Titania to continue. "There's an item I've been searching for quite some time, centuries really, and I have finally tracked it down to a collector. Wherever it's been hiding all this time, I don't know, but this guy has not made it that much of a secret that he now possesses it in his collection. He's willing to show it off; he loves to be the center of attention, after all, but unfortunately, we've had a bit of a misunderstanding in the past, and he won't have anything to do with me. Which is why I need you. Well, you and maybe some friends."

It became obvious quickly what exactly Titania had in mind for this favor. "I'm not a thief, Titania," she said bluntly.

"Anymore, maybe," Titania responded without missing a beat. She laid a well-manicured hand over Catherine's on the tabletop. "You're the only one I trust to do this for me, Mir. You are one of the most brilliant thieves I know, and I've known many thieves. You can have anyone you like to assist, and as payment, you can pick any item from my own collection. Please say yes, Mir." Her face was eager and her cerulean eyes were pleading.

Catherine sighed. Her rational brain said no, screamed it really. Maybe in a past life, she had been a thief. Okay, maybe in several past lives, she had been a thief. But being a thief had cursed her with immortality, and who knew what kind of trouble she would find herself in taking on a job after so many decades? Still, Catherine had never been able to say no to Titania. And the magic of a debt was binding, so even though she wanted to decline, the magic would not allow it. Once the debt was called up, there was no way out.

"What is the item I am to steal?" Her tone was defeated, and that's how she felt, her choice taken away.

The bright, if slightly malevolent, smile on Titania's face would have quelled a lesser person. "I'm so glad you asked. You've heard of Pheme's trumpet, I presume? I would expect you have, Professor." Her tone toed the line of mockery, but Catherine let it pass. Of all Catherine's career choices in her life, Titiana held little regard for her current role as an educator. Well, former role since she had not been back to the university in some time. All that was left was to officially tender her resignation.

"The trumpet used by the goddess Pheme to spread the gossip she overheard? That trumpet?" Catherine deadpanned.

Titania clapped her hands together once in delight. "See, I knew that big brain of yours wouldn't fail. Yes, that trumpet." Her face turned serious, the playfulness gone. "I need it."

"What for?" Catherine asked, wondering why Titania would want magic like that. The trumpet itself had no other magical properties other than to spread rumors to everyone who could hear its call, but Titania was already a master of that herself.

"I have my reasons, Mir. And like I said, I've been after it a long time, and I don't want anyone's help but yours." Titania didn't have to appeal to Catherine's ego since the magic would already hold her to the job, but still, she could not help the boost to her self-importance at Titania's words. She had been great once; perhaps there was still a little of that skill left.

"I don't have much of a choice, so I'll do it. Just this once though, Titania. I'm coming out of retirement only this one time. You're the only one I would ever do this for, even if I wasn't compelled to. But as you said, I'll pick my team, no interference from you." Catherine leveled a glare at the fae.

Titania feigned insult with a hand over her chest. "I would never."

"You absolutely would. It's your nature to manipulate and interfere. But that's one of my conditions," Catherine retorted, sitting back in her chair and picking up the nearly empty cup of stone cold tea in front of her.

Titania shrugged as if to say *so what*, and then spoke. "One of your conditions?" She lifted a perfectly shaped eyebrow. Everything about Titania was perfectly shaped, at least to Catherine.

"Yes. Besides me picking my team, you are not to mess with the plan. We do it my way or no way." Catherine's face was stern, the tone and look she usually reserved for the classroom.

"Very well, we have a deal, though it does take away some of the fun." Titania pouted. A flow of magic whooshed through Catherine's veins in that moment. A bargain was made, a debt in the process of repaying. She would feel the hum of magic until her task was completed.

"Your fun tends to end in disaster. Now, send me the details, and I'll keep you informed on what we're doing once I know what I'm dealing with and who will be assisting." Catherine rose from her seat, deciding that staying in Titania's presence any longer would be a bad idea. The fae queen remained seated.

"I'll have my assistant send over an email later today. Now, Mir, we can still have some fun today and save the business for later." Her eyes said *come hither*, but Catherine found she wasn't in the mood for an amorous time with the queen of the fairies, or anyone, for the time being.

"I'm rather tired, Titania. I'll have to take a raincheck." Catherine shouldered her bag and began to leave, pushing the feeling of the magic within her to the back of her mind, letting it become a dull thrum easily ignored.

"Mortality has softened you too much," Titania muttered as Catherine walked away, and maybe she was right. But that didn't change the fact that all Catherine wanted at that moment was the quiet of her flat, a place where old lovers wouldn't bother her. She had had enough of that lately.

The email from Titania's assistant came at four PM sharp. There were no pleasantries, just the facts of the job, including the address where the item was held. Catherine would have to see if she could acquire the blueprints, which depending on the age of the building, would either be easy enough or virtually impossible.

"Are you fucking kidding me?!" Catherine yelled into the quiet flat as she read through the message. The mark was a name she recognized.

Arruk.

The minotaur was a friend of hers back when she was in Greece for the brief time Ezra set up shop there back in the 1560s. They had to leave not long after the Ottomans lost the battle of Lepanto in 1571, and the Greek ships carrying Ezra's good started to be constantly attacked by pirates. It wasn't a good time to be in Greece, so Ezra packed up and moved elsewhere, Catherine following close behind.

But in the time she spent there, Arruk and she had become fast and good friends. Never anything more. It broke her heart to leave him behind since few understood Catherine like he did. But he was bound to the land by obligation, and not even the love of a friend could compel him to leave. He was too fiercely in love with his city.

That, however, wasn't the worst part of it. Arruk's collection was housed in the very place where Ezra's shop once stood. The magic Ezra brought with him wasn't directly there anymore, but every place that had once housed that much magic always left something behind, a magical residue of a sorts, and that meant powerful magic would still linger there, even this long after the source had left. Not to mention that Arruk was no fool, and if he truly valued his collection, which Catherine knew he did, there would be even more layers of magic, newer magics, protecting the place and items within.

"That conniving bitch," Catherine mumbled, picturing Titania's grinning face. The fae queen knew exactly what she was doing, and it was abundantly clear why she had to have Catherine do the dirty work. Arruk trusted her. Had trusted her, anyway. It would be easy to gain access to the trumpet during the day. Taking it out without being caught would be another matter altogether.

Her stomach dropped and she felt sick. It had been so long since she had worn the mantle of thief. Had it been a random collector, someone that Catherine had no ties to, she might have had no qualms about robbing them. But this? Arruk had been important in her life once, and it felt like another betrayal, just maybe not as horrible as leaving him was.

Not that the two of them had kept in touch over the last hundred years. Once Catherine had immigrated to Connecticut, changed her name for good, and started over as a professor, she found that many of her old friendships took a backseat. It was hard to keep up with everyone after centuries and count-less trips around the globe, especially when she was finally settled.

But Arruk was special, even if they had lost touch. He had seen her for the scared human she had always been, even now. He saw her soul and had cherished every bit of it. And now Titania was asking her to betray that for a piece of treasure that the queen was sure to misuse.

The magic, though, wouldn't let her blow off this job. And Titania had made sure the mark information was given only after the deal was set. The faerie queen knew exactly what she was doing to Catherine. Cruel as ever, she didn't care who she hurt in the process of getting what she wanted.

As much as Catherine wished for a way out of the deal now, there was no hope for it. All she could do now was to assemble her team and plan. Luckily, she knew a bit about the old magic on the building, and what she didn't, Ezra could tell her. But she would need to know more about what was there now. She would need a ward breaker, obviously, and someone who could run interference. There would be no doubt that Arruk would have hired security to protect his collection; he had them even back when they met. Besides the magic, Catherine didn't know if he would have mortal security measures, like cameras or alarms. When she went to scope the place out, that would be one of the things she looked for.

Some magical creatures only relied on magic, but many had advanced with the times and found both mortal and magical means to be useful. Catherine was one of them. So having someone who could run interference and was good with computers was probably her best bet.

Three was a good number, but a fourth would give her peace of mind. Catherine could plan and steal herself, but without any power of her own save her skill and cunning, it would be better to have someone more adept than her to make the actual grab. Catherine would have her own part to play in scouting and get them a way in.

A warder.

A tech wizard.

And a thief.

Now she just needed to call in some favors.

CHAPTER 3

Catherine left London early on a Wednesday morning. It was early fall and already there was a chill in the air. At least San Francisco would be warmer, one of the perks of leaving London for California. Not that she would be there long. Her one purpose was to find her tech wizard and be on her way.

But first, she had a layover at JFK for three hours before her flight to SFO. That was after an eight-hour flight already, and then it was back on the plane for another seven hours. She really shouldn't have booked so last minute. Maybe then she could have caught a direct flight.

The captain announced that they would be landing soon, and Catherine took the time to lift up her window cover and look out at the Hudson Bay. As the plane banked, she caught a glimpse of the Statue of Liberty below. She rested her head against the cool window as memories bubbled up.

The first time Catherine saw the Statue of Liberty was from the steamship *RMS Aquitania*, sailing to America from Liverpool in 1920. Ezra moved the shop from London following the Great War. With Europe left in a disastrous state, Ezra thought it would be safer to set up where war had not touched.

Though both she and Ezra voyaged on the *Aquitania* in first class, they did not interact with one another. While Ezra had always tolerated Catherine's presence in his life, he wasn't forced to be her friend. They kept their distance as polite acquaintances.

On board, they only saw each other at meals in the first-class dining room, which was as grand a social event as any back in London before the war. Each night she was decked out to the height of fashion in drop-waisted dresses with straight lines and handsewn beadwork, her long brown hair pulled up and teased in the back with curls hanging in the front to mimic a bobbed hairstyle. She acted the part of a widowed heiress, which suited her just fine after spending the previous few years as a nurse.

War had touched them all, even the magical community, despite it being a human conflict. It was one of the few times she and Ezra worked together without conflict. He opened his shop to those fleeing their homes, and both cared for the sick and wounded. They were lucky the magic of the shop kept them all hidden and safe.

When Ezra informed her that he was moving to the Americas to open a new shop, he told her she could come with him or stay. Not that Catherine had much of a choice. It was her duty to follow him whether either of them liked it or not. His announcement left her little time to get her affairs in order, but at least he was gracious enough to book her passage on the *Aquitania* at the same time he was leaving.

As the ship sailed into the harbor that summer day, Catherine remembered standing on the port side of the ship on the first-class promenade looking out as they passed the tall figure of Lady Liberty, a beacon of hope to the many immigrants on board. Not long after, they disembarked the ship at the port on Ellis Island, where Catherine passed off her newly forged citizenship papers, and she and Ezra made their way into New York City.

She could see it so clearly, her neck craned back to stare up at the towering statue, already with her green patina. There had been a pang of regret that there was still daylight, as Catherine would have loved to seen her lit up with her torch shining brightly with the electric lights installed a few years previously. Still, Lady Liberty was a sight to behold.

Even now, as she now looked down upon the statue, Catherine still felt a spark of awe. So many people had been given hope upon seeing her for the first time as they entered the land of opportunity. And Catherine had experienced plenty of opportunity in her hundred or so years living in the country.

The view of the statue was gone a few minutes later, and soon the plane touched down at the crowded airport. Her first stop was to get a coffee and bagel while she waited. The Kindle in her bag was well stocked and would provide her ample distraction while stuck in an uncomfortable terminal surrounded by people.

After what felt like a whole second day, Catherine finally landed that evening in San Francisco. She was beyond exhausted, despite sleeping on the plane for most of the seven-hour journey, and all she wanted was to get to a hotel and sleep until late the next morning.

Coming out to baggage claim, she noticed a man not far from the escalator holding a sign—a sign that had her name on it. As she took in the handsome man holding the sign, she realized immediately that she knew him.

Sidatih was tall, broad shouldered with muscular arms, and his black button down was rolled up so his tanned firm forearms were proudly displayed. His deep brown hair, so dark it was nearly black, hung in loose curls around his ears with a few streaks of gray shot throughout, and his chocolate eyes sparkled with mischief. He had a single gold hoop through his nose, and a boyish smile on his full lips. The sign in his large hands simply said *Mir* with a clumsily drawn heart next to it.

Despite her exhaustion, Catherine felt her body lighten, and a huge smile spread across her face at seeing the man, or more accurately, the ifrit waiting for her. Not that she had called him or even texted him to let him know she was coming.

As she stepped close to him, he dropped the sign to the ground and reached out to pull her close to his body by her waist. Neither had a chance to say any-thing before he crashed his lips against hers and kissed her deeply. To Catherine, it felt like coming home, though it had been several years since she had last seen Sidatih. While his hands stayed on her waist, she placed hers against his chest, feeling the beating of his heart as they kissed passionately.

After what felt like an eternity, but was no more than a minute, they pulled away and rested their foreheads together. "How did you know I was coming?" Catherine finally managed to speak, though her voice sounded breathy and high.

Sidatih chuckled and pulled away, though he grabbed her hand and twined their fingers together. "Oh albi, there is very little that happens in this city that I don't know about and see. It's amazing what technology can uncover in an instant. Cell phones are convenient beacons we willingly carry around with us."

Plenty of immortals were resistant to changing technologies, but when one was trying to blend in with the human world, it was better to embrace the habits of others around them. And Catherine really was fond of her cell phone. She didn't miss the days before the internet or the ability to have knowledge with a few quick taps on a screen. Sidatih had certainly embraced technology with open arms and found his calling in varied coding languages and hacker communities.

"You certainly are good at what you do, Sida," Catherine said as she pulled him toward the baggage claim. She felt giddy at being around Sidatih again.

"You should have heard my talk at DefCon this year on large language models. It would have blown your mind." They waited by the turnstile along with other passengers on the lookout for their bags.

"I highly doubt I would have understood a word of it, especially since I have no idea what a large language model is," Catherine said with a laugh. She was right; the whole concept of whatever Sidatih was talking about was lost on her as he explained the general idea of his talk while they waited.

They held hands all the way to where Sidatih had parked his Tesla. He placed her bag in the trunk before sliding smoothly into the front seat. "Why don't I treat you to dinner first?" Sidatih said, his voice deep and honeyed.

"I thought I would get a hotel first, but we can do dinner after," Catherine responded, staring out the front window as they hit Highway 101.

"Absolutely not!" Sidatih said firmly. "You are in my city, and you will stay in my home as long as you are here. There's space enough for two of us to have our own floor if you need. Though, I hope you won't need too much space." He grinned at her, two perfect dimples on display as he turned toward her. Catherine hoped he had his autopilot on, or she was going to slap him for not paying attention to the road.

Sidatih turned back to the road as the hillside with white lettering spelling out "South San Francisco" loomed up before them, the picture of seductive leisure. His white smile, his burnt sand skin, everything about him was still so enticing to Catherine.

"Still a flirt, I see. Some things really never change." If her smile was coy, well, that couldn't be helped.

Sidatih raised an eyebrow suggestively. "I only flirt with people I have enjoyed fucking or would like to fuck, and both apply to you, albi."

Heat spread through Catherine's body in an engulfing inferno. The way this man could still set her blood on fire after centuries was staggering. "I'm here for business Sida, not pleasure."

"Why not both, Mir? There's always time for both," he said with a lascivious grin. Catherine very much wanted to agree with him. She was in the city for a day or two, so there was definitely plenty of time for both. And why should she deny herself some fun with an old lover? It wouldn't detract from her plans, especially since he was her plans.

But reason cracked through her lust. Sidatih would be part of her team, and they had a job to do. Sleeping together again would only complicate things and take her mind off repaying the debt to Titania. "I know how this goes, Sida. If you had your way, we would never get to the business, and I would be wasting a trip out here."

Sidatih seemed to pout as he frowned at the road. "So, you didn't come to see me because you missed me. I see how it is, albi. You don't care how I've suffered from missing you all these years."

Catherine rolled her eyes at his dramatics and turned her attention out the window. They passed Candlestick Point on the right, indicating they were entering San Francisco proper. The last time she had been in the city, the stadium had still sat there. It was long gone now, replaced by a newer baseball stadium in the city and a new football stadium down in Santa Clara. If Catherine remembered correctly, the last time she had been in San Francisco, she and Sidatih had gone to a Giants game there, but she mostly remembered the taste of overpriced beer and Sidatih's lips during the seventh-inning stretch.

Catherine let out a long-suffering sigh but still smiled to herself. "Sida, you know I've missed you dearly. We've had many good nights together. That's just not the reason I'm here."

"I figured as much, but you can tell me all about the real reason you've come to my city over dinner. I won't discuss business without a glass of wine in front of me," Sidatih said, and Catherine agreed. She was exceptionally hungry, and it was safer to talk in a crowded restaurant than the intimacy of Sidatih's home. There was no way Catherine could trust herself if they went straight there.

After thirty minutes of driving, Sidatih finally pulled up to a parking lot in the Mission District, and they exited the car. He grabbed her hand the minute they started to walk, and he led her down Mission Street to a small Italian place called La Traviata.

The intimate setting had cloth-covered tables filled with diners, despite it being a Wednesday evening, and signed pictures of opera casts and singers adorned every inch of wall space. The space was cozy, and the food was some of the best old-world Italian outside of Italy, or so Catherine remembered.

They were seated immediately despite the waiting crowd. "This place is always busy, so I made sure to get us a reservation." Sidatih flashed her a smile as they took their seats. He ordered a bottle of Chianti for the table, knowing full well it was one of Catherine's favorites.

They spent a few minutes going over the menu and quickly placed their orders when the server returned with the wine. "Now, to business I suppose, unless you've changed your mind about going straight to my home," Sidatih said once their server left again.

Catherine tried to level a sober look at him, though there was no will behind it, not when she was looking into his handsome face. "I need your skills outside of the bedroom right now. I need someone who is good with technology and can be my eyes."

Sidatih leaned toward her, his attention completely on her words. He looked eager, a smirk playing on his full lips. "Ooo, are we stealing something? Is it heist time?!" He asked the last question loudly enough that several diners looked their way.

Another sigh escaped her, and she massaged the spot between her closed eyes. "Yes, Sida, it's heist time." Catherine was already regretting the whole meeting with Sidatih, maybe even regretting recruiting him for the job altogether. But he was the best techie she knew, and more importantly, she trusted him with her life.

Their food arrived minutes later. The gorgeous plate of gnocchi set before her was almost too perfect to eat, but it tasted even better. Throughout the meal, they chatted about their lives. It had been many years since they had seen each other. Sidatih was thriving in the tech boom in Silicon Valley, he had started many companies in the time he spent in San Francisco, and he was currently running a company focused on artificial intelligence.

Catherine couldn't understand half of what he talked about but nodded along when it seemed appropriate. When he asked about what she had been up to, she recounted her time in Connecticut and her career as a university professor, leading up to her decision to give up her immortality to her mentee, Brie.

"So that's it? You're done with the whole living forever thing?" Sidatih's glass paused halfway to his mouth, and he stared at her over the rim. There was shock there, but was that a hint of sadness as well? Catherine couldn't be sure.

She shrugged. "I've lived a long time. I'm tired." It was the same answer she gave everyone, though Catherine still wasn't sure if that was the whole truth. Three years after giving up her curse, she wasn't entirely convinced she had made the right choice.

Sidatih scoffed at her pronouncement. "Albi, you are but a baby to me. I've lived five times over what you have, and I'm still loving life. How could you possibly be tired of immortality?"

And there it was. Sidatih would never understand what it was like going through the centuries and never having power. She was simply a human who had lived a long time. There was no underlying magic in her; she wasn't born a magical creature. As an ifrit, Sidatih had always been what he was and always would be.

"I guess we have different outlooks on the thrill of life," Catherine said noncommittally. "My shortened life aside. You still never gave me a definitive answer. Will you help me with this job?"

"Albi, you know I would do anything for you. But I have a lot on my plate here. I have a company to run. I'm on several boards of directors, not to mention my social obligations. I can't be taking the time to galivant around the world in a grand heist adventure."

He looked truly remorseful, like he was physically pained to turned her down.

Catherine's heart sank. She had figured Sidatih's involvement would be guaranteed. There was nothing the ifrit loved more than mischief and chaos. There were others she could ask, skilled in technology, but Sidatih was the best, and she wanted only him. She hated to admit she hadn't prepared for a backup in case Sida couldn't do the job.

"Oh" was the only thing she could say. Her mind was reeling, trying desperately to think of anyone else she could call on.

The remorseful look on Sidatih's face fell away, replaced by a wicked grin. "Ha! Got you! Mir, albi, did you seriously think I would let anything get in the way of a heist? Especially with you? And here I thought you knew me better than that." He laughed, and Catherine couldn't decide if she wanted to kiss him or punch him in his perfect face.

"I'm going to kill you, Sida," Catherine said with a level glare.

"Only if you fuck me first so I can die a happy man," he retorted before shoveling a large bite of lasagna into his mouth.

"You're incorrigible, Sida," Catherine said a small smile. His flirtations did have her reconsidering her resolve to not mix business with pleasure. Why shouldn't she take as much as she could get when her time was running short?

He answered with a wide grin, sipping his wine much more seductively than he needed to. It wasn't like Sidatih acted like that with everyone. It would be easy to write him off as an unabashed flirt, but that really wasn't his style. Ifrit were not known to be creatures of seduction and romance or even of sexual pleasure. Their realm lay in the underworld and with the spirits of the dead. The fact that Sidatih lived in such a busy and populated city as San Francisco was outside of the norm for his kind. Not to mention that Sidatih only felt sexual attraction to those he felt a strong emotional bond to first. He and Catherine didn't become lovers until they had known each other for quite a while after he had helped her find her way in Istanbul after she was newly made immortal. The fact that Sidatih still felt that attraction toward her, despite the time away, was something that Catherine cherished immensely.

Sidatih didn't bring up sex for the remainder of the meal, instead choosing to focus all his energies on having his moment with the dessert. "Listen, I'm not saying I would marry a cannoli, but the passionate love affair I'm having with this one in particular is one for the ages," he said, not even bothering to look up from his plate.

Catherine couldn't fault him, of course; she was exercising immense control in not shoveling her own tiramisu into her mouth as fast as humanly possible. No matter how long she lived, great food was something Catherine never took for granted.

When their dinner was finished, and they could barely move, Catherine and Sidatih made their way out into the night. The walk back to his car was much slower, and this time he put his arm around her waist and kept her close to his body.

"Now, you're coming home with me, and you'll stay there until you are ready to leave, albi." Sidatih left no room for argument as he opened the passenger side door for Catherine. She was too content to even try to refuse, not that she would anyway.

When they arrived at his home, Catherine could see it was one of those tall, narrow, picturesque San Francisco connected houses. If she had to guess, Sida had bought it for next to nothing decades ago, and it was likely now worth millions.

Sidatih led them up to the door, unlocked it, and pushed it open, gesturing for Catherine to go inside. She stepped past him into the dimly lit entry. The door clicked shut once Sidatih followed her, and then she found herself whipped around and pushed up against the door, Sidatih caging her in with his hands on either side of her head, pushing her against the flat surface. Dark eyes wide and shining with lust, he held himself inches away from her face. But he made no further move to close the space between them. Instead, he waited for her move. That was the thing about Sidatih. He never took what wasn't freely given, never wanted to cross a boundary he wasn't invited to cross. So, he waited for Catherine to give him a sign.

Pressed against the door, heat flooding her body, Catherine had a choice to make. She could try to hold onto her conviction that nothing should happen with Sida until the job was done so as not to complicate anything between the team. Or she could yield, let the simmering heat between them grow into an inferno, and give into what she knew would be an exquisite night of passion. And probably the next morning. Probably all the way up to when her flight left.

What the hell, she thought before surging forward and slamming her lips against his. He tasted like cinnamon and desert sun, and it was intoxicating. With a light grip on her neck, he tilted her head back to deepen the kiss. A knee nudged between her legs, putting pressure just where she needed it.

Before their kisses could turn too frantic, Catherine pulled away long enough to murmur something about a bed. Sidatih picked her up as if she weighed nothing, quickly replacing his lips on hers, and carried her to his room, slamming the door behind them. Clothes came off in seconds, and they fell together onto the bed, hands exploring, reacquainting themselves with each other's body.

At least she had the first member of her team.

CHAPTER 4

Kyoto was always best in the early morning, right as the sun was rising. Nobody was out, the bustle of the day not yet started between people going to work and the tourists off to see the cultural marvels Japan had to offer.

Catherine slipped out of her ryokan before anyone else was awake to simply walk the streets. Later she might visit some favorite sights like the Nijō Castle and its *uguisubari*, the nightingale floors. She loved the way the wood sang under her feet. But the time for that was still hours away, and by then the place would be crowded with tourists. Maybe after she found who she was looking for, she would spend some time around the city to people watch.

For now, though, she would enjoy the quiet streets and prepare to find her thief.

A cool wind whipped through Catherine's gray-streaked dark hair. It was newly cut back to where she kept it sharply bobbed at her shoulders. Traveling as she had been, her hair had gotten too long. Wanting to make a good impression on her would-be team, she had finally visited a salon. The grays she kept, though, a reminder to herself and others that her life was now fleeting, and she wasn't going to waste a single day she had left.

Kyoto in the autumn was unlike any other. It wasn't yet cold enough to drive people indoors but not hot enough where she had to carry a cloth to constantly wipe the sweat from her face. Catherine felt perfectly comfortable in the dark gray leggings and knee-length fitted black sweater dress, heavy enough to keep her warm in the cool morning air.

As she walked, seemingly without direction, she passed by a man who was sitting half asleep on a bench at a bus stop, a hat sitting low over his eyes. He took no notice of her, and she didn't look at him. Instead, she stopped near the bench to consult her phone. To anyone looking at them, it would appear as if two people were merely waiting for the bus.

"Mizuno Yuwa. *Fushi no josei kara*," Catherine said, her voice low. The man on the bench made no acknowledgement other than a slight twitch of a finger resting on his thighs. It could have been a twitch to anyone else, but Catherine accepted the gesture. She put her phone away and continued down the street without a backward glance at the man on the bench. Not that he was really a man, but oni messengers had to blend into their surroundings.

After an hour of wandering the city on foot, as the sleepy people of Kyoto began to move about their day, Catherine decided to head back to her ryokan for breakfast.

At the door, the stern looking owner, a diminutive woman well into her seventies, greeted her. First, the woman chastised Catherine for leaving so early as Catherine slipped out of her shoes and put on the slippers provided for inside and then directed her to the table where breakfast was already being served to other guests.

"*Gomen nasai*," Catherine said humbly with a deep bow toward the woman. The owner threw up her hands and, with a dismissive noise, turned away and went back to the kitchen. Nobody looked her way as Catherine settled one of the chairs at the large table. She picked up a discarded newspaper from the table and started to read.

"Do you read Japanese, or are you just looking at the pictures?" a scratchy voice next to her asked. Catherine looked up and over at the middle-aged man sitting next to her. He had thin blondish white hair, a barely there mustache, and extremely pale skin that looked like it had never seen the sun. It was like he was white-washed, and he could easily blend in with the background. By the accent, he was probably American.

"I can read it just fine," she returned in a clipped tone. She was not in the mood to deal with men today. But the guy sitting next to her didn't seem fazed by her response.

"First time in Kyoto? I'm sure I have time to show you around the city today. Been coming twice a year for six years now, so I probably know it better than most." This guy was so full of himself. He cocked his head toward Catherine, giving her a look that said he would like to show her many things, none of which she had even the slightest interest in.

"Thanks, but I used to live here; I doubt it has changed so much that I require a tour guide who I assume neither reads nor speaks the language." Catherine pulled the paper up to cover her face, sending a clear signal that the conversation was over.

She could hear his chair creak as he leaned back in it. "Don't need to be such a bitch about it. I was just trying to be nice." Catherine rolled her eyes behind the paper. She folded up the news, not really reading it anyway.

"Actually, I do have to be a bitch because that's the only way men like you will take the hint," she said bitterly. The man reeled back in his chair like she had physically struck him, and Catherine grinned internally.

Breakfast was quiet after that; the man finished his quickly and left without another word to anyone. Catherine left the table feeling optimistic about the day. Determined that she would leave Kyoto with the second member of her team, she headed out into the crowded streets of a city waking for the day.

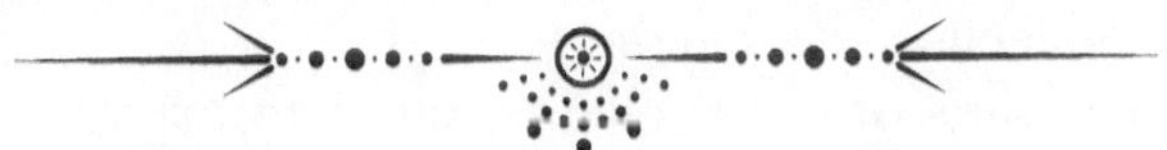

Finding her thief wouldn't take much time, or so Catherine hoped. Large though the city was, the magical community of Kyoto was insular, and nobody came into the city without their council knowing. And with her message left with the oni that morning, the chances of Mizuno finding her sooner rather than later seemed high.

The best thing for Catherine to do was make herself visible. She could spend the day in the ryokan if she felt like it, but when meeting with a thief, especially one of Mizuno Yuwa's caliber, it was best to be in a public space.

Which is how she found herself striding around the compound of Nijō Castle. The place was crowded with tourists, not surprising considering the weather was fair and the castle was one of the most popular sights in Kyoto.

As she passed into a hall made of dark wood and bronzed panels, the floorboards beneath her feet began to sing. The castle was well known for its nightingale floors, and while some found the noise grating, Catherine had always thought the sound held a certain charm. Her steps were soft and careful as she walked, not in any rush, giving herself time enough to let the history of the room soak in.

Halfway across the hall, she felt it: the prickle at the back of her neck that indicated she was being watched. Her feet stopped moving, the noise of the nightingale floor ceasing with it. There was no sound in the room, but the feeling was still there.

The slide of a cool blade came to rest against the side of Catherine's throat. She didn't bother to turn to face her assailant. "Impressive, but I heard the first board slightly as you entered. Not altogether clumsy but still room for improvement." Catherine directed her comment straight ahead in English, letting the woman beside her decide when and if she would remove the knife.

"I doubt that, Miriam. You would have had a weapon on me the second I was beside you," the melodic voice responded with only the hint of an accent.

Catherine chuckled. "Look down, Mizuno." Catherine had drawn her weapon the moment she heard the faint noise and felt the eyes. Her own small blade was pressed lightly against the side of the woman's belly. Mizuno's eyes traced the blade, though her face was blank.

"It would take longer to gut me than for me to slice your throat. Especially now that I hear you are mortal, Miriam," Mizuno purred softly.

This time Catherine smiled. "Yes, you certainly could. But you won't." She waited, keeping her blade pressed against Mizuno's stomach.

"Confident of yourself. But you are right." She withdrew the blade from Catherine's throat and slid it into a hidden pocket. "What do you want with me now, Miriam?"

Catherine turned just enough to take in Mizuno's appearance. Mizuno was not a particularly tall woman, a few inches shorter than Catherine's average height. Long shiny black hair hung like an elegant curtain around her shoulders with shorter pieces framing her face. Her deep dark eyes, hidden below blunt bangs, shone brightly against her light flawless skin. One look at Mizuno, and no one would think she was a thief. A blue and white flowered fashion kimono peaked out from beneath a calf-length red coat that draped elegantly over her shoulders. Natural looking makeup adorned her face with a pop of red lining her eyes to match the coat. On her feet were delicate wooden sandals. The overall look was a blend between traditional Japanese and high fashion. No, rather than a thief, Mizuno looked as if she just came back from Tokyo Fashion Week.

The sound of people moving into the hall spurred the women to move on. They said nothing as they exited the hall and moved out of the building altogether. The gardens in the castle complex were extensive and wide open enough for them to talk without being overheard by unsuspecting passersby.

After a few moments of silence in the cool air, Mizuno broke the quiet. "Why are you here, Miriam? You know that Aritoki is dead. He cannot repay his debt from the grave."

Catherine kept walking, leading them around without any intentional direction. "I know about Aritoki. Your master was a good friend, and his death brought me much pain. But as his protégé and heir, his debt falls to you. And I've come to collect."

The light tapping of their footsteps filled the pregnant silence between them as Mizuno absorbed Catherine's words. Magical debts were not easily dissolved, even when the debtor was dead.

"What would you have me do?" Mizuno finally asked, her gaze focused on the middle distance.

Catherine smiled internally. Out of the three she had in mind for the job, she expected Mizuno to put up the most resistance. Her willingness to listen from the start boded well. "We all have debts to pay, Mizuno. And one of mine has been called up. I need a team to extricate an object, and that means I need a skilled thief. You were Aritoki's greatest pupil, so I need you."

Mizuno stopped walking, and she turned toward Catherine, the light breeze drawing tendrils of her midnight hair across her face. "Why does a thief need another thief? Were you not the one to instruct Aritoki? You are a far better thief than I, Miriam."

To hear those words filled Catherine with a sense of pride she had long forgotten. "I'm afraid my thieving days are long past, and besides, I'm too familiar with the target. I need a shadow. I trust no one else for this job."

Aritoki Chuichi had long been a friend to Catherine, a pupil of hers in the art of thievery several lifetimes past. The fox spirit was one of the best, not simply for his sleight of hand, but because he was charming. He was so skilled, he didn't even need to rob people outright. He had a way of making people want to hand over their valuables. His untimely death under mysterious circumstances stood to prove that immortality isn't always guaranteed.

Still, he had trained Mizuno well. Very well. And she had made a name for herself beyond the legacy of her master. As a jorgumo, Mizuno had the ability to change her form from the gorgeous woman that stood beside Catherine into a spider capable of weaving silk and slipping in where others could not.

With an air of indifference, Mizuno turned away and resumed walking, Catherine matching her steps. "Is the job here in Japan?"

"No, Greece. Will that be a problem?" Catherine knew Mizuno stuck close to home, rarely leaving her country for a job or even pleasure. But she counted on Mizuno holding to the terms of a debt, even if it wasn't hers.

Mizuno was silent for a minute or so, continuing her leisurely pace through the gardens. There was no sign of emotion on her face, nothing to suggest she was thinking over the proposition. Just a cool mask of indifference.

After a time, she finally spoke. "I do not like to leave my home, but it is my duty to take on my master's debts. You have your thief, Miriam."

Catherine kept her own countenance flat, not daring to show her excitement and her relief. "Excellent. I have one more I need for our team; I will be in touch when I need you."

Mizuno nodded. "And where will we be meeting to plan this job?"

"Connecticut. I'm sure you remember Ezra," Catherine responded grimly.

CHAPTER 5

Catherine left her tiny car at the bottom of the hill in the half-full parking lot. No vehicles were allowed on the streets of Orvieto, and Catherine didn't mind the hike up to the picturesque city in the Umbrian countryside.

Her warder was somewhere in the city, and out of the three of them, this one would be the hardest to face, though the easiest to recruit. Their history ran too deep, rooted under her skin, flowing through her veins, and wedged into her very soul.

Though she lacked any real magic, there was one that was passed down through her ancestors that she called upon now to find who she was searching for. It had led her to Italy, and she summoned it again while standing on the narrow cobbled streets. She followed the glow of magic within her, passing tourists and locals without a second glance.

Up ahead, she saw the rising spires and gables of the Orvieto Duomo, an impressive cathedral made of alternating layers of white travertine and dark basalt with a gold façade. Catholic church designs fascinated

Catherine. The opulence of them and the intricacies of the statuary and stained glass were staggering.

The temple she had grown up in was simple. The only ornate thing about it had been the tabernacle that housed the beautiful Torah her father joyously carried out for Shabbat services. The Torah and the temple were long gone now, just as many Torahs that were cared for by communities that no longer existed.

Her own shtetl was completely destroyed, long before the terror of the Einsatzgruppen came to Ukraine, when the Cossacks came a hundred years after Catherine left. Most of her family members were long gone by then, but her community, her home—the invaders massacred them and left nothing behind. She had never been able to bring herself to return, not once in over five hundred years. Not that there was anything left to see anyway.

A dull ache started in her chest, clutching at her heart as she thought of all that her family and her people had lost over the centuries. This meeting was already beginning to dredge up painful memories of her human life, and it hadn't even begun.

The thrumming magic led her toward the cathedral but veered off at the last minute to the terrace of a restaurant. And there she saw them, sitting at a small table by themselves with a half-empty coffee and a novel cracked open.

To anyone else passing by, they would appear as a large unremarkable man with light curly brown hair and a darker beard. But Catherine could see through the glamour as only one with her bloodline could. While they were indeed large and man-shaped, bulky with defined features due to the sculpting skill of her great-grandfather, they were comprised of hardened clay and quite genderless. Around their neck hung the *shem emét*, the means which brought them to life. Nachem, as they were called, was a golem, crafted by her great-grandfather to care for the family.

The golem only answered to one person now, and that was Catherine. She was the only one left. Her family had remained in Ukraine long after she was gone, but her entire line, everyone who bore the Kokush name, had been wiped out in the Shoah. It was surprising that Nachem had survived beyond them.

"Shalom, Nachem," Catherine said as she stood before the table.

The golem raised their eyes from the book. It was easy enough to tell where the eyes looked, though they too were made of clay and were unpainted. Their eyes roamed over her features, taking in gray-streaked hair, the simple fitted jeans, and relaxed blue t-shirt under a well-worn dark leather jacket she had picked up in Florence in the 80s. Catherine looked a far cry from the eccentric professor persona she had cultivated in her time in New Britain.

"Shalom, Miriam. It has been so very long." Nachem spoke English, which Catherine had not expected.

"May I sit?" she asked. They waved toward a chair, and she sat down heavily, dropping the bag she was carrying next to her on the ground. "How have you been?"

Nachem placed a bookmark in the novel they were reading, a clincher romance from the look of the cover, and set it on the table. "I have been well, though quite bored since my charge insisted on staying in the New World for some time." Their voice was like gravel, but a grin spread across their well-crafted face.

Catherine had always admired the level of detail her great-grandfather put into creating Nachem. She had seen other golems in her life, and few had more than vaguely human features that exhibited little to no emotion. It was unnerving at best. But Nachem was more animated; her great-grandfather had been very talented.

"You knew about my own charge. It's hardly my fault Ezra barely left his little haven. Angels are such creatures of habit. I suppose you know that he is no longer under my guardianship. And that—"

"That you are mortal now. Yes, word has reached even me, Miriam. I felt the line of your life shorten some time ago. Which I suppose means that my days are coming to end as well, seeing as I will no longer be needed." There was no judgement in their words, but a wave of guilt crashed over her all the same. She hadn't thought about Nachem when she gave up her immortality. If she was being honest with herself, she hadn't thought of the golem in general in years. That thought only served to heighten her guilt.

But they waved her off, one large hand coming off the table to rest gently atop one of her own. "It matters not. My purpose is nearly fulfilled, and I am content to return to the earth in which I was created."

Their words did little to assuage her guilt, but she could appreciate them anyway. "I assume your visit is because you require something of me and not a simple friendly visit," Nachem continued, and it was like they were punching her with guilt.

It wasn't that Nachem was being unkind. They weren't capable of that kind of emotional response. They were, however, making a poignant statement that Catherine couldn't deny. "You do not let me get away with anything, Nachem. You never have." She smiled, thinking of when she was a child and how anything naughty she did around the village somehow always got back to her parents thanks to the golem keeping watch over her.

"But yes, I have need of someone well-versed in warding. Since I know that is one of your specialties, I thought you might be open to helping me. Specifically, deconstructing wards." She sucked in her bottom lip because she knew what Nachem would ask next.

They leveled their gaze at her, though still no judgement was there. "Am I to assume this need is for some kind of criminal activity?" And they got right to it.

Catherine tried not to fidget in her seat like a chastised school girl. It was amazing how such a short conversation with the golem could make her feel like a child again. "Criminal activity? I wouldn't go that far. More like rehoming an item. Does that make it sound better?"

Nachem actually chuckled. "It does not. But tell me about your crime plan anyway, *sheifale*."

Keeping her explanation brief, Catherine gave Nachem the rundown of her plan for the heist and what part she had in mind for them. The building would no doubt have layers of warding both outside and on the items themselves. Arruk wasn't a fool and had been a collector for centuries before crossing paths with Catherine. The wards from when Ezra occupied the building should be easy enough to dismantle once they spoke to the angel, but Arruk would undoubtedly have added more over the decades for extra safety as his collection grew.

When she finished, Nachem sat back heavily in their chair, a contemplative look on their face. They rubbed at their chin as if to help facilitate the thinking process. "Stealing from a friend is quite the sin, Miriam. But then, I do not see you caring much about one more black mark on your soul." Another blunt statement, though not untrue. "I believe this will be one of the last acts of service to our family, and so, despite the legalities, I will help and serve you, as always."

Catherine wanted to throw her arms around the golem and hug them tightly, but despite their years, Nachem had never gotten the hang of affectionate physical contact beyond patting heads and hands. So, Catherine opted to lay her hand on theirs and thanked them. "I appreciate everything you have done for me, and everything you are willing to do now."

Nachem only nodded and waited for her to say more. But Catherine was at a loss for words. Nachem knew what was expected of them now, and all that was left was for the full team to come together and form their plan. If she stayed in Orvieto for a while and spent some time with the golem, she knew she would have to face the memories of her youth, of her family, of what was lost to not only her, but Nachem as well. And Catherine realized she wasn't ready for that. Not yet. Soon enough she would have to think over the entirety of her life, especially the painful memories of her first family, of all they had lost. But she couldn't bear to do it now. Not with so much else on her mind, not when she still had a few more decades of life left in her.

"We are convening in—"

"The angel's place in the New World. Yes, I will be there in one week's time. Good bye for now, *shei-fale*." And with that, Nachem picked up their book and went back to reading without another glance up at Catherine.

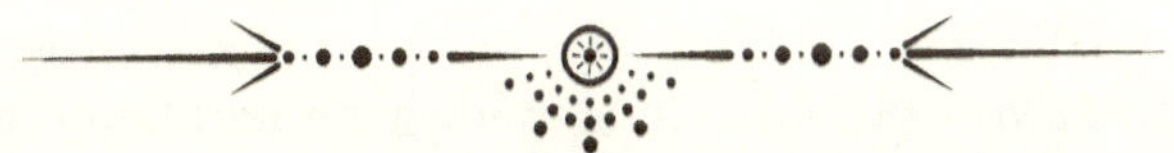

The flight back to London was short and uneventful—unless she counted the fact that the air conditioning on the plane wasn't working, and the flight staff made up for it by giving everyone as much alcohol as they wanted. The man sitting next to her passed out on her shoulder, which was definitely not part of the first-class experience. Not to mention the tea was one of the worst cups she had ever had, which was astounding considering she was on British Airways.

So maybe not all that uneventful. But certainly, one she didn't want a repeat of.

Her plan was to spend a few days in London before heading to Connecticut. Once she landed and had settled in, she would contact Sidatih and Mizuno to let them know the meeting details. That should give them enough time for travel arrangements.

Before leaving Italy, she had contacted Ezra to let him know they were all coming, telling him rather than asking. It was the best way to deal with Ezra, and it was something he was used to. She also let Brie know she was visiting. Catherine had meant to visit her mentee after the trip to Thailand, but that hadn't panned out.

Brie's response came quickly and with far too many exclamation points, yet it still filled Catherine with a quiet joy. Catherine had had so many students over the course of her academic career, but every now and then, a student appeared with whom she connected. Even before Catherine gave her immortality to Brie, she was invested in the girl's future. Another young mind she helped shape had been sent off into the world to do great things, or so Catherine thought. There was something incredibly rewarding about teaching, and maybe she would go back to it once she had finished her travels. That is, if she lived through her travels. Survival was no longer guaranteed. She could easily fall victim to a horrible accident or face the consequences of a past slight like what happened in Thailand. Even disease was now something to worry about.

She had taken things for granted in her immortal life, but she was so fragile now.

Once she was back in her flat in London, she dropped her travel bag in her bedroom and flopped down on the large bed. She purchased her lovely little flat in Parsons Green in the 1850s, and it had always been a safe haven to come back to whenever she needed. Even after Ezra packed up his shop and moved to the Colonies, and thus forcing Catherine to follow, she couldn't bear to give up the space she had called home for over twenty years.

The expanse of stark white ceiling filled her vision as she emptied her mind of all thoughts. There would be time for planning the job soon enough, but what she needed was a blank brain and a lot of sleep. Traveling the last two weeks had taken enough out of her, considering she had been every which way over the globe. And she had more travel ahead of her and far more beyond that.

CHAPTER 6

The bell above the door tinkled as she entered. Spirit Antiques looked to be completely empty, even behind the heavy wooden counter across the room. Within seconds of Catherine's entrance, though, the only door behind the counter opened, and a young woman with ginger hair tied back into a ponytail with several pens sticking out between the elastic appeared.

Brie St. James appeared almost exactly as she had when Catherine saw her nearly four years ago: medium height, pale skin with freckles, and decked out in an emerald green long-sleeve dress with black leggings to stave off the cold. The thin gold wedding band on her left ring finger was still a shocking sight, though that was mostly because Catherine never saw Ezra getting married, and certainly not to one of her former students. Still, their wedding had been beautiful, intimate with only a few friends, and a joyous day.

"Dr. Fry, you made it!" Brie shouted across the room before rounding the counter and bounding over to the older woman. She threw her arms around Catherine's shoulders and pulled her in for a tight hug.

After a second's hesitation, Catherine put her arms around the other woman and held her close.

"Sorry it took a little extra time. I ran into a bit of trouble on my travels," Catherine responded when the two finally pulled apart.

But Brie only beamed, unfazed by Catherine's tardiness. "No worries. You're here now, and that's all that matters. You look different. What happened to the squirrel sweater vest and glasses?" The younger woman appraised Catherine's appearance.

Catherine's casual look was now worlds away from the professor persona she had taken on for so many years. She was well aware that the woman Brie knew as her mentor appeared much older than Catherine looked without the glamour. For one, she had ditched the ridiculous sweaters with crochet animals and long skirts for more comfortable jeans and fitted shirts. And of course, her leather jacket. The absurdly thick coke bottle glasses she used to wear were gone too, and for that, she was thankful since they were dreadfully annoying to wear.

"To be honest, I hated the whole look, but it helped me blend in better in the academic world and left enough of an impression on my students." Catherine laughed.

Brie chuckled in return. "Oh, it left an impression. I definitely saw a few undergrads years ago dress up as you for Halloween. It was a surreal experience to see a six-foot-three dude in a skirt and knitted sweater vest staggering down the street."

The image in Catherine's head was all too realistic and wildly entertaining, and she told Brie as much.

"Come on. Ezra is in the back, still working on inventory. I'm sure he'll be excited to see you." Brie led Catherine behind the counter, pushed the number two button on a side panel next to the door, and waited until she heard a snick before opening the door.

The two women stepped through the doorway into an impossible room. The space was cavernous with rows upon rows of shelves that were stuffed full of every matter of items and large crates. Despite the hanging lights, there wasn't enough illumination to make out the ends of the room. It was a space that could not possibly fit into the back room of a medium sized shop in the middle of a city.

But the Storage Room of Spirit Antiques did not adhere to the rules of physics. Magic rarely did. And everything from the items on the shelves to the room itself, and even the owner of said room, was teeming with magic.

"Hey, sweetie, we need a ride to Ezra," Brie called out, seemingly to the Storage Room. Barely a second later, an ornate rug zoomed around a corner and hovered next to the small raised platform the two women were standing on. "All aboard," Brie said over her shoulder before stepping onto the rug and sitting down.

"I do love a magic carpet," Catherine said with a grin before climbing onto the rug herself. She was barely seated before the rug zoomed off again, careening around the corners of aisles, skirting past rows and rows of shelves. Without thought, Catherine gripped the side of the rug with one hand while her other scrambled for purchase on the fabric in the center, coming up empty as the rug was flat. Beside her, Brie let out a delighted squeal, not even bothering to hold on. Clearly, the younger woman was much more comfortable on flying objects than Catherine was.

It took perhaps a full minute of the rug flying around the Storage Room before it finally came to an abrupt stop in a random aisle far back from the entrance. Standing before a shelf with a tablet in his hand was Ezra. He was large and lithe, light brown skin with dark hair styled in an undercut. His clothing was all black, the only color a stitched golden torch above his left breast pocket, which was his personal work uniform.

"Hello, Aunt Catherine," he said without looking up from his tablet. Not that Catherine expected a warmer greeting; that simply wasn't Ezra's way. But she felt a bit of delight that he still referred to her as Aunt Catherine, despite never wanting her to be his watcher for centuries. Not to mention he was far older than she was. That didn't seem to matter to Ezra. Their relationship had much improved once Brie had come into his life, and he had reconnected with his mother, who was, in fact, a god. She should ask after his mother since they had not spoken in some time.

"Hello, Ezra. It's good to see you," she responded. Years past, she had stopped referring to him by his original name Arakiel, per his wishes. Instead, she used the name he had chosen for himself: Ezra. Catherine could appreciate him wanting a new identity after so much tragedy in his life.

"Don't mind him. He's been working on this for years, and it's never ending. I'm not sure why he bothers. The Storage Room keeps moving things around just to mess with him." Brie laughed, and Catherine saw that Ezra smiled just a little. There was a man who adored his wife because he never smiled for anyone else. Never had for as long as Catherine had known him.

Ezra finished whatever he was working on and set the tablet aside on one of the crates sitting out. "I have unlimited time to finish this. Eventually, the Storage Room will see this is a good thing. But that's not why you are here, Catherine. And it's not just to see my wife and have a friendly visit. So, to what do we owe the pleasure?" He crossed his arms as he turned toward the women.

He knew very well that Catherine wouldn't visit without something happening. Sure, she had wanted to connect with Brie and even see him, but if she didn't have need of him, Catherine wasn't so sure she would have visited them yet, despite her plans to do so earlier in the year. "You've caught me. I need your help. Your knowledge, actually."

Brie clapped her hands together. "Why don't we take this to our place where it's more comfortable?" A large round silver object fell off one of the shelves onto Brie's foot. She yelped in pain and looked up, like she was addressing the ceiling. "Not that you aren't comfortable. You are the best room ever. But I also like my home, and it has tea. And before you start, I want to go make it myself, so you leave your tea set alone." The air in the room seemed to shift, like the Storage Room was accepting her words, and the round object that had hit Brie rolled away and disappeared back into a shelf.

"I love this place, but it does love to throw tantrums when it doesn't get its way," Brie mumbled as an aside to Catherine. The older woman chuckled, and the three of them climbed onto a much larger rug that had appeared after Brie had addressed the Storage Room.

The apartment was large. Catherine had only been in it perhaps twice in the last century, but it was definitely much larger than it had been the last time she was inside. There used to only be one bedroom, the kitchen, bathroom, and living room with a short hallway leading into it. Now the hallway was much longer with framed pictures covering nearly every inch of space, depicting Ezra and Brie's family and friends, their wedding photos, and a portrait in a place of honor that showed Brie's adoptive mother Maddy with a younger Brie and her brother Wes. Two more bedrooms had been added, the living room had expanded, though it still felt like a living forest, and the kitchen was enormous. From what Catherine could see, another door led into a greenhouse that should not be able to exist given the space, and as Brie pointed out, a set of pocket doors opened into a newly created library.

The wonders of magic never ceased to amaze.

Brie motioned for Catherine to sit before shuffling off to the open kitchen to make tea. Catherine settled herself on one of the chairs made of woven wood with forest green cushions. Ezra took a seat on the large couch fashioned to match the chairs. The two of them sat in silence while Brie moved around the kitchen.

Catherine took the time to inspect the space more. The bookshelves that used to be in the living room were gone, most likely off to the library. It allowed the space to feel more like a forest; the wind softly blowing through the leaves caused the walls to appear to move like living wallpaper.

"So, Dr. Fry, what's going on? Is Ezra right, and you need us for something?" Brie asked, placing a tea service on a coffee table in the center of the room. She poured out three cups and passed them around, giving everyone a chance to fix their tea before sitting down.

The warm liquid was soothing as Catherine took several sips before beginning. Might as well be lubricated before diving into her request.

She began with little preamble, just facts. "In my life, I have accrued certain debts. Recently, one of those debts has been called up, and as you know, a magical debt cannot be broken until fulfilled. In short, I've been tasked with retrieving an item. The current owner of said item is a collector, and he houses his wares in one of your old shops. I need your knowledge of the wards and magics put on the space so we can infiltrate the space and retrieve the item."

"Arruk or Terrance?" Ezra asked, speaking over the rim of his cup before taking a sip.

"Arruk," Catherine said with a flinch. Ezra leveled a knowing gaze at her. He knew about her history with the minotaur and how much their friendship had meant to her.

But it was Brie who spoke next, not knowing what the look meant. "Wait. Hold up. Are you saying you need to steal something? And there's a *we*? You have like a team or something, or are you wanting us to steal it with you?"

Catherine held up her hand. "No, no. I do have my own team. They will be meeting me here at the shop soon if all goes well. I have a warder; they will handle breaking whatever magic lingers and the new magics Arruk has set up. But it would be easier if they knew how to dissemble them rather than trying to pick them apart while we're there."

Ezra nodded thoughtfully. "That shouldn't be a problem. My wards change with each location, but I keep records from each one. It shouldn't be too hard to give them over to him."

"Them. Nachem is a golem, not a man," Catherine corrected. A single bob of his head was Ezra's acknowledgement.

"Can we go back to the part where you have a team that is going to steal something?" Brie asked, incredulous. Of course, she wouldn't understand; she didn't know the life Catherine led long before she became a university professor. To the young woman, she had always been a teacher.

"Brie, dear, I have had many professions in my life, and not all of them were the most ethical. Before my immortal days, I was a thief. And it was because of my thievery that I ended up cursed to be an immortal babysitter to your husband." Catherine settled in for what was likely to be a lengthy discussion. Or more accurately, a recounting of her life.

So, she began her tale of a young woman in Crimea over five hundred years ago.

Miriam sat in a tree at the line of the forest watching the stack of stones that made up the crumbling temple. She had been watching the temple for a week now, observing the comings and goings of the few worshippers and one priest come and go. Really, it would be all too easy to go in there and take anything she wanted, but Catherine never did any job by halves and thus conducted a thorough scouting before she made a move.

Why there was a half-ruined temple deep in the woods she had no idea, especially since it clearly wasn't dedicated to Hashem or the Christian god; instead, it was for some Lady Ania or other, a god she had never heard of. Whatever was worshipped deep in the forest, Miriam didn't really care. All that matter was what was inside the temple. An ancient golden statue stood in a place of prominence at the center, watched over by the one old priest, while the upkeep, the little of it, was done by the devout few.

Miriam had been given a job to retrieve the statue and bring it back to her client for a hefty sum of coin. It was a job that she couldn't turn down. It should have been easy. There was no security to speak of and few people. Really, she could walk in after dark and simply take the statue and be done with it. And that's exactly what she planned to do in the next two hours once the sun was down and the priest retired for the night. She almost felt bad charging Zevi for the job considering how little work was going into it. But that didn't mean she wouldn't anyway. She had acquired enough items for him over the years that she didn't mind gouging him as often as possible.

He always paid in the end, anyway.

Within the hour, the last of the worshippers slipped off into the forest and returned to wherever they came from. The priest began to extinguish the lamps around the temple before making his final prayers and heading to the small cottage behind the building. There was no chance he would hear anything coming from the temple, not the way Miriam moved around.

She could have gone in any night, but she planned for this one particularly because there was no moon. No moonlight meant less chance of being spotted, and she was taking no chances despite the remote location and lack of people.

The temple was dark and silent, but Miriam had excellent night vision. She wished she had the chance to scope out the inside before, but with such a small number of worshippers who all appeared to be the same every time, she would definitely be noticed as an outsider. Luckily for her, there was a small fire built up in the center of the temple, an everlasting light to illuminate the statue of the god. Miriam knew from her observations that the priest would wake sometime in the night to feed the fire before returning to bed. But she had plenty of time before that happened.

As she approached the statue, she pulled the rough woven sack she carried on her back off, ready to place the golden treasure inside. She set it on the floor just below the stone crafted pedestal the statue sat upon, opening it to await its booty. With a quick swipe of her palms against the men's leggings she wore, Miriam placed a hand on either side of the statue and lifted. Her arms buckled slightly under the weight. Though it wasn't large, it was much heavier than she anticipated. It was going to be a real shitty walk back to town with that thing slung across her back. But the thought of the money and a hot meal at the end of the hike made it all worth it.

The statue nearly tumbled from her hands when a voice spoke from behind her. "Do you often come into sacred spaces to steal, little thief?" The voice was feminine and deep, though there was an ethereal resonance to it as well.

Fuck, Miriam thought. There wasn't supposed to be anyone around. Why would there be when it was already well past dark? And the priest was an old man, so he definitely did not fit the voice.

Miriam slowly turned around. In the dim light of the fire, she saw a beautiful woman. Her skin was so dark she nearly blended in with the night around her. Her hair, from what Miriam could see, was nearly white and wavy. The strands seemed to move in a wind that was all her own. The dress she wore was simple white with a colorful hem like that of a rainbow. Eyes of gold that glowed from far more than firelight stared unblinking at Miriam.

There was a faint glow all around the woman, and Miriam knew without a shadow of a doubt that this woman wasn't human. Not really, anyway.

"Who are you?" she asked, not sure she wanted an answer.

The woman's face remained unchanged, just a flat look that signified she was awaiting answers and would give away nothing else. "I think the real question is: who are you? You are in my temple, after all," the woman said in an even tone. There was no accusation or judgement in her voice.

"I... I'm..." Miriam found that she wanted to be truthful, something she never was anymore. "My name is Miriam Kokush." If there was a waver to her voice, she didn't want to acknowledge it. Confidence was something she always exuded, whether she truly felt it or not. But right now, she felt the furthest thing possible from confident.

"Miriam Kokush, who absconded from her shtetl twenty years ago at the tender age of eighteen to escape a marriage contract, leaving her rabbi father, mother, siblings, and a betrothed behind. Now a sought-after thief. You seem to be doing well for yourself. That is, until you decided to steal from my temple." The woman rattled off her life story like she knew everything about Miriam. How did she know so much? Miriam had never met the woman before; she certainly would have remembered if she had. And there had certainly been none of her relations in her small shtetl growing up since it was made up of the only four or five extended families, all of whom were Jews and as lily-white as she was.

"How do you know me?" was all she could think to ask. It was the only thought in her mind at the moment. She was scared, more than she wanted to admit to herself.

The woman took one step toward Miriam, so Miriam took one step back. There wasn't much space behind her though. She had turned from the pedestal, so now it was directly behind her, stopping her quick exit that way.

Pausing, the woman looked over Miriam, her glowing eyes seeming to bore into Miriam's soul. "I know you, Miriam. When you came into my temple, I saw your heart. While I find no evil lingering there, you would still steal from me. It is a slight I cannot let go unpunished."

Miriam took another step, realizing finally that she still held the statue between her hands as her arms began to scream in pain from the long minutes spent holding it. "Look, I'll put it back. There's no harm done." She hefted the statue back up onto the stone pedestal, despite the pain in her arms. The sack lay forgotten at her feet.

"See. Now I will leave, and I promise not to return." Miriam took a step to the right, hoping to skirt around the woman and exit slowly.

"No," the woman said sternly. Her voice wasn't loud, barely above a whisper, but it still held power enough behind it to make Miriam freeze in her tracks. "No, Miriam Kokush. You still chose to steal a sacred object from a god, and there must be a punishment. For so long now, you have shirked your responsibilities. What good have you done for the world in your life? Nothing."

Miriam felt the sting of her words in her heart. It wasn't like Miriam wasn't aware of the mark she left on the world; she had just convinced herself she didn't care.

"So, Miriam Kokush, I curse you to a long life of servitude. From this day until I see fit, you will serve at my discretion. As such, you are charged with the guardianship of a wayward soul, and for the rest of your days until I release you, so shall you be tied to this duty." The woman's words were a proclamation. And once she finished speaking, Miriam suddenly felt her whole body start to heat up.

At first, it was a gentle warming, like the sun hitting first thing in the morning. But then it didn't stop heating. Soon, it felt like her whole body was on fire, and she had to look down at her hands to make sure there weren't visible flames. A scream tore out of her throat, and she slammed her eyes shut, unable to focus on anything other than the pain. It was the worst kind of heat and pain she had ever endured, and Miriam felt she was going to die from it.

Then just as suddenly as it started, everything stopped. Miriam's body still tingled from the sensations she had experienced, but that was all. Though now she found she was kneeling on the hard stone floor, doubled over herself without any idea of how that happened. "What did you do to me?" she sobbed, unable to comprehend anything that happened.

The woman stepped close to Miriam and crouched down, offering her hands. With trepidation, Miriam placed her hands in the woman's dark ones and let herself be hauled up. The woman didn't release Miriam even once they were standing. "No one crosses a god, Miriam. No one. And punishment must be dealt, even if the theft is incomplete. Let this be a lesson for you to ponder over your long life."

Leading Miriam by the hand, the woman took her to the entrance of the temple. "You must seek out a man named Ezra at a collector's shop in Istanbul called Ruh. He will be your charge. You have one month, or else you will feel the fires burn you each day you are late." The woman's hand pulled Miriam forward until her feet touched the grass beyond the temple, only then releasing her.

When Miriam turned to question her, the woman was gone, leaving only a dark and empty threshold.

Her nerves shaken, her body still feeling the aftershocks of whatever happened, Miriam fled into the night. Without a shadow of a doubt, Miriam knew that she had just met the god to whom the temple was dedicated, and that she had to get to Istanbul as quickly as possible if she wanted to avoid that fire and pain.

Not that she particularly wanted to believe what just happened, but Miriam was very much concerned with her own self-preservation and wasn't willing to take the chance of angering a god further. So, she headed back to town, prepared to pack up her things, sell off what she couldn't carry, and skip town before Zevi realized she never finished the job. It wasn't like he would follow her to the Turkish Empire, and Miriam had plenty of money to finance a trip. Though it hadn't been in her plans, Miriam knew there was plenty of adventure ahead of her.

As she ran through the forest, though, she couldn't help but fret over the words the god had said. She had cursed her with life immortal. Did that mean she would never die?

"So, your mom cursed her because she tried to steal a statue? Like didn't even actually remove it from the building, just tried, and your mom decided *hey, curse her forever and make it unbearably painful if she doesn't listen?* Your mom is really messed up sometimes." Brie crossed her arms tightly and leaned back against the couch. The lights in the house flickered, and an earth-shaking crack of thunder ricochet around the room. Clearly, the god had heard her.

"If you're going to smite your daughter-in-law, just do it already. But you know I'm right!" she shouted at the ceiling, like the god was above their heads, listening. After a few seconds passed and Brie still sat untouched, Catherine figured the young woman was in the clear.

Ezra massaged the spot between his eyes, exasperated by his wife's outburst. "She's mellowed out a lot in the last few centuries. She was going through a rough patch around that time, if you remember."

Catherine nodded in agreement. "She has. Though it's been a few years since we spoke. I asked her not to interfere in my life while I'm traveling, though I've regretted that decision a few times." She smiled, but she didn't elaborate to Brie and Ezra. They didn't need to know about her near execution in Thailand just now.

"I think we should get back to our original topic. You need help stealing this artifact, and you have a team of people coming to my shop to plan. Is that about right?" Ezra flung an arm to rest on the back of the couch behind his wife's head. Brie scooted closer to him, and he let his hand drop to her shoulder.

"In short, yes. I'll need you to provide the details of the wards and assist Nachem in learning how to deconstruct them. If you would permit me to use one of your spaces for planning, we will come up with a general idea before setting off for Greece. If you have the blueprints of the building, that would also be helpful. We'll do the rest of the planning from a place in Athens." Catherine hoped that Ezra would agree. He was always willing to help others in the magical community, but this was on the gray side of things. More than gray, really, but Catherine didn't want to think about that.

"I don't approve of stealing things from Arruk. He purchased the building in good faith from me, and it would be wrong to betray that," Ezra said, his face clearly showing his disapproval. Catherine's heart sank. She could pull off the job without Ezra's help, but it would be infinitely easier with it.

"However," Ezra began again, and Catherine perked up, "Arruk has been in possession of something of mine that was left behind in the move for centuries and hasn't bothered to give it back. I will help you under the condition that this item you are after is the only thing you take. It'll make Arruk and I even, at least in my book, which is the only one that matters."

"You don't want your own item back?" Catherine asked, not really wanting to steal more from Arruk than she was already obligated to.

Ezra shook his head. "It doesn't matter. He can keep it; he's had it longer than I ever did at this point. I simply feel like being petty about it." Brie burst out laughing at this, and she quickly covered her mouth with her hand while she tried to control herself.

Catherine enjoyed how much Ezra had relaxed into himself since meeting Brie. Though he still wasn't a particularly warm man, except with his wife, he was softer and joked more easily. The young woman had rounded his edges, and in return, Ezra had given her the home and family she always hoped for. Catherine was happy they had found each other. More than a few times she had found that happiness with someone else, or something close to it, though it had been a lonely few years as of late before she spent the night with Sidatih. Maybe after the debt to Titania was repaid, she could spend some time with him in San Francisco and see if they couldn't bring each other a little happiness for a time.

"You can use my office for your meeting. I'll see if I can find the plans for the building and the notes on the wards. Stay out of the Storage Room and don't harass my customers. If you are bringing any more thieves into my place, keep them in check. I'll know if something goes missing." Ezra leveled a pointed glare at her but let it fall flat again when Brie gave him a soft backhanded hit to the chest.

"Be nice. You definitely won't notice if something goes missing since you don't even know half of what's in this place," Brie said, leaning her head on her husband's shoulder.

Catherine nodded. Not that she thought Mizuno would steal anything, but she would reassure Ezra if it meant keeping the peace. With nothing further to say, Catherine stood, thanked them for everything, left their home, and headed out through the antique shop. With nothing else to do the rest of the night, Catherine decided to head to the small home she had lived in while in New Britain, one that she hadn't given up even though she hadn't been back in years.

The house was dark when she entered, but with a few flips of light switches, the house was illuminated in a soft glow. Everything was still clean since she continued to pay someone to come and clean it regularly, in case she decided to come back at some point. It was still early; the light outside had only just started to dim. Catherine couldn't decide if she wanted to venture out again to get something to eat or order in and not have to deal with people. She had forgotten to inform her housekeeper she was returning, so there was no food stocked.

The one issue with going out was the possibility of running into old colleagues from the university, and she simply didn't feel up to discussing what she had been up to, if she was coming back, or really, even the idle small talk that came with meeting people she had a forced acquaintance with.

That thought pretty much settled her decision to order a pizza and stay in. She was a simple woman after all, and simple food like pizza pleased her just as much as any elaborate meal. In fact, she enjoyed simpler foods, streets foods, the things people often referred to as peasant food far more than anything upscale.

Her mother's dark bread, made to go along with whatever they had put in a stew, was a favorite comfort. She could almost smell the delicious scent of it baking, filling their home with warmth. While other memories of her life before her curse had faded and were now only vague fragments, the smell of her mother's cooking never quite left her.

She shook her head, trying to clear it. Too often in the last few months she had found her mind wandering to memories of a time before immortality. Maybe it was the idea that now she was mortal again, she would soon be reunited with her family in whatever came after this life. Not that she knew what that meant. When a person lives forever, she doesn't really think about what comes after life. Then again, maybe it was her inevitable death that was making her think of everything she had lived through.

Whatever the reason, she didn't like it and tried to push the memories away. Instead, she pulled out her phone and ordered her food, then opened her laptop to see if she could do some research on Arruk and his warehouse.

She found him easily enough on social media. Not that a minotaur would be on normal human social media, but there were plenty of magical folks who kept up with technology, people like Sidatih, who used their talents to create their own space on the internet for people like them. Which, thanks to Mystagram, meant she could easily track Arruk down and study the life he posted in pictures.

There were plenty of images of his collection available online. He wasn't shy about showing off the more rare and intriguing pieces in his possession. Lucky for her, this meant she could start to piece together a layout of the building. Not that it would be easy, even with Ezra's plan. Magical buildings didn't always stay the same shape they were supposed to. Still, it would allow her to have a better understanding of where she needed to be and where the exits were.

Catherine continued to scroll through his feed, hoping perhaps to find an image of the trumpet. Easier said than done, considering Arruk posted a lot. Like all the time. It seemed like the guy was addicted to social media and showing off his vast collection. She had been scrolling for easily fifteen minutes and had hardly cracked even a third of his posts. Why did anyone need to post so much? Did people not care about their privacy online?

Catherine had her own account on Mystagram that she often forgot about. She also had her accounts on human social media that she posted to more frequently to keep up with appearances as a university professor, like when she published a new paper or book or when she gave lectures outside of her classes. But even those had fallen by the wayside lately as she traveled, her posts showing a generic vista from wherever she went and only after she left.

Her social media investigation did give her some good information though. While it wasn't a picture of the trumpet, she did see that Arruk was opening his collection for a gala coming up in a few weeks' time. But before that, he was hosting a smaller party, invitation only, but that hardly mattered to Catherine. She had her ways of getting into parties she wasn't invited to. She could use the party as a means to scope out the interior while the gala would be the perfect opportunity to get in and take the trumpet. It was much easier to hide in plain sight than risk tripping more wards and alarms in the dead of night. She would be able to keep Arruk distracted while Mizuno took the trumpet. The thought of seeing Arruk again did give her a small leap of her heart and a pang of anxiety at the same time. It had been so long. What if he hated her? Or threw her out on sight? She wanted to see him as much as she wanted to find out where the trumpet was located.

No, that wasn't true. She wanted to see Arruk more than she wanted to find the trumpet. Actually, if she could skip anything to do with the trumpet and only see her friend, that would be even better. But then she wouldn't have even bothered to think of Arruk if it wasn't for Titania's stupid scheme, so that wasn't an option.

A few weeks until the gala didn't give them much time, though. She had to get them all assembled, go over what she had planned, and then get them all set up in Greece. Maybe she should have had them all meet up in Athens rather than at Ezra's shop, but she needed a familiar space to work, and she did need Ezra's help. All of them would benefit from Ezra's knowledge of the building, and Catherine would rather him explain than to try to pass along the information.

Strategy and logistics were what she was good at, and she would make it all work with the time she had available. This was going to be her last job; after this, she would retire the thief persona once more, never to be picked up again. Even if it meant dying with a debt still over her head. But only after this one was complete. She didn't want to risk the wrath of Titania, not when, no matter what, she still held fondness in her heart for the fae queen.

CHAPTER 8

Nachem was the first to arrive at Spirit Antiques the next morning, not that it surprised Catherine. As they were duty bound to serve her family, the magic wouldn't allow them to be late. They were dressed in human clothing, a simple white button down and black slacks, the glamour up until they crossed the threshold of the shop.

Mizuno arrived a day after, looking resplendent in one of her high fashion kimonos, this one in fall leaf orange, with a brown wool coat draped elegantly over her shoulders. She was so put together, her black hair shining and her makeup perfect, there was no way to tell that she had traveled across the world in the last day.

The three of them adjourned to Ezra's office to wait for Sidatih and have a bit of brunch. Ezra and Brie were elsewhere and promised to attend to them once the whole party was assembled.

Four hours later, Sidatih finally waltzed into the shop, and Catherine met him at the counter, a disapproving look on her face. "You're late, as usual," she said crossly.

Sidatih gave her a wide grin, like he didn't have a care in the world. "Albi, you know me. I would be late to my own funeral. If anything, I tried to be as punctual as possible for you," he said, reaching out and pulling her by the waist until her body was pressed against his.

As he leaned in to kiss her, Catherine placed a hand against his lips. "Nope, no kissing until after the meeting. Had you been here when you were supposed to, there might have been time. But now, you've missed out on the food and the kissing." She shoved him toward the door and pressed the number one on the keypad. After the click of the door, she opened it and walked in, not waiting for Sidatih to follow.

Catherine resumed the seat she had vacated to go get Sidatih and crossed one ankle over the other. The ifrit sat down on a leather couch in front of her, on the far end away from Nachem. From an end table next to her chair, Catherine pulled up what looked like a clam shell and wrenched it open. Both halves of the shell glowed faintly with magic. Holding it up to her ear like a phone, Catherine spoke into the bottom half. "Ezra, Sida finally arrived, if you want to come to your office."

From the other end, she heard Ezra tell her just a minute, and then she snapped the shell phone shut and placed it on the table to give back to Brie later.

It took less than a minute for Ezra to arrive with Brie trailing behind him. More leather chairs were pulled into the circle, and a fire crackled cheerfully against the wall next to Catherine's chair. She relaxed into the warmth of the fire as she waited for everyone to situate themselves.

Catherine gazed at the people around the room and thought it was quite the unusual grouping: an angel, an immortal, a golem, a jorgumo, and an ifrit. And then there was Catherine. She wasn't like any of them, not anymore. Yet they looked at her expectantly because she was the mastermind behind it all.

Gathering her thoughts, Catherine began, "I have met with each of you individually and explained the job, and you have all agreed to lend your services."

"Not that we had much choice when you were calling in debts," Mizuno murmured in English, accent light, and only for the benefit of those around her.

Catherine could only nod because hadn't she done to them exactly what Titania was doing to her, holding a debt over their heads? "We are fortunate that the mark will be hosting a small party for his collection in about a week, giving us the perfect opportunity to infiltrate and get a feel of the location. There will be a larger gala the weekend after for a wider *paying* audience, which is when we will complete the job. I know that's not a lot of time, but you are the best of the best, and I trust in all of your skills." She held up a hand toward Sidatih when it looked like he might speak. The time crunch wasn't ideal, and no doubt Sidatih had planned to complain, but he would listen, and he would show up when he was needed.

"Ezra has agreed to provide whatever blueprint, plans, and information about the wards available since the collection is housed in one of his shop's previous locations. The magic there will be both old and new. The older magics will be easy enough to deal with since we have Ezra, and Nachem knows everything there is to know about warding. As for new wards, that's where I need you, Sida. You know everything there is to know about mortal security, and you keep updated on emerging warding magic, so that's what you'll be focusing on. With the plans Ezra provides of the physical layout and from what we can scout out while at the party, Mizuno, you should have no trouble taking the trumpet and getting out without anyone noticing during the gala." That covered most of what Catherine needed to say. They all knew the risks of the job, but Catherine hoped there wouldn't be any cause for concern once they were in.

"And is there anything in it for us or just a debt wiped clean?" Sidatih asked once Catherine had finished.

Catherine cocked an eyebrow at him since there was no debt hanging between them. She knew very well that Sida would do anything for her if she asked, and she would do the same in return. "What do you have in mind?" she asked, unsure of what she could give him. It wasn't like Sidatih needed money or treasures. He had plenty of money, and he wasn't much for holding onto trinkets that he didn't need.

The small shy smile that spread across his face made Catherine's heart pound. "The same thing I will always ask of you, albi."

A warm feeling rose within her, and she swore there were butterflies in her stomach. The one thing she knew Sida wanted from her was time together, a life together. But Catherine had to push past her hope and focus. "We can discuss that later," she stated, not looking at anyone other than Sidatih. The smile on his face widened; he clearly was enjoying himself.

The room felt warmer suddenly, and it had nothing to do with the crackling fire. "If you have something in mind as your payment in addition to the debt cleared, you may speak with me about it." She knew Sidatih would gladly take advantage of the offer, but Catherine was uncertain of what Mizuno could want from her. Nachem would take nothing as they saw it as their duty to serve her since that was exactly what they were created for.

"That offer doesn't extend to you, Ezra. I kept watch over your brooding behind for over five hundred years, and you are doing the bare minimum here. So, while we are not exactly even, I'll still tip this in your favor." Catherine had to turn her attention away from her team, so as not to have to look at expectant faces.

Ezra shrugged. "I expected nothing, Aunt Catherine. You have done more for me and mine than I can ever repay anyway." His tone was flat, but he turned an affectionate gaze on Brie, who smiled brightly back at her husband.

"So, this is the miracle worker who has managed to tame Ezra?" Sidatih sat forward in his chair, genuine interest on his face.

"I don't know if I would call myself a miracle worker. Ezra is a big cinnamon roll once you get past his broody exterior. It's all show," Brie said with a giant smile on her face. She placed a hand on her husband's knees and gave it a squeeze while Ezra scowled.

Catherine turned her attention toward Mizuno and Nachem. "Ezra and Brie are married. Brie was one of my students at the university until she met him while he was still under my guardianship." She then pointed to the other two, indicating for Ezra and Brie's sake. "Mizuno is a pupil of one of my former protegees. And Nachem is my family's golem. They have been in service to my family from the time of my great-grandfather."

"Now that we are all acquainted and have an overview of the plan, we can adjourn. I will make the plans for travel to Greece. Once Ezra provides everything, Sida, Nachem, look over the list of wards Ezra has on the building. Mizuno, study the blueprints. They are rudimentary and probably outdated, but it will give you a better idea of the layout. I've also put together a slightly more updated layout based on my research that can be used to compare against." Now that everyone had a task, Catherine stood. "We can meet here again tomorrow once I have the travel set."

She headed toward the door, confident that everyone could handle things from here. As she opened the door, she turned and saw that Ezra had already handed over the parchment with the blueprint and the papers Catherine had assembled to Mizuno. The thief was rolling the papers together and grabbing her own bag to leave. Sida and Nachem sat next to each other on the couch, each grabbing a packet of pages Brie handed over.

"I'll find you soon, Mir," Sidatih called as Catherine gave them one last look and left. She waved a hand over her shoulder to acknowledge him, but the heat was back in her cheeks. Nothing was ever just about sex with Sidatih. He wanted more from her, and he was very selective about the people he felt sexual attraction to. Lust she could handle, but the thought of something more than that with Sidatih was enough to warm her heart.

But first, she needed time to arrange for four people to get to Greece and accommodations for all of them. The home she once had in Athens was long gone, destroyed some three hundred years previous. It wasn't a great loss to her since she hadn't set foot in the country since leaving with Ezra, and Ezra had been the one to purchase the house anyway.

As she headed back to the house she kept in New Britain, her mind began to wander again to days long past, as it had been doing often as of late. Her time in Greece was several lifetimes ago, but she could picture perfectly the busy streets of Athens as they were in the sixteenth century. By then, the city was much more diminished than it had been in centuries previous or in centuries after, cast off as the yoke of civilization and democracy under the rule of the Ottomans. Still, that didn't stop the Athenians from continuing to move about the streets at all hours of the day.

Arruk would take her to the ancient amphitheater, and they would watch whatever orator or play was passing through with Ezra as an unwilling chaperone posing as Catherine's brother. The minotaur would talk to her for hours about the Athens of centuries past, of when it was the center of democracy and modern thought. For Arruk, Athens was the center of the universe, and he obviously still felt the same way since he was still there occupying the same space for centuries.

"You should have seen it, Miriam. The streets were paved with gold, and any philosopher worth his salt debated upon the stages of Athens. Parties that lasted into the dawn, flowing with wine and formulations for the birth of democracy and science. There was nothing like it, nor do I ever think there shall be again," Arruk would tell her enthusiastically, though Catherine doubted the streets were actually paved with gold. Plenty of trade flowed through her streets, but Athens was also a practical city.

Whenever he spoke like that, Catherine wished dearly that she had been there to see it. When she lived in the ancient city, it was but a shadow of what it once was. As a student and now teacher of history, she could only imagine it through her research and from the friends who had been there all those centuries ago.

As she entered her house, Catherine pushed away the memories. If she let her past with Arruk cloud her judgement, she would never get through the job, and who knew what would happen if she broke her contract with Titania? Maybe nothing too horrible save for Titania's wrath, which admittedly, was considerable indeed. But magical debts did not work like that, and usually the consequences were severe.

Still, Catherine had come too far now to back out, especially since she already had a team assembled and ready to go. She wouldn't have them think she was unreliable and wasting their time.

Sitting down heavily at her desk in the small office of her house, she pulled up flights and available locations near the warehouse Arruk owned. While tickets and the spacious loft she booked for their stay were not cheap, money wasn't a concern for Catherine. Live long enough, and wealth just started accumulating by itself if invested correctly.

With that finished and the details and tickets sent off to her team, Catherine ordered herself dinner and settled in one of her favorite chairs with a book. This would probably be her last night of quiet and peace, and she wasn't going to let it go to waste.

In the next two days, she would be in Athens, and there were more than a few demons from her past she would have to face. Until then, she would gather her thoughts and try to focus on the tasks ahead of her.

CHAPTER 9

"I'm so jet lagged," Sidatih complained as they set their bags down in the apartment Catherine had rented for the month.

"Do you not travel frequently?" Mizuno asked, not bothering to look at Sidatih as she settled her compact suitcase near the plush couch in the center of the room. The woman looked pristine as ever, which baffled Catherine since she herself felt like she looked haggard and had a headache forming. Mizuno had a grace about her and seemingly let nothing bother her, like the world was beneath her notice, though Catherine was well aware that Mizuno was ever vigilant.

Nachem was completely unphased by the hours of travel, but that wasn't surprising considering their nature. They did not feel the discomforts that flesh and blood experienced. The golem could sit still for years, unmoving, and would feel nothing.

Only Catherine and Sidatih seemed to have any adverse effects from traveling, though only Sidatih was vocal about it. "Yes, I travel tons. I'm just usually on either a private jet with a bed, or a quick jaunt through the underworld gets me to where I want to go much faster. Commercial flying is not nearly as comfortable or quick. It's a literal hell."

"You flew first-class. It wasn't like I put us in coach, Sida." Catherine rubbed her temples and pulled her carry-on bag forward so she could find her bottle of ibuprofen. She could really use a nap after the flight, but they needed to get settled first, and she really should start getting them all ready for the work ahead.

"You should get some rest, Miriam," Nachem said, their tone even. They looked at her, assessing her as if they could scan her body for ailments. The familial magic certainly gave them an edge into her mood and feelings, so she wouldn't be surprised if they knew exactly how exhausted she was. Not to mention how utterly stiff her body felt.

"I can rest tonight. We should get to work now and not waste time," Catherine said matter-of-factly. She found the bottle of pills, poured out two, and swallowed them without anything to drink. The bitter taste on her tongue made her wish she had taken the extra step to grab her water.

"No, Mir, Nachem is right. Some rest would be good for all of us. Can't use our full brainpower if we're passing out at the planning table. So, let's say two hours to nap and refresh and then we'll do dinner?" Sidatih forgot his own woes for a second and glanced around the room for everyone's answer. They all nodded their agreement, and Catherine couldn't help but breathe a sigh of relief. She really wanted the rest but also wanted to appear to be a good leader. But that also meant knowing when her people needed to take some time. Now that she was no longer immortal,

Catherine couldn't push her limits too much, lest she collapse under her own exhaustion.

Though her head was full and her body sore, Catherine barely remained awake long enough for her head to hit the pillow. Her dreams were filled with another Athens, one now five hundred years gone, and of the young woman she once was.

"The party is next week with the gala being the week after; that gives us time to get an idea of the building and plan escape routes for all of us. Ezra's blueprints will be helpful only to a point; we don't know any of the modifications Arruk may have added over the years. It will also give us a chance to monitor the normal security measures he has on the outside." Catherine waved a hand at the faded parchment that served as a blueprint for Arruk's warehouse, the other hand clutching the generous glass of red wine Sidatih had poured for her.

The four of them sat around the apartment's main living space, worn yet comfortable chairs pulled in a circle around a large coffee table stacked with parchment, wine glasses, and what was left of the dessert they picked up on the way back from dinner.

"Why don't we hit the place after the gala is over? Seems like there would be less security," Sidatih said, his focus on the joint he was rolling between his fingers.

"It is clear that you have never done something like this. Security will be doing more sweeps before and after the event to ensure the safety of the items. Yes, there will be an increased security presence during the gala, but also enough people will be there to cause distraction," Mizuno said with steel in her voice. She leveled a glare at Sidatih as she watched him work. "You're doing that all wrong. Give it here." She reached for the half-rolled paper and flower.

Sidatih made a noise of protest but still let Mizuno take every from his hands. "I have been rolling joints for centuries before you were born, and it's been working perfectly well for..." He stopped to stare as Mizuno's long delicate fingers expertly rolled the barely-there paper into a tight shape, perfectly smooth and even. She handed the joint back to Sidatih, who stared at it for several long seconds.

"It is one of my specialties," Mizuno said by way of explanation.

"Take that to the balcony. The smoke will scramble my brain if I inhale too much." Catherine pointed to the pair of doors that opened to a tiny balcony. Sidatih got up, walked over to the doors, and stood next to them while he lit up the joint in his hand. Mizuno rose as well and joined him, standing against the opposite door. The two of them passed the joint between them while Catherine continued.

"The party will be used to get a feel of the inside. Two of us will attend as guests. I'll distract Arruk while Mizuno takes the chance of scoping out the open areas." Catherine took a swig of her wine, letting the rich nutty flavor fill her mouth.

"Why Mizuno? I thought I would escort you," Sidatih asked from across the room.

"Because Arruk knows you, and I don't think he would be pleased to see you," Catherine shot back.

"How does he know me? I haven't been to Athens in forever." Sidatih looked as if he was trying to recall, though Catherine knew his memory tended to be hazy at best. When one had lived as long as Sida, the centuries tended to blur together.

"You may have forgotten, Sida, but I don't think Arruk would ever forgive you for what happened during Thargelia. You did ruin his sacrifice to the gods." Catherine smirked, for a moment picturing that day. Those who worshipped the old gods of Athens were few, and even in the magical world, worship had to be done in secret. That didn't stop Arruk from hosting and carrying on an entire celebration to the twin gods Artemis and Apollo.

"Oh no! That was Arruk. I had completely blocked that year from my memory. It was for the best. Very well, a fair point, and Mizuno will undoubtedly do a much better job than I would." Sidatih took a long drag from the joint before handing over the nub to Mizuno.

"What happened that would make him remember you all these years?" Nachem asked, their voice deep and gravely, sounding unused, though even when they were their chattiest, Catherine knew their voice always sounded that way.

Sidatih blew smoke out into the night air. "Long story short, I ate a bunch of stuff I wasn't supposed to, and maybe saved a person meant to be sacrificed off a cliff. Which to Arruk meant that he would not receive the blessing of the gods for the year and that their wrath upon his head was imminent."

"You cursed him. It took nearly five years for his business to recover," Catherine piped in.

Sidatih threw her a look. "That had nothing to do with me, and everything to do with the Ottoman Empire, and you know it, Mir. The gods of old were long weakened and nearly gone by the time I arrived for my brief stay in Athens. It was fine."

"I believe we can all agree that the ifrit will not be attending. I will be your companion for the evening and map out my route if I am able," Mizuno said, snuffing out the last of the joint.

"Why can't Nachem take you? They are literally your family bodyguard." Sidatih asked, shooting a glare toward Mizuno.

Catherine rubbed the spot between her closed eyes, but it was Nachem who spoke. "As this gala will be attended by mostly magical beings, they can easily see through my glamour. There still remains a prejudice when it comes to golems such as myself. I would be more a distraction and a hindrance than an acceptable companion."

Catherine swirled the dregs of wine left in her glass. "Nachem is right, though I hate that you are. Mizuno, you should attend as my wife. Fewer people will try to talk to us if they believe we're married."

"Less men will hit on you, you mean," Sidatih quipped.

Catherine rolled her eyes and nodded. "That too. We should get something to wear for the party and the gala. I figured we could do some shopping first and do any modifications for weapons or equipment concealing."

"I have brought plenty that would be suitable, all created to my specifications for my work," Mizuno said, resuming her seat. She crossed her ankles and tucked them to the side, hands placed demurely on her lap.

"Are you a fashion designer as well as a thief then?" Sidatih asked, plopping down in his chair with less grace.

Mizuno reached for her wine glass and took a small sip before responding. "Actually, I am. My work is a combination of traditional Japanese pieces working in synergy with contemporary looks. I aim for modern elegance while honoring my heritage."

"That sounds lovely and a tribute to your ancestors, I'm sure." Nachem's tone held a note of reverence. Heritage and remembrance were important to Nachem. After all, they were created on the magic of familial blood; it was crafted into the very fiber of their being.

Nachem carries on the family legacy more than I do, Catherine thought, her gazed fixed on the golem.

And it was true. When she left Crimea, she left behind being Miriam Kokush. The only person to carry on the Kokush legacy was Nachem, crafted from the dirt and rock of her home and infused with the magic and blood of her great-grandfather.

Mortality really was making her more nostalgic and maybe even a tad regretful.

"I will take you to procure a dress, Miriam. I do not trust these two to pick a suitable ensemble for you." Mizuno raised a lazy hand toward Sidatih and Nachem.

Sidatih sniffed indignantly. "I take offense to that. I don't see anything wrong with my taste in clothing.

I would see Mir dressed only in the finest of things if she let me."

Mizuno narrowed her eyes at him. "You arrived here in sweatpants and a sweatshirt from Yale, a university we all know you did not attend since you went to Oxford. Now you are wearing jeans that are not tailored, and French cuffs that are rolled up, wrinkling the fabric. I do not find your taste to be acceptable to pick the correct gowns for Miriam's form."

Sidatih looked down at what he was wearing. Catherine saw nothing wrong with his clothing choices; in fact, she was a fan of the rolled-up sleeves that showed off his wonderfully toned forearms. Sida's body was something that should be admired with less clothing to impede the view. Not that she should be thinking that way, not when they were preparing for the job ahead. There would be time for that after, once they had retrieved the trumpet and got it back to Titania.

"I wore the sweatpants to make traveling more comfortable. But I concede your point. Dress our girl up and make her sparkle more than she already does." Sidatih shot a smile toward Catherine, care and admiration in his eyes.

She smiled back. How had she let so much time pass without seeing Sidatih? He always made her feel so special and so safe, even at their very first meeting. And she knew without a doubt that she made him feel the same. Sida didn't open up like he had without feeling that complete emotional connection to her. That was his nature, and it was something she worried she had taken for granted for a long time.

The four of them finished their planning for the evening and retired to their separate rooms for the night. As Catherine climbed into the sumptuous bed, she considered for a moment walking across the hall to Sidatih's room, climbing into bed with him, and making love to him. But she quickly dashed the thought away.

Only after the job was done. If she allowed herself this now, her focus would be all screwed up, and she couldn't let her feelings get in the way.

Instead, she flopped back against her pillows, put on a sleep sound app on her phone, placed it next to her on the bedside table, and tried to sleep.

The morning sun was too bright as it cut through the gauzy curtains of Catherine's room. Still, she felt refreshed for once, sleeping better than she had in a while. Sleeping was one thing that Catherine wasn't great at. It never came easy for her even before she was made immortal. All the traveling lately must have taken its toll on her, and her body decided it was time to fully relax.

The smell of something cooking filled the room, mingled with the rich scent of espresso brewing. Forgoing real clothes, Catherine shrugged on a robe she found in the closet, its material silky and luxurious against her skin, and headed out into the common area.

Standing at the stove, Nachem concentrated on whatever was cooking in the pan, and Mizuno sat at the island sipping from a small espresso cup. "Good morning," Catherine greeted them as she made her way to the expensive-looking espresso maker sitting on the counter near Nachem.

"Good morning, Miriam. I will have sfakianopita ready for you in a moment. There are some tomatoes and olive oil along with fresh fruit on the counter should you wish to eat before this is finished." Nachem gestured behind them with the spatula, though their focus did not leave the pan on the stove.

Catherine grabbed her full cup, took a seat next to Mizuno, pulled one of the waiting plates toward her, and filled it with the flatbread and tomatoes while she waited for the cheese pie Nachem cooked.

"Sida not up yet?" Catherine looked around, searching for some evidence that Sidatih had already come and gone.

"I heard snoring from his room when I passed. I assume he is still wasting the day away in bed," Mizuno responded, tearing off a piece of flatbread and taking a small bite. "It is good that we will not be conducting business in the morning hours, lest we find our hacker unavailable."

The sound of loud footsteps came from down the hall with Sidatih appearing moments later. "I'm available whenever needed, but sleep is important for growing boys," he said with a wide yawn and a stretch with his arms high over his head, giving Catherine a peak at his tanned stomach. She had to turn her head away quickly.

"Are you not the oldest among us? I do not quite grasp how that makes you a boy," Nachem said, putting a large platter with the sfakianopita down on the counter in front of Catherine.

"Hush you. Let's not bring age into this. I'm not ashamed that I enjoy my sleep and getting plenty of it. I also like to eat, so what are we having?" Sidatih slid onto the stool next to Catherine and let his eyes wander over the breakfast spread. He wasted no time in filling his plate with a bit of everything while the other two took a portion of the cheese pie.

Nachem stood on the opposite side of the island and watched them eat, a pleased smile on their face as everyone mumbled praise and thanks for the food around mouthfuls. Though Nachem could eat, they mostly only did so when out in public to keep up appearances. The golem didn't actually require sustenance, being only a construct of magic.

None of them spoke beyond that until plates were cleaned and seconds were had. "That was an exceptional breakfast, Nachem. Thank you," Catherine said brightly. This earned her a bashful dip of the head from Nachem, who turned away and started to clean up the minimal mess they had made in the kitchen. Catherine knew better than to offer to help clean up, as Nachem would take it as an offense that they could not serve the family correctly.

"Okay, let's lay out the plan for today. Mizuno and are I going shopping. Sidatih, I want you to do some research on the area surrounding Arruk's warehouse. We'll need entrances and exits, escape routes around the building, and anything else you can find that will make getting in and out easier. Whatever you can find. Nachem, you will take a walk. See what you can feel around the building but don't get too close and don't stop unless you need to. Whoever is out there securing the place will be able to feel the magic around you, so be careful." Catherine doled out the tasks with an authoritative air, as if she were back in her classroom lecturing her students.

For a moment, she wished she was back there, back in the comfort and safety of her university lectern and shaping the minds of the future. But for now, her life was on a more exciting turn, and maybe she would go back to teaching later, end her days tucked in her little office, sharing the history she had lived through. Or maybe she wouldn't. She had grown too comfortable over the years; her life lacked the excitement she used to crave. Either way, life was short, and she wasn't going to waste it being unhappy.

They all left the island counter and headed to their respective rooms to get ready for the day. As Catherine walked down the hall, Sidatih reached out for her and pulled her close to his body, her back pulled up close to his chest, out of sight of the others. "Pick something red for me. You always look gorgeous in red," he whispered, ghosting his lips across the shell of her ear. Heat flared throughout her whole body, and Catherine fought hard to suppress a shudder of delight.

"What about being inconspicuous? I'll stand out in something that bold," she said, tilting her head back and resting it against his shoulder. Sidatih's lips were in her hair, placing soft kisses there.

"Albi, you will stand out in any crowd no matter what you wear. You shine like the stars, and even the blind would feel your radiance." He spun her around and pressed a sweet kiss to her lips. Catherine's eyes fluttered closed as she fell into his kiss, letting the feeling of adoration sweep through her. Unlike many of her partners over the centuries who were creatures of lust and passion, Sidatih was a romantic. He was not an overtly sexual person; instead, he sought the soul within her, seeing her body as the case to hold her vibrant spirit.

Sidatih pulled away all too soon, then rested his forehead against hers. "After we complete this job, Mir, I want to talk about a future. I want what time you have left to be with me. Don't think about it now, but when this is over, let's talk."

"Okay." The word came out breathy and hot, and she cupped his cheeks, placed a fleeting kiss on his lips, and walked off into her bedroom, flushed, her heart beating fast. They would have that talk, and Catherine couldn't stop herself from imagining what a life with Sidatih would be like, short though it would be. The idea was far too tempting, knowing that until the end, she would be loved unconditionally.

"What about this one?" Catherine held up a floor-length gown in a shade of pale olive. It was simple, very little adornment other than a few pieces of lace and a modest slit. She could easily blend in with the crowd. Nobody would pay her an ounce of attention.

Mizuno eyed the piece as if it were personally offensive and scoffed. "Absolutely not. It would be no better than a cotton sack." The woman wasn't even looking at any of the dresses that lined the store. In fact, she seemed bored and uninterested entirely.

"Is there anything that is acceptable here?" Catherine asked, a bite to her tone. She was annoyed that Mizuno wasn't being more helpful. When she asked the thief to come along, she thought she had made the right choice in shopping partner, someone whose life partly revolved around fashion.

But it seemed Catherine had been wrong.

"There is nothing in this shop that I will approve of you wearing. Now, I have let you waste our time enough. Come with me." Mizuno didn't wait for Catherine's reply. Instead, she grabbed Catherine's hand and pulled her from the shop.

Mizuno was shorter than Catherine, yet her stride was long and quick, causing Catherine to nearly be pulled along. "Where are we going?" she asked, correcting her steps so she didn't stumble.

Mizuno didn't even spare her a glance, instead focusing straight ahead like she was on a mission. "I have a friend in this city that has a few dresses for you. I won't accept anything else on you but her work." That was all Mizuno would say as she dragged Catherine for what felt like half the city, though it was only a few blocks.

The building Mizuno brought her to was a small place, the shop little more than one window and one door. The sign above was small yet neat and simply said "Arachne."

Spider.

It made sense that Mizuno would bring Catherine to a place called Arachne since the thief herself was a jorōgumo, a spider demon, though Catherine had never seen the other woman's spider form.

Inside the building, there was one large mostly empty wooden room and a back wall with a single open doorway. Woven tapestries hung on the walls in starbursts of color. Some depicted scenes from mythology with spiders heavily featured. Others seemed to be more abstract, simple patterns of colors, though these too all seemed to form the shape of a spider.

From the doorway, a woman appeared. She was tall and curvy in all the right places, soft and rounded with golden hair wrapped in a braided crown around her head. Glistening black eyes shone, though Catherine was surprised at first when she realized that the woman had no irises, no whites of her eyes. They were all black. Her olive skin had a golden undertone that made her seem like she was lit from inside. A simple shift dress made of white linen hugged her curves.

"Mizuno!" the woman shrieked with delight, crossing the room in a few long strides to pull Mizuno close and kiss each cheek. The smile the woman wore as she pulled away was wide, bright, and transformed her face into pure happiness.

"Singa, it has been too long. How are you?" Mizuno returned the kisses and held the hands of the woman, speaking in Greek. Their affection was sisterly, and it was the most animated Catherine had ever seen Mizuno.

Singa squeezed Mizuno's hands. "I am so well. I have your order all ready. Is this the canvas?" Singa asked, turning to Catherine. The woman lunged forward and pressed a kiss to each of Catherine's cheeks before sliding her hands down Catherine's arms and pulling her arms out to her side.

Singa appraised Catherine's body in a calculated way which caused Catherine to feel completely exposed and left wanting. The woman before her was a goddess in proportion, and Catherine suddenly felt so plain standing next to the two glamorous women.

"Oh, my gods, if you aren't completely gorgeous. Yes, Mizuno, you were so right. The colors are perfect for her complexion, and the structure for the gala dress is going to show off her figure perfectly. If only all canvases could be as perfect as you," Singa said as she dropped Catherine's hands, grabbed at her waist as if she were measuring, and gave Catherine's sides a squeeze.

Catherine didn't know how to react to Singa's words or the fact that she was being manhandled by a complete stranger, but she had learned long ago to mostly roll with whatever was happening until things became dangerous. There didn't seem even a remote chance that anything like that would happen in this shop, especially not with Mizuno around, so Catherine allowed the touches for now.

"You ordered a dress for me?" Catherine asked, turning her gaze toward her companion.

"Not just any dress but probably one of my best creations. As well as a simpler gown suitable for a small gathering. I'm Singa, by the way. Mizuno is so rude sometimes and didn't bother to introduce us. And as you could probably guess from, well, everything." She gestured to the tapestries on the wall and a sign that matched the one outside above the door on the back wall that said the shop name. "I am a descendant of Arachne, you know, the one who out-weaved Athena and got turned into a spider. That one, which makes my family some of the best weavers and now designers in all of Greece."

Singa spoke so fast and so enthusiastically that Catherine couldn't help but be taken in by the energy of the woman. Not to mention she found Singa's family history fascinating.

"Catherine. I should have introduced myself sooner. I'm eager to see what Mizuno has commissioned from you! She told me absolutely nothing and instead let me shop around to no success," Catherine said with a laugh.

Singa gasped and turned back to Mizuno. "You let her walk around a store like a common shopper and didn't bring her straight here? I'm disappointed, Mizuno." Though Singa's face didn't actually show an ounce of disappointment, and Mizuno smiled at her in return, one that actually reached her eyes.

"I was having a bit of fun, and it allowed me to spend extra time with her," Mizuno said without a hint of remorse.

Singa seemed to accepted this and nodded her head. "Can't say I blame you. Catherine, you really are a beauty." And with that, Singa flounced away, back through the doorway into the back room, probably to retrieve the dress.

"I don't know what she's talking about because I am clearly the old hag in the room compared to the two of you," Catherine said with a self-deprecating laugh. Not that Catherine thought of herself as unattractive; she knew she was pleasing to look at. But compared to statuesque Mizuno and the goddess that was Singa, Catherine felt old and plain. That might be her vanity talking since she was already starting to see new wrinkles lining her face—faint, but they were still there. She should be grateful for them; for five hundred years, her face had remained unchanged, and Catherine was now earning those lines.

Even though it had been her choice, Catherine still struggled with the idea of mortality. She probably would until the day she died.

"I can hear you thinking from here, Miriam. What is on your mind?" Mizuno's smooth voice broke through her thoughts.

Catherine turned toward her companion and gave her a small smile. "Mortality and my aging body," she answered truthfully, not sure why she decided to be open with Mizuno. They weren't friends, and Catherine couldn't be sure if the other woman held any resentment at being called up on her master's debt. Not that she questioned Mizuno's integrity. She would no doubt consider it her duty to fulfil the debt.

Mizuno regarded her for a long moment, saying nothing. "I do not understand what it feels like to be mortal, but I do know that you will age with only grace and beauty."

Catherine chortled. "I don't know about that, but thank you for saying so anyway. It does wonders for my ego."

Mizuno's elegantly shaped brows furrowed slightly. Even then her beauty remained unchanged. "Even in my youth, I thought you beautiful. I do not see that changing even as you change with the years." She sounded so sincere, and Catherine thought she detected a note of reverence in the other woman's voice.

But Mizuno looked at her with open awe as her features settled into her smooth look, and Catherine felt a blush rise to her cheeks. She had always found Mizuno to be more than simply attractive; she was absolutely gorgeous. Catherine had been with many beautiful men and women in her life, but only Mizuno seemed to exude grace and power while looking delicate as a flower.

It was lucky that Singa bustled back into the room carrying two large garment bags and a stand on which to hang them. The interruption chased away the heat that had started in Catherine's belly and any wayward thoughts toward Mizuno. She shouldn't be thinking of her team as anything more than her cohorts right now. Catherine definitely shouldn't be thinking about sleeping with not one but two members of her team.

"Okay, you need to try these on to see if there's anything I need to alter." Singa unzipped the first bag, letting the long swaths of fabric spill out.

"Right here?" Catherine asked slightly incredulous. She had no problem with nudity, but it just seemed strange to undress in the middle of a shop.

"Yes, so drop them. Modesty is for prudes and has no place in my shop," Singa said, already pulling at the sleeve of Catherine's leather jacket. The other woman wasted no time undressing Catherine without waiting for help. In seconds, Catherine stood nearly naked in the middle of the shop front, her black underwear the only stitch of clothing she wore. Even her bra was discarded on the floor with the rest of her clothes since Singa insisted a bra would not go with the gala dress.

As the silky material flowed over Catherine's body, she couldn't help but think she wasn't an old hag after all.

CHAPTER 10

"**D**o you have any idea how easy it is to get into people's schedules? And it's not just his schedule. I've got his email, too. Honestly, it's like nobody cares about security these days," Sidatih whined, leaning over his computer to stare at the screen.

Catherine sat in the chair next to him, her legs tucked up and crossed over the cushion. "Not everybody cares about online security like you do, Sida. Now, what's his schedule look like tomorrow?"

Sidatih studied his screen. "Looks like he has a lunch meeting at some café called Kafenion. I think we can arrange a meet cute, and hopefully you can snag a party invite." That was the plan anyway. Catherine would stage a "coincidental" run in where she would be on her way out of the café as Arruk arrived. There wouldn't be enough time for catch up, so she could keep it brief. Then the hope would be he would offer her an invite so they could better catch up. If he didn't offer outright, Catherine would find a way to steer the conversation toward the warehouse and prompt him to it.

If all else failed though, she and Mizuno would simply crash the party if, or more accurately, when Sidatih hacked the list and put them on it.

"It seems that a lot of this plan hinges on chance. Are we sure this is the best course of action?" Nachem asked, setting down cups of tea for them.

"You're not wrong. A lot rides on the hunch that very little about Arruk has changed in centuries, which really isn't that outlandish. He is a generous person, and it's been..." Catherine sighed deeply, "a very long time since we've seen each other. I have confidence that he will extend an invitation." And she was confident. Arruk had remained largely unchanged in their original acquaintance, and she doubted much had changed about his personality.

"Well, you'll try tomorrow, and if it doesn't work out, we'll just find another way," Sidatih said with certainty.

"At least the gala will be easier to get into. That's just buying a few tickets, which we've already done," Catherine said, standing up from the chair and stretching. Her whole body felt stiff lately, and she felt much older than she looked.

Sidatih made a noise of agreement. "Not cheap, though."

Catherine chuckled. "It's not like we don't have the money. Besides, it's for charity."

Sidatih dismissed her words with a wave and turned back to his computer. Catherine considered their conversation over and wandered from the room. She went down the hall back to the bedrooms, intending to go to her own room and rest for a while. But the sight of Mizuno's cracked door had her veering off course.

She knocked on the threshold to keep from moving the door. "Come in," Mizuno's voice called out from within. Catherine pushed open the door the rest of the way and stepped inside the room, closing the door behind her but not moving any farther into the room.

Mizuno sat on the floor, her eyes shut, her back ramrod straight with hands resting on her knees. She was clothed in a silk robe of deep purple with delicate blossoms covering the fabric. It was tied loosely, exposing a large swath of smooth skin down to her navel. Her straight black hair was tied back low, showing off the planes of her face, unadorned and free of makeup.

Not wanting to disturb Mizuno further, Catherine leaned back against the door and focused her gaze on the woman on the floor. Mizuno didn't stir, didn't acknowledge Catherine's presence for several minutes. From her spot at the door, Catherine tried not to fidget while she waited, even one minute was a long time to just watch someone meditate. It felt very much like she was intruding, even though Mizuno had invited her in.

Just as she was contemplating leaving the room, Mizuno spoke up, though she kept her eyes closed. "I can practically feel how troubled your mind is, Miriam." The sound of her voice, though she spoke softly, seemed so loud in the room after the minutes of silence. It jarred Catherine away from the door and finally pushed her to move closer to where Mizuno sat on the floor.

"Sit with me and clear your mind," Mizuno urged, patting the spot next to her on the floor. She did not look at Catherine, her eyes still shut as she moved her hand back to her knee, assuming her earlier position. With careful steps, Catherine moved to sit next to Mizuno, leaving several inches between them. She crossed her legs and let her hands fall limp on her own knees, a more comfortable position for her than Mizuno's more rigid posture, and her eyes fell shut.

Meditation was nothing new to Catherine, and usually she was quite adept at clearing her head and finding a peaceful connection between mind and body. She fell into an easy breathing pattern, focusing on each breath, slow and even. Her whole being knew what to do, and with each exhale, she imagined she was blowing all thoughts and worries out of herself.

The only sound for a long time was her own breathing and Mizuno's. Faint sounds from the street below, or of Sidatih or Nachem moving around from the other rooms filtered in, but they were dulled and barely penetrated Catherine's consciousness. The dim light of the room kept her from being distracted by any brightness and naturally made her eyes want to remain shut.

Slowly, stress eased from her body, her shoulders relaxed, and the knot of tension in her stomach loosened a little. Catherine might have been happy sitting like that all day, but already she could feel the pin-pricks of her foot falling asleep. Reluctantly, she began to shake the appendage, and while that helped, it also broke her concentration.

"You fidget too much for someone who is supposed to be a master thief," Mizuno quipped next to her. She had remained perfectly still through their entire meditation session; one could almost mistake her for a statue. But she moved now, her beautiful dark eyes opening and a serene smile gracing her pale pink lips.

"I was a master thief once. Now I'm finding it harder to remain still," Catherine responded, turning her head to regard Mizuno fully. There was a look of understanding in the woman's eyes, even if she couldn't relate. The two women regarded each other in silence for several heartbeats, and Catherine found it was easy to get lost in the dark pools of Mizuno's eyes.

Mizuno stood up suddenly, all fluid grace as she did so, and held out her hand to Catherine who took it and let herself be pulled up. "Come. Kneel on the bed and let me give you peace. My master was trained in the art of anma before the Tokugawa shugonate decreed it a profession only for the blind. He taught me eventually, only after the Meiji Restoration, of course."

Catherine didn't move. She stared at Mizuno instead, unsure of what she should do. Mizuno easily read her unease. "It will help your body and mind. You do not need to take off your clothing. Though I warn you, it can be quite ... aggressive ... to promote the blood flow."

With a sigh of relief, Catherine followed Mizuno's instructions and climbed onto the bed, situating herself until she reached a comfortable position. The thought of being even partially unclothed in front of Mizuno was too great a temptation, so she was glad for the layers of clothing between them.

Mizuno took up a position behind Catherine, and her cool smooth hands started by gently touching over Catherine's shoulders. It was soothing caresses at first, then she gripped Catherine's left shoulder forcefully with one hand while the other was placed flat against the shoulder blade, and she pulled back on Catherine's shoulder. It didn't hurt exactly, but it was by no means the type of massage where she posed the risk of falling into a leisurely sleep.

With practiced hands, Mizuno continued to work her way down Catherine's body, pushing and pulling, kneading, tapping, and pressing against her at specific points on her body. Skin warming with the increased circulation, Catherine hovered on the border of pleasure and pain and marveled at the way the tension fell from her body. It seemed she breathed a little easier, aches that she didn't even realize she had began to fall away, and her mind was blissfully blank for once. The jorgumo had been right; it was exactly what Catherine needed.

"There. How do you feel?" Mizuno's voice was soft, cutting through the haze of Catherine's brain.

"Hm? Oh, better. Much better. Thank you, Mizuno. Truly," she said, craning her head to look back at Mizuno, the muscles in her neck feeling much looser now. She saw Mizuno nod and then remove herself from the bed, the weight on it barely shifting as she did so.

Not wanting to overstay her welcome and potentially do something stupid, Catherine thanked Mizuno again and left the room, finally making it to her own space and shutting the door behind her. She rested her head against the door, unsure of what was happening to her. Maybe she had gone too long without a lover, but she found herself not only wanting to reconnect with Sidatih, someone she always kept coming back to, but she felt the pull of lust toward the graceful Mizuno. The attraction to Sida was understandable, and they had been lovers over the centuries and had constantly found each other again. But her draw toward Mizuno was confusing, though not unpleasant. Was she really so starved for affection that she couldn't keep her mind from wandering to her companions?

CHAPTER 11

The café wasn't particularly crowded that day. Catherine had been sitting for nearly forty-five minutes. The plan was to look every bit like a casual diner, and then the moment she spotted Aruk, she would move to the exit, casually bumping into him.

Her eyes were trained on the sidewalk. Sitting at one of the outside bistro tables despite the chill had been the better idea. She could keep an eye on both ends of the road and position herself to be most visible. There was less chance of missing Arruk if she was right there before the door. The café was located in the magical sector of the city, a safe guarded place where creatures didn't have to use their glamours to move about, so Arruk should be easy to spot.

Right on time, she saw the hulking frame of the minotaur approach the café. He was tall, easily over seven feet, and covered in hair. While his physique was humanoid, and he wore a well-tailored and expensive tuxedo, his head was definitely not human. Instead, he had a fuzzy snout with a shining diamond ring through his nose. Expressive black eyes glittered in the sunlight, and atop his head sat a pair of polished and gold-capped horns.

Arruk had not changed at all since Catherine had last seen him.

Standing, Catherine stalled as if she were taking her time collecting her things. Arruk made for the door, but his eyes briefly glanced her way. He took half a step forward and stopped, doing a double take at her.

"Miriam?" His deep voice sounded like the thunder of an oncoming storm, and it sent a shiver down Catherine's spine, though she wasn't sure if it was from fear or elation at seeing her old friend again.

Probably a bit of both, especially since she was there to find a way to rob him.

"Arruk. It's been a long time," Catherine kept her voice pleasantly surprised, determined not to let the encounter break her. Maybe all her mental preparation hadn't been enough after all.

There was a small, if a little sad, smile on Arruk's face. His dark eyes seemed a little watery as he gazed down at her, taking in her features. "A very long time. Several centuries I believe. What brings you back to Greece?" he asked, the small smile staying on his face.

"I've been doing a bit of traveling the last few years, visiting old friends and some of my old haunts. It seemed inevitable I would end up here." It wasn't even a fabrication. Before Titania's job came into the picture, Catherine had every intention of making it to Greece for the very purpose of seeing Arruk. She had just hoped to put it off a little longer, knowing their reunion would hurt more than many of the others from her past.

And oh, it hurt so much worse knowing that she wasn't really there to see him, to mend old wounds, and to try to reignite an old friendship. No, instead she was going to rob him and hope he never found out it was her. She would let him down once again, just as she had all those years ago. Only this time, it would be so much worse than just leaving and never returning.

Arruk made a humming noise. "I heard you had been making your way around the world. I was wondering when you would find yourself my way or if you had forgotten me entirely." He said it with a smile, though it continued to look more forced than genuine.

Catherine felt like hanging her head in shame. She had thought about him and how she was going to avoid him for as long as possible during her walkabout. Not that she wouldn't see him. She had honestly planned to make her way to Greece... eventually. "I could never forget you, Arruk," she whispered, remorse coloring her words. Not that he knew the feeling was partially due to her avoidance of him but also of what she was planning to do to him.

Damn Titania and her stupid fucking debt.

The minotaur gave her a look, like he was unsure if she was being sincere, but then his face returned to something more amusingly even. A chime sounded between them, and Arruk turned his face away from her to pull out his cell phone from his pocket. "Shit, I'm running late for a meeting. Listen, Miriam, it's great to see you, and I would like to take the time to catch up. I'm having a party this weekend before a gala I'm hosting. I would love to see you there at my warehouse. I have some new treasures I want to show off. I'll add your name to the list with a plus one, of course."

Just as she planned, Arruk had extended the invitation. Catherine's smile was genuine when she responded, "Of course. I would love that very much."

Arruk nodded, his smile broadening. "Brilliant. Seven o'clock on Friday. I will see you then, Miriam." She returned his smile, and then he was gone with another nod, disappearing into the restaurant with one more backward glance, like he couldn't believe she was really there.

Once he was out of sight, Catherine sighed deeply, feeling the prick of tears at her eyes that she hadn't expected. She quickly dashed them away and headed away from the café. Phase one of their plan was complete, and it was time to prepare for the next step.

CHAPTER 12

"So, there's two guards posted at two entrances. The whole place is a safety violation. You would think there would be more doors in case of emergency," Catherine said, poring over the sketch of the warehouse Sidatih and Nachem had created the previous week.

"I don't think there's like a magical OSHA to fine you if your building doesn't have the proper amount of emergency exists here, albi." Sidatih laughed.

Catherine made a harumphing sound. "Well, maybe there should be. There's going to be around five hundred people at the gala in a few days, in a gallery of highly volatile magical items, of which I'm sure something explodes. Could be devastating."

"Really selling the whole job here, Mir. Maybe it's too dangerous for you to be going in. We can always send in Mizuno on her own." Sidatih wasn't trying to be patronizing. Catherine was well aware of that. But it still stung a small part of her heart to think that Sidatih might question her ability to hold her own. Just because she wasn't immortal anymore didn't necessarily make her more vulnerable in a situation like she was heading into.

"Miriam can handle herself fine, ifrit. And I will be by her side throughout the night since we are attending as a married couple," Mizuno said in the bored tone she had started reserving for Sidatih alone.

The ifrit narrowed his eyes at Mizuno. "Doesn't mean I trust you to keep her safe. Truth of the matter is that I don't know you well enough yet to know how you operate, Mizuno. I've met many a thief with no integrity at all."

The slim knife embedded itself into the back of the chair scant inches from Sidatih's head, the blade flying faster than even Sidatih could track. His eyes were wide as he registered what happened, but Mizuno looked as if she hadn't moved at all. "Never question my integrity again or my loyalty to Miriam. It is unwavering."

The ifrit reached up and pulled the knife from the chair, holding it between his fingers for a moment before disappearing it in a puff of dark smoke. "Noted," he said solemnly.

"If you are all finished acting like jealous children, I suggest the ladies adjourn to dress for tonight's activities," Nachem chimed in, clearly exasperated by the whole ordeal. Catherine imagined they felt like the only adult in the room sometimes. Poor Nachem had endured centuries of petty squabbles between members of the Kokush family. It was a wonder they hadn't begged to be released from the magic long ago.

The three of them said no more, and Catherine and Mizuno followed Nachem's instruction and filed off to their respective rooms to dress. The gown Mizuno had made for the party was a simple black dress, the bodice fitted with a deep v-neckline and an even deeper v-cut down the back. The skirt flared from the waist down to her ankles, and she added a pair of red heels for a pop of color. She placed silver bands on each wrist and diamond studs in her ears as the only adornment she wore. It was definitely more party dress than formal event gown.

When she finally emerged from her room, she saw that Mizuno had already finished getting ready and was waiting for her in the living room with Nachem and Sidatih. The thief was dressed in a more elegant, if that was possible, version of one of her designs. The top was a traditional houmongi in a deep red with a delicate floral pattern. The bottom, however, flared out into a wrap skirt just past the knees in an imitation of the houmongi bottom half. A thick obi in black with white flowers bisected the two parts of the dress with a red tie that matched the dress color wrapped around the center. Her dark hair was pulled back into an elegant updo behind her head. She was a stunning mix of traditional and contemporary, and Catherine found she couldn't stop staring at Mizuno.

"Mir, you look breathtaking." Sidatih's voice cut through her ogling, and Catherine shyly looked down at her own dress. Sure, she felt good in the dress, and it was a far cry from the ensembles she sported as a professor for years. Those outfits were a cry for help but good camouflage for what she needed to do while in New Britain. Few people asked questions if the frumpy professor didn't seem to age at all. Now she felt powerful, like she was back in her own skin again.

She did a little twirl on the spot, letting the skirt swish around her ankles, and she couldn't help the smile spreading across her face. "We should probably go before I decide to stay and let you compliment me all night," Catherine said with a laugh.

"I wouldn't mind that at all," Sidatih whispered, placing a tender kiss to her temple before ushering the women out the door.

The sleek black car dropped the two women off in front of the door to the warehouse. Valet in crisp uniforms were there to help guests from their cars. Arruk had done some remodeling to the warehouse in the intervening years. The storefront was now more of a grand entrance with elaborately carved columns holding up an archway. Real fairy lights hovered in the air above them as Catherine and Mizuno linked arms and walked into the building. At the door, an imposing gryphon stood, holding a tablet in one claw, taking the names of each guest before consulting the list on the screen. There weren't going to be more than fifty or so people, and Catherine hoped Arruk had remembered to put them on the list.

Her fears were quickly assuaged as they walked up, gave their names, and were ushered in without another word. A few of the other guests filtered in around them as they walked into the building proper, and the sounds of a string quartet drifted as they made their way inside. In previous days, the front of the building acted as a functional shop with the back housing the magical Storage Room, much like it did in the one in New Britain. The space here had been converted into a grand foyer, decorated with human works of art like a regular gallery, but the magic could be felt radiating from behind a wide set of French doors that were flung open wide to invite guests to the heart of the Storage Room.

As they approached the doors, Catherine took a deep fortifying breath and straightened her spine. The biggest challenge tonight was overcoming the ghosts of her past, and she could do that. She had been doing that for the last three years. This would be, while not exactly easy, manageable.

But what had once been the Storage Room was hardly recognizable now. The shelves that had once filled the entire space were long gone, their utilitarian uses no longer needed. Instead, glass cases and protective clear boxes on plinths dotted the floors. The room itself was so large, magically enhanced so that no walls could actually be seen. Catherine wondered how much of the area was actually filled, but knowing Arruk, what space he did have left would be artfully arranged so that no empty space remained.

Dozens of people in party finery milled about carrying crystal glasses of wine, glancing over the artifacts in the cases, and talking amongst themselves. As she and Mizuno made their way deeper into the room, eyes turned toward them, some appraising and others hungry and heated as they took in the forms of the two women.

A waiter in a simple outfit of black slacks and white shirt with black tie came up and offered them a tray of red wine, which they took to at least keep up appearances.

A quick scan of the room and Catherine saw no sign of Arruk. There were a few minotaurs in attendance, but she figured Arruk would either be doing the rounds by now or waiting to make a grand entrance himself.

"Let's take a walk. See if we can locate the trumpet. Pick a direction but stay within sight. It would be easy to lose each other here even with this small crowd." Catherine pulled her arm from Mizuno's and scanned the area around them to decide where to go.

"This place is much larger than the plans we have would suggest," Mizuno said quietly, her gaze wandering off in the opposite direction of Catherine, deciding her own route to take.

"It's been several centuries since Ezra was last here, and the same goes for me. Clearly, Arruk has expanded since then," Catherine responded. "Let's meet back in thirty minutes, but signal if you need an extraction from meddling people."

Catherine turned to head off, but Mizuno caught her wrist in a firm but loose grip. She turned back to face the thief. "And what should I do if the minotaur becomes suspicious?"

There was only a hint of concern on Mizuno's face, and Catherine felt a pang of guilt for making her worry. "Do nothing unless you think you have to."

Mizuno's eyes narrowed. "And what will you do if faced with his questioning?"

Catherine drew in her bottom lip and bit down, unsure of how to answer that question. Mizuno's eyes followed the movement, gaze drawn to Catherine's mouth. "I'll figure it out if and when it happens." She pulled away from Mizuno again and turned, a heated feeling pooling low in her belly at the look she got from Mizuno. There were too many conflicting emotions with her team lately, and Catherine had to wonder if she had just been alone for too long or if she was longing for a connection that would last.

No time to think of that now. She had a trumpet to find and a minotaur to hopefully placate.

It was like walking through a museum. Each piece was set in a specific spot, lights illuminating them with placards below giving details on each item. Catherine could feel the magic radiating out of the displays, and like a film over it, layers of newer magic, warding magic. Arruk really took his security seriously. Maybe she should have brought Nachem instead of Mizuno, so that they could have gotten a firsthand look at the wards. Though it was true that many people held an extreme prejudice against golems.

But Catherine did come prepared. From a tiny concealed pocket in the front drape of her dress, she withdrew a small coin, the engravings rubbed clean from centuries of use. The coin had once been part of a halsgezeige, a neck band her family members used to ward off the evil eye. But with just the one coin and a bit of tinkering with the magic, it worked as a way to siphon a sample of the magic from the wards, something that Nachem would be able to analyze and hopefully, subvert.

Palming the coin, she kept it concealed until she needed to use it. There was no way for her to know if the wards were different for each case or if each had the same layers of spells, so her best course of action was to find the trumpet and use the coin on that particular case.

She mingled around the various cases, eyes scanning quickly to find the trumpet, but there was nothing even remotely close to what she was looking for. Turning, she caught Mizuno's passing silhouette a few yards away. Mizuno gave a small shake of her head and continued walking, and Catherine's heart sank a little. It was going to be nearly impossible to locate the trumpet tonight. There was simply too much in the collection to find one item easily.

If only a locator spell had been feasible, it would have made everything so much easier. But with the wards and just the sheer amount of magic in the place, a locator spell would not only give them away but would be completely useless once it was in the collections.

Barely managing to hold back a growl of frustration, Catherine turned a corner around a large case and nearly ran into a large body. An oversized paw reached out and steadied her as she started to teeter on her heels, and she was righted and held firm. Catherine looked up at the person she nearly collided with. Arruk stood towering over her, a small grin on his maw. He was in a well-tailored navy suit that was very broad across the chest and tapered down to his much narrower waist. The ring through his nose was gold and matched the expensive gold and crystal watch on his wrist. His gold-capped horns glittered under the lights of the gallery.

"Miriam, good to see you again." His deep voice sounded like the thunder of an oncoming storm, and it sent a shiver down Catherine's spine, though she wasn't sure if it was from apprehension or elation at seeing her old friend again for the second time in as many days.

Probably a bit of both, especially given what she planned to do.

"Arruk. It's wonderful to see you. Thank you again for inviting me. I know it was so last minute and probably threw off your count." Catherine kept her voice pleasant and even, determined not to let this encounter break her. It was her role to distract him.

He waved her off with a giant dark fur covered hand. "It was no trouble at all, though my secretary might not say the same. Come. Let me show you around. This is a far cry from the humble collection I had in my youth." He placed a hand on the small of her back, warm fur against the chill of her exposed skin.

There was nothing Catherine could do but let Arruk guide her around the room, indicating with the hand holding a half-full glass of champagne at the various objects behind the glass. It was exactly what she needed to do anyway. From the corner of her eye, Catherine spotted Mizuno keeping pace with them from a distance while also seeming to be interested in whatever was in front of her. It would only take a small gesture to signal to the thief she needed an exit strategy.

"So, tell me, Miriam, what has been going on with your life since we last met?" Arruk changed the conversation quickly away from the displays.

Catherine was unsure of how to answer at first. Did she tell him about her mortal state? Or did she keep that fact to herself? She didn't want to see the pitying look on his face if she told him she would soon die. Arruk valued his immortality, loved living as long as he had. But keeping as honest as possible would be the best course of action. The more she kept to the truth, the fewer lies she would have to keep track of.

"I've been teaching history at a university in the States. A few years ago, my curse was lifted, and I was made mortal again, so I've been taking the time I have left to revisit old friends," she said, her tone light, conversational, instead of giving in to the swirl of emotions within.

Arruk arrested his movement, stopping before another case to turn his gaze on Catherine. "Now that I had not heard. You had eternity and you let it go? I don't think I understand."

Few immortals did, so Catherine wasn't surprised by Arruk's response. She shrugged. "It felt like it was time. I have been released as Ezra's keeper. He has a wife now and is speaking to his mother again. There was no need for me anymore. So, I had no purpose to keep going on with a long life." It wasn't that simple, but Catherine wasn't about to go into detail about why she chose to become mortal, not that she was entirely convinced her decision had been the right one.

To her surprise though, Arruk chuckled. "Ezra married—now that is quiet the revelation. His poor wife."

Catherine couldn't help her own small laugh that escaped her. A few years ago, it did seem absolutely absurd that Ezra would marry, but he and Brie were good together, especially since Brie had brought him out of the darkness he had lived in for many centuries. She helped him see the truth behind the lies his old mentor had weaved and brought him back to his mother, to his family. In Catherine's mind, they were a perfect match.

"Oh, I assure you, Brie is more than up to the task. And she loves him, so I'm sure that makes it easier for the both of them." Catherine let herself smile, a genuine smile as she thought of the two.

A slender hand snaked around Catherine's waist from behind, and an instant later, Mizuno pressed her body against Catherine's. "Darling, are you going to introduce me to your friend?" Mizuno's voice whispered in her ear, loud enough for Arruk to hear, but soft and sensual as well, as if they really were lovers.

Catherine turned her head, her nose brushing against Mizuno's as she looked into the other woman's dark eyes. "Of course, love. This is Arruk, the owner of this collection and an old friend. Arruk." She turned away from Mizuno to look at the minotaur. "This is my wife, Mizuno." Catherine's arm wrapped around Mizuno's waist so that the two women were pressed close together without an inch of space between them. Mizuno's body was cool against hers, but it was a grounding sensation; the churning in her stomach eased a little.

"Pleasure to meet you, Arruk. Your collection is unparalleled." Mizuno was a natural at cavorting with these types of crowds, and she knew exactly how to stoke Arruk's ego it seemed. His chest puffed up a little in pride, and Catherine knew he was already charmed.

"The pleasure is all mine. Your wife is absolutely stunning, Catherine. I wish you both many happy years together." His smile was bright; he was genuinely happy for them. A pang of shame shook her to her core. Another deception to add to the list.

"What do you have here?" Mizuno asked, using her free hand to point to the case next to them. Arruk brightened further at the chance to continue showing off his collection. It took a moment for Catherine to realize exactly where they had stopped in their chat.

"Ah yes, Pheme's Trumpet. It was created by the goddess Pheme and was used to spread widely the gossip she heard, and trust me, there was a lot of gossip to spread. Lucky for me, she misplaced it centuries ago, and I happened to come across it in a marketplace in Marrakesh of all places. Not my most impressive piece but a fun story behind it all the same." Arruk beamed at the treasure, like he took personal joy in each piece.

"How fascinating. Do you have many pieces from the gods in your collection? I would love to see if you had any from my home country." Mizuno spun her web of charm, and Arruk was falling right into it, eager for the chance to show her everything he had from Japan.

"You two go along. I'm going to use the washroom and get another drink," Catherine said, pulling away from Mizuno.

"Come find me when you are done," Mizuno said before planting her lips on Catherine's. The kiss was soft, but there was a surprising passion behind it. Mizuno hadn't let go of Catherine's waist, instead pulling her closer as her pillowy lips claimed Catherine's. It set off a heat low in her belly, and even as Mizuno pulled away and followed Arruk, Catherine had to pause for a moment to clear her head. That kiss felt a lot more than just for show.

When she had recovered and Mizuno and Arruk were out of sight, Catherine pulled out the coin she had tucked away and held it up to the glass case. The tiny pulse of magic as the coin gobbled up a sample piece of the magic reverberated through her hand. It took only seconds for the coin to heat up and signify it was full. Catherine quickly and discreetly tucked the coin back into the pouch of her dress and walked through the warehouse to the washrooms at the front.

Not long after, she found Mizuno and Arruk speaking in front of a collection of masks, worn with age, but identifiable as Kabuki costuming. Mizuno held out her hand to Catherine as she approached, and Catherine placed her hand in the other woman's and laced their fingers together. "Are you enjoying yourself, love?" she asked the thief.

Mizuno nodded and smiled at Arruk, who was completely off his guard under Mizuno's gaze. "Oh yes, very much so. Your friend has shown me some of the most magnificent artifacts, many of which I have only ever heard about in stories. He has quite the collection." She was far more animated like this than her normal countenance. And while the charming Mizuno was a wonder, Catherine found she much preferred Mizuno's stoic nature. It suited her more.

"Would you like to stay longer? I know you have a long day tomorrow," Catherine asked. Now that they had finished what they came to do, Catherine was hoping to make a quick exit without looking suspicious.

"There's so much still to see, and I would love to stay, but you are right. I will hate myself in the morning if I do not get enough sleep," Mizuno said, batting her lashes at Catherine, really playing up the act of being in love.

"It was lovely to meet you, Mizuno. Miriam, it was wonderful to see you again. Perhaps you would like to take lunch with me sometime this coming week. To catch up and where we can actually talk for longer than a few minutes." Arruk looked at her expectantly.

That was something Catherine hadn't considered. She was prepared to meet Arruk at the party and gala, but she never suspected he would want to spend additional time with her. She really must be out of practice when it came to friendships, or former friendships—she wasn't quite sure where they stood.

"I would like that very much," she found herself responding.

Arruk nodded, a large smile on his maw. "Excellent. Let's say Tuesday at eleven? It's one of the few times I have before the gala next weekend. You are welcome to meet me at my home in Kifissia. There are many fantastic restaurants in the area and we can walk." He reached into his pocket and produced a business card and pen, quickly writing down the address before handing the card over to her.

Catherine nodded, keeping the card in her hand. "Sounds perfect. I will see you then." Mizuno threw a wave over her shoulder as she led Catherine by the hand out of the warehouse and onto the street. Their hands remained laced together as they waited for the car to arrive, and even as they drove back to the apartment, they kept pressed close together in the backseat. It was a silent ride; there were too many thoughts going through Catherine's brain for her to say anything.

It had been hard to see Arruk again but so easy to talk to him, which only served to make her feel more guilty since in just a short time she would be stealing from him. This felt so much harder than it did even earlier that day.

"Come along, Miriam. Let us get you upstairs." Mizuno's voice broke through her introspection, and Catherine allowed herself to be led out of the car and back to their homebase.

Nachem and Sidatih were sitting in the common room waiting for them, Nachem with a book in their hand, another romance, and Sida with his laptop spread across his thighs. "Get what we needed?" Sidatih asked, closing the laptop. "Are you alright, albi?" His gaze settled on Catherine, his brows furrowed with concern.

"She needs rest. Seeing the minotaur has taken much out of her emotionally," Mizuno said, giving a warning glare at the other two to contradict her. Neither did. One look at Catherine probably told them everything they needed to know.

"I have the ward sample," Catherine managed, pulling the coin from the pouch in the front of her dress. She vaguely registered Sidatih's cheeks turning red at the sight of her reaching between her cleavage.

The warm coin was handed off to Nachem who accepted it with a nod.

Mizuno tugged on her hand and led her down the hallway toward Catherine's room with no protest from Catherine. The two slipped inside the darkened room, and Mizuno turned on the lamp next to the bed.

"Come. Let me get you out of that dress so you can rest," Mizuno said, turning Catherine around to release the zipper that curved over her bottom. The silky dress fell off her shoulders slowly as Mizuno gently pushed the gown down, her small fingers brushing delicately over Catherine's skin. Catherine shuddered at the cool caress but composed herself long enough to step out of the dress and let Mizuno hang it up properly. She stood clad in only a pair of underwear, her shoes, and the jewels from Sidatih.

Mizuno turned toward her, gaze growing heated the longer she looked at Catherine's nearly naked form. "Sit," she commanded, and Catherine wasted no time in perching herself on the edge of the bed. Mizuno knelt before her, legs tucked under her as she began to remove Catherine's shoes.

When the shoes were off and set to the side, Mizuno stood slowly, letting her eyes rake over Catherine's seated form. "Lean forward," she said, pushing Catherine's hair off her neck to reach the clasp of the necklace. With slow reverence, Mizuno removed every piece of jewelry, fingers lightly touching Catherine's skin. In her bare state, Catherine felt the sensual gestures, and despite her state of mind, she felt heat pool between her legs.

After placing the jewelry back in the box on Catherine's vanity, Mizuno rifled through the dresser in the room and pulled out an oversized sweater Catherine used to sleep in. She crossed back to Catherine on the bed and indicated that Catherine should raise her hands. With deliberate movements, Mizuno pulled the fabric over Catherine's head, her fingers brushing against the side of Catherine's breasts as she pulled the sweater down over her body. A small gasp came out and goosebumps spread over Catherine's skin.

Placing a finger under Catherine's chin, Mizuno raised her face up to meet her dark eyes. She leaned in and placed a soft, quick kiss on Catherine's lips before retreating. "Sleep well, Miriam."

And then she was gone, leaving Catherine overheated and an emotional mess.

CHAPTER 13

"There are three layers of warding, all very basic. The first is a simple sticking charm which keeps the object from being physically removed and attaches itself to the plinth. The second is an alerting ward. It will alert the caster or the designated person that the item was touched. And the third layer is an offensive spell, meant to shock the thief into unconsciousness, presumably until someone arrives to apprehend them."

The next morning after breakfast, Nachem sat them all in the common room and explained what they found in the ward sample. Catherine still felt tired, but she listened intently, keeping her focus only on Nachem and not on Mizuno or Sidatih, though she could feel both of their gazes on her periodically.

"Can you break the wards on the trumpet from a distance?" Catherine asked, her fingers clutched around the empty cup of coffee between her hands.

"No, these will need to be broken where I can reach. The wards surrounding the building are more complex with six layers of wards including those Ezra placed, but a few of those can be deactivated from a distance. Even opening and maintaining a small hole will take considerable effort and won't last long—just enough for you to slip out once it's time. I can devise a tool that will allow you to remove the wards on the object, but you must be within a limited distance, and it will draw energy from you. There would be only enough for the thief to slip through quickly, unless you would like me to enter the building as well." Nachem spoke with no inflection, more like they were giving a simple presentation. They were methodical and looked at the facts of the job only.

Catherine thought for a moment, placing the mug on the coffee table to free up a hand to rest her chin on. "The more people we have on the inside, the more complicated things can get when it's time to leave. Mizuno and myself will already be in the building, and we won't arouse suspicion since only the two of us are expected."

"So now you are going to do more than simply be a distraction? You're going to be a conduit for ward breaking magic now, too! What is the point of the thief then if she can't handle a few wards?" Sidatih's outrage mixed with fear.

Catherine turned her attention toward him. "Because someone has to take care of the wards while Mizuno is taking the trumpet. She needs to be completely focused and not have to worry about ward-breaking draining her. Nachem will already be opening them from the outside, so we need a second person to hold the ones on the inside. The point is to not get caught, so we'll need to replace them before anyone finds out. It's more like opening a hole for us to slip through the wards. But we have to keep people distracted while also letting Mizuno do her work without worrying about tripping an alarm."

"Send Nachem anyway! They already said they can break the exterior wards from a distance. They can do that from inside the building. At least then it doesn't put you at more risk!" Sidatih stood abruptly, his lovely golden eyes glowing crimson. His ifrit nature had started to surface.

"Did you not just hear what I said, Sida? Nachem can remove the wards from a distance, but it takes considerable time and concentration. A dead giveaway in the middle of a party full of magical creatures. Not to mention being a golem around a bunch of magical creatures who don't take well to constructs. Someone needs to do the same on the wards surrounding the trumpet. And Mizuno will have to focus on not tripping anything while she's removing and replacing the trumpet. We have to keep the penetration of the wards to a bare minimum; we don't know if Arruk will be alerted if there's a disruption." Catherine wanted to massage her temples; a headache was building behind her eyes. But she stopped herself because she knew Sidatih would fuss over her, and the rest of their discussion would be lost.

"We're swapping items?" Sidatih asked.

Next to Catherine, Mizuno pinched the bridge of her nose. "Do you simply not pay attention? We have covered this. The better to remain undetected until we are safely away from this country. We will replace the trumpet with a similar, ordinary one."

"I have a miniaturizing spell from Ezra that will shrink the trumpet for an hour, and I'll put it into the warded pocket Mizuno had made for dress. Then we'll just walk out the door," Catherine added.

"And what about Mir? What happens if things go to shit, and you need to get out quick? You can't just become a spider and disappear up the wall like Mizuno!" Sidatih still stood, seething.

"I have my ways of getting out," she said, not elaborating.

"That's a bullshit answer, and you know it, Mir. I want details. I want to make sure you'll be safe!" Sidatih was nearly shouting, which was unlike him. He wasn't overly emotional and never one to give into anger. Catherine sat very still, shocked at his outburst.

"I have a transportation spell Ezra gave me before we left Connecticut. It will work only once and can cut through wards just in case Nachem is unable to hold them open long enough." The spell was extremely rare magic since few things existed that could cut through properly placed wards without tripping them. Catherine had hoped she wouldn't have to use it, but since Nachem could only concentrate on the outside wards, she might have to use the spell to quickly get out of the warehouse and remain untraceable.

Sidatih seethed for a moment longer, his breath coming heavy, his eyes blazing red. But slowly, he started to calm, and his normal even demeanor returned, eyes fading back into gold. Slowly, he sat back down and rested an ankle on his knee. "I don't like this, but I trust you, albi. I just don't want to see you in harm's way. You are so fragile now."

"Maybe, but this is still my job, my debt to pay. I can't rely on the three of you to do everything for me.

We've all put ourselves in dangerous situations before. This shouldn't be any worse than any of those other times." She looked at them each in turn, and all three nodded. She didn't know each of their histories completely, but she knew enough through personal experience with each of them that they had been in far more dangerous situations throughout their own long lives. This, she hoped, would be the last one for her.

"Now, where are we with the modern security measures?" she asked Sidatih, who reached for the laptop on the coffee table.

He opened it up and started to click around the screen after it booted up. "From what I've been able to get into, there are security cameras surrounding the building and inside. Not surprising. They are spelled for recording and image enhancement or so Nachem has been able to detect. There are no less than two guards at the front entrance, and there's a back entrance with another two guards. They rotate every six hours. All of the windows are facades and not real, so if you try hitting one to break in, well, you're getting a shower of brick on your face." He turned the screen around to show off a picture of the building with camera placements highlighted.

"The security system is pretty robust, but it's nothing I can't handle. I can splice the feed so that it shows an empty street, and nothing will show up if you have to escape. Same goes for the inside hallway leading out to that exit. And, of course, the trumpet. It'll be like you aren't even there, at least on camera. But if everything goes to plan, you won't need to disappear. You can just casually leave a party." He spun the laptop back around and closed it with a satisfied click.

"You watched *National Treasure* again, didn't you?" Catherine asked, a smile on her face. "You know that's not an instructional documentary."

Sidatih huffed and set the computer back on the table. But when he straightened in his seat, he was smirking. "One man's treasure hunting movie is another's instructional video. If it works, it works."

"If it works," Mizuno mumbled next to Catherine. She had a copy of the blueprints, once again updated based on the knowledge they gained the night before, pulled up on a tablet.

"You seriously have no faith in my abilities. I am a world class hacker, thank you very much," Sidatih said indignantly. "I've been doing this since computers were invented!"

"That does not automatically make you good at what you do," Mizuno sniped back.

Catherine held up her hands. "Okay, enough of that. I brought you all on board because you are the best at what you do. And that includes Sidatih. Mizuno, I trust his skills implicitly, and I hope you trust my judgement. So, whatever issues you have between each other, I suggest you work them out so we can cooperate as a team."

Sidatih looked properly chastised, but Mizuno glared at him, defiant. "I don't have a problem with the thief. She seems to have a problem with me." He refused to look at the other woman and kept his focus on Catherine.

"Maybe I simply do not trust you." Mizuno crossed her ankles and continued to glare at the ifrit, who pretended not to notice.

Sidatih threw his hands in the air, exasperated. "Well, that makes two of us. Listen, Mizuno, you want to help Mir and so do I. She trusts the both of us, and I trust her. So, let's work together, get through this, and then when it's over, you don't have to see me anymore."

Mizuno didn't seem happy at his declaration but nodded anyway. The tension in the room, which had been building slowly over the last several minutes, finally began to dissipate.

"I am going to make some snacks for everyone," Nachem said, standing from their chair quickly and disappearing back into the kitchen. The golem tended to avoid drama as much as possible, though they had seen more than their fair share of familial drama throughout the centuries. Instead, he did what any Jew—or Jewish creation—would do in a tense situation; they fed everyone.

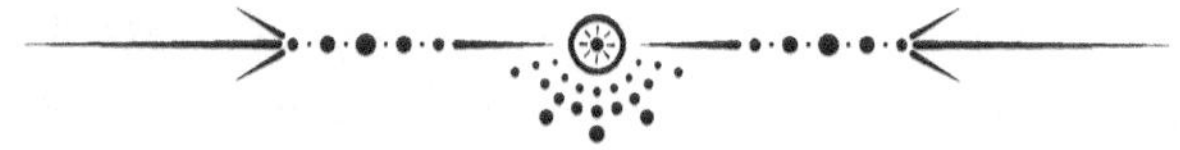

Working on the plans for their operation kept Catherine occupied all week. They took turns scouting the building throughout the day, observing guard rotations and any blind spots for cameras. There would undoubtedly be more security during the event, but likely they would keep a similar rotation.

Finally, Tuesday morning came, and the anxiety that Catherine had been trying to push away reared its ugly head. She was having lunch with Arruk that day, and she didn't know which was worse: the dread or the guilt.

"Do you want one of us to come with you?" Sidatih asked, handing Catherine's bag to her.

"He thinks Mizuno is my wife, and again, he most certainly still holds a grudge against you, so if I were to take anyone, it would be Mizuno, and I really feel this should just be between me and Arruk." Catherine thought about taking the other woman to keep up appearances, but she really did feel like the time should be spent with only her and Arruk. This wasn't part of the operation, this was personal, and Mizuno was part of the job. She didn't want to mix the two outside of that.

"So, take Nachem with you. Arruk knows about them, and it wouldn't be weird to take the family golem with you around town," Sidatih said with conviction.

Catherine stepped toward him, cupping his face between her hands. "I'm going to be fine meeting with Arruk. We're old friends, and as far as I know, he doesn't suspect me of anything. I'm not thrilled about continuing to lie to him, but it's something I am good at, and I don't need anyone else complicating that. Please, Sida, don't worry about me. I can handle this." She placed a small kiss at the corner of his mouth, waved to them all, and left, shutting the door firmly behind her.

Arruk's place was too far to walk, and Catherine did not want to be disheveled upon arrival, so she opted for a car. The ride over was quiet, and she stared out the window at the bustling city around her. It had changed so much in the centuries she had last visited. It was truly a metropolitan place now, swarmed with tourists and locals alike.

Her stomach twisted with nerves the whole way. After living so long and being in countless messy and dangerous situations, she thought she wouldn't be bothered by a simple meeting with an old friend. The thought did nothing to ease her anxiety. If anything, she was more anxious than if she had been meeting a stranger.

Catherine was a skilled liar; she had to be after switching her identity so many times. But lying to someone she used to be so close with, someone she shared her secrets with, well, she wasn't sure if she could handle it. Not without giving something away.

Unless the time had dulled Arruk's ability to read her emotions. He used to be so good at it, but it had been so long since they had shared that kind of platonic intimacy, and the minotaur didn't know Catherine, the persona she had crafted over the last decade or so. She was a completely different person from the woman who left Athens centuries ago. Arruk only knew Miriam, and she hadn't felt like Miriam Kokush in a long time.

Before she had a chance to calm her nerves, the car pulled up to a large villa, one of the old constructions. Catherine stepped outside of the car to see Arruk already waiting out front. He wore a glamour, which was unsurprising. While the magical community in Athens was large, and his community was predominately magical creatures, a minotaur walking around the streets and dining in a café would definitely cause more than a little upheaval.

Much like how Nachem appeared when they wore their glamour, Arruk kept his height and bulk. His human appearance had dark brown skin the same color as his fur. His gray trousers were expertly tailored, and his crisp black button down had the sleeves rolled up his muscular arms. His long wavy black hair, styled exactly like his mane, was swept back into a half bun on the back of his head. An expensive gold watch with crystal inlay wrapped around his right wrist, and Catherine could just make out the stamped gold medallion with an image of the goddess Artemis peeking out from under his shirt where the top two buttons were undone. The chain had changed, but it was an amulet Arruk had worn forever.

"Miriam, you look lovely," he said by way of greeting, pulling her in for a bone crushing embrace. It took her a moment to return the gesture, and when she finally did, her arms could barely wrap around his sides.

"You look quite dapper yourself, though I must say, I much prefer your natural form," she said, plastering on a smile as she pulled away.

Arruk let out a deep chuckle. "It's true. I am far more glorious as my true self. But I don't want to overwhelm the humans with my magnificence, so I try to blend in."

Catherine let out her own small laugh. "Nothing about you blends in, Arruk. Not just because you stand a good foot taller over everyone else." The minotaur smiled, a bright twinkle in his eye.

The tightness in her chest began to loosen, though her stomach still swirled. They were falling back into an easy repartee, almost as if no time had passed since they last spoke. Catherine didn't know if that was better or worse for her situation.

"Shall we?" Arruk asked, holding out his arm for Catherine. She nodded and looped her own arm through his, and they began to walk down the street. Arruk kept his stride shorter to match hers, a gesture she was grateful for as his long legs would have had him dragging her along otherwise.

They didn't speak as Arruk led them down to a small bistro in Kifissia. The suburb was flashy, old and new constructions showing off just how affluent the area was. It wasn't surprising that Arruk chose to live there.

Once they were seated at their table and Arruk had ordered them a bottle of wine, they got down to talking.

"I'm surprised you didn't send me a notice you would be passing through my city. I would have made better arrangements for us to catch up. How long are you here for?" Arruk asked, taking a sip from his glass.

Catherine took her own glass in hand and let the rich flavors of the wine sooth her nerves. It was best to stay as close to the truth as possible. "It was a bit of an impromptu trip. I was visiting Ezra and his wife in Connecticut and somehow, we got to talking about Athens and I realized I hadn't been to visit yet in my travels. I convinced Mizuno to join me. She's always busy so we rarely see each other, and well, here I am. Though I haven't decided how long I'll stay. Perhaps another couple of weeks just to see a few more places and meet with a few old friends in the area."

"Well, I won't get to monopolize your time like I want, then. I understand you have plenty more places to see, more than enough friends to reach out to. I'm sorry to hear about the mortality affliction. You had so much more living to do," Arruk said as if it was some great tragedy and not something Catherine had chosen for herself.

Another fortifying gulp of her wine helped her find her voice. "It was my decision, actually. I willing gave up my immortality to my protegee Brie, Ezra's wife. I've accomplished plenty with the life I've led. I'm not sure what else I would do with immortality now that I'm not bound to a duty."

Another truth. With her responsibility toward Ezra, she could easily stay in one place and live out her life there until it was time to move on. And then what? Create another persona, another Miriam to be or a Catherine, or a Mir, and start the cycle all over again? "I think I'm ready to rest."

Arruk leaned back in his chair, swirling the wine left in his glass nonchalantly, as if they weren't discussing mortality. "You *think*. Which means you are not entirely sure. And in the time you've spent revisiting your old haunts, seeing friends and lovers you have long since left, has it not once crossed your mind that you are giving it all up? That you are ripping yourself out of their lives permanently?"

His words felt like a stab to the heart. Catherine realized in that moment that no, she hadn't thought of anyone else, hadn't thought about what her death would mean to others. There had been so many people in her life, so many adventures and misadventures, passionate love affairs, and casual flings, but every one of them had left an imprint on her, and maybe she had left something of herself behind with them. Was her wish for mortality selfish? And was it wrong to be selfish when it was her life to choose whether to keep going or not? Was mortality even what she really wanted now that she thought about it?

It was too much for her to contemplate now, and she certainly wasn't going to while having lunch with a long-lost friend. She would have to wait until the job was done, and she was in a safe space alone to really contemplate what she saw for the future.

So, she shrugged and set her glass down. "That's really my decision to make. We all die eventually, even if it's not the conventional death of mortals. One day, Arruk, you will grow tired of existence and will fade away, too."

The air between them was charged and heavy. Luckily for them both, their server appeared with the food Arruk had ordered with the wine. After that, they lapsed into comfortable light conversation while eating, both steering clear of any more heavy topics.

After they had finished their meal, Catherine felt no better than she had when she first arrived. It was possible she felt even worse, actually, because now she felt the weight of judgement from Arruk, even if he hadn't intended it that way. She knew very well her actions and choices had consequences—knew that better than many. But the job would get done, the trumpet retrieved, and Catherine knew this would likely be the last time she ever saw Arruk. After this, she would not return to Athens, especially once Arruk discovered the trumpet missing. He would know she had taken it, and Catherine would not be around long enough to even ask for forgiveness.

"I had a wonderful time catching up with you, Miriam. I hope you think about what I said. I hope to see you at the gala this weekend." Then, surprising her, he dragged her in for another tight hug and placed a soft kiss on her temple. "Take care of yourself, Miriam. I hope you come to your senses soon."

He released her and reached around her to open the door of a black car that had pulled up without her noticing. Catherine gave Arruk one last lingering look, said a quick goodbye, and slid into the backseat of the car. Arruk shut the door behind her and stood by the road, watching as the car pulled away. Catherine turned to look out the back window as his form quickly became smaller with the distance.

When the car took a turn and Arruk was no longer visible, only then did Catherine sit back in her seat and let out a deep sigh.

CHAPTER 14

Catherine was wrung out when she stepped through the door of the apartment a few minutes later. Emotionally, she was fried, and physically, it felt as if her body was weighed down by large stones. It was only midday, but the thought of curling up in her bed and sleeping was enticing. Despite the light fare from lunch, her stomach felt as heavy as if she had consumed a Thanksgiving feast by herself.

"How did it go, albi?" Sidatih appeared from the hallway. His gaze turned to concern in seconds as he took in her appearance, what could only be tired eyes and drooping shoulders. In a few quick strides, he was across the room and pulling her into his arms. Catherine let her head drop into the spot between his neck and shoulder, her breath heavy and warm against his skin. She melted into his warmth, wanting his arms to take away all the feelings swirling within her.

"Miriam, is everything alright?" She heard Mizuno's voice from behind Sidatih, and moments later, the woman was slowly pulling Catherine out of Sidatih's arms to cup her face and look into Catherine's eyes. Catherine was a tall woman and had several inches on Mizuno, but with Mizuno staring at her like that, searching her face for all her emotions, Catherine felt so much smaller.

Off to the side, coming from the kitchen, Catherine heard the heavy footsteps of Nachem. They did not approach but stood watching from the archway. "We are taking her to rest, Nachem," Sidatih said as he wrapped his arm around Catherine's waist and led her out of the entryway and down the hall to her room. Mizuno followed so closely that Catherine could feel her body heat on the other side of her.

Once they were ensconced in her bedroom, the door shut behind them, Sidatih and Mizuno began to work in tandem to make Catherine more comfortable. With a look, Sidatih kindled a fire in the grate. Mizuno crossed the room, drew the curtains, and then returned to Catherine's side to take her bag and set it off to the side.

"Let us take care of you, albi. I can only imagine the emotional drain you just went through." Sidatih's words came from just behind her, and with her small nod, his hands came up and brushed the hair from one side of her neck before he placed a kiss just below her ear. His warm body pressed up against her back, and Catherine leaned into his warmth.

In front of her, Mizuno grabbed one of Catherine's hands and threaded their fingers together before drawing closer and pressing her own mouth on the other side of Catherine's neck. The moan that escaped Catherine's lips was loud and unexpected. She closed her eyes and let herself feel the press of their bodies against hers. Between the comforting presence of

Sidatih and Mizuno, she felt safe and cared for. She would let them wash away all the turmoil in her mind, let herself surrender to whatever they gave her, and come out better from it.

Their kisses on her neck were feather soft, neither one becoming too heated. As if by some unspoken direction, they both pulled away seconds apart and began to slowly, reverently undress her.

Sidatih's large soft hands skimmed up the side of her ribs as he pulled her top up and over her head from behind while Mizuno's long delicate fingers slipped inside the waistband of her skirt and pushed it down to pool on the floor.

When she stood between them in nothing but a lace bra and underwear, Catherine let out another moan as their hands returned to her body, working over soft flesh and tight muscles. Her underthings hit the floor moments later until she was completely bare, Sidatih pushing against her back, his growing erection against her backside, and Mizuno's cool fingers tracing the bones of Catherine's hips to her front, their chests pressed against each other. The feel of the silky fabric from Mizuno's blouse against her exposed nipples was almost too much to bear. Her moan this time was softer, and she didn't dare open her eyes for fear they would both disappear. A throbbing began at her core, and heat rushed through her. She needed this. She needed them.

But a thought cut through the building lust within her. One that stopped her moans for a second. "Sida, are you sure? I know this is something you are comfortable doing with me. But you don't know Mizuno well.

You two don't even like each other. You don't have to do this." Her words were breathy, and she didn't want them to stop, but both ceased their movements against her as she spoke.

Sidatih placed a sweet kiss against her hair. "Don't worry, albi. We knew today would be taxing on you, so we have agreed this is what you need, that the focus is all on you. The thief and I will not be engaging each other at all."

"But—" Catherine began, but Sidatih cut her off.

"I am comfortable with that arrangement, Mir. But you are sweet to think of me when you should be focusing on feeling good. Now, no more thoughts. Let us give you pleasure instead." Sidatih returned his lips to her neck, sucking on her pulse point, and all her concerns and worry fled.

Mizuno's kisses began to move from Catherine's neck up to her jaw and then slowly toward her lips. She pressed her body even closer to Catherine's, one hand coming up to knead at the flesh of her left breast. Catherine gasped into her mouth, and Mizuno took the opportunity to slide her tongue against Catherine's.

With her body so heated and her mind all but absent, Catherine let herself feel every movement, every stroke and touch. Sidatih's warm hand wrapped around her body to grab at her free breast, teasing her nipple mercilessly. Catherine nearly shrieked with pleasure into Mizuno's eager mouth.

While the sensation of being touched on her sensitive breasts, one hand cool and small, the other large and warm, the differing temperatures sending her to wild places, she wanted more for the rest of her body.

She felt empty and achy and desperate to be touched between her thighs. As much as she loved the friction against her naked flesh from their clothes, she wanted to feel their skin against hers, but the last functional part of her brain new that it would be a step too far for Sidatih. There was too much vulnerability in being naked.

Gently, she pulled her lips from Mizuno's, and the other woman turned her attention to kissing Catherine's neck again. "Please. I need more," she gasped and panted; there didn't seem to be enough space in her lungs to get enough air. Every inch of her body was buzzing with need.

She cried out in desperation when Sidatih and Mizuno pulled away from her, leaving her feeling chilled where their bodies had been pressed up against hers. "Get on the bed, albi," Sidatih said gently, directing her to lay back against the headboard in the center of the large bed.

Catherine did as she was told, the quilt soft against her bare skin. Sidatih and Mizuno kept their eyes only on Catherine. This was not a seduction; instead, they seemed prepared to give her everything she wanted. Everything she needed to make the aching in her heart go away.

Sidatih moved around the bed to sit next to her on her right while Mizuno did the same on her left. They both remained clothed while she lay between them without a single scrap of fabric, and Catherine had never felt so vulnerable as she did now. She was an emotional wreck after spending time with Arruk. For a while, she had been fighting with herself over whether to allow herself to become closer to Sidatih again, to start to become close with Mizuno.

But in that moment, when the two of them slid their hands over her body again, hot flesh pressed against her on her right side and cool soft skin on her left with gentle lips and searching tongues, she let it all go. There were no worries, no complicated feelings, no guilt about Arruk, no anxiety over the job, no damn debt hanging over her head. There was just the feel of two people using hands, lips, and tongues to bring her pleasure.

Soft moans filled the room, some Catherine's, but just as many belonging to either Sidatih or Mizuno. The two of them didn't touch at all, nor did they even look at each other, their focus completely on Catherine. Somewhere in the haze of her lust, Catherine was grateful for what it took for Sidatih to participate. Physical intimacy was something he could only share with a person he had a deep emotional connection with, which wasn't Mizuno. They were barely able to be civil to one another. But there they were, working together for her, and Mizuno respected Sidatih's boundary. Not once did the woman's eyes stray to take in Sidatih's body, nor did she even brush against him as they both moved their hands across Catherine's skin.

Sidatih's lips trailed down her shoulder while Catherine turned her head the other way, her lips captured by Mizuno's. With one cool hand, Mizuno again began to massage and tease Catherine's breast. A loud groan escaped her mouth when she felt Sidatih's hand slide between her legs, cupping her and pushing against the slick heat there.

Catherine didn't know what to do with her hands. There was an ache within her to touch everywhere she could on their bodies, but she didn't know where to start, couldn't think about what to do, or how to maneuver her fingers under clothing.

"Get out of your head, albi, and feel," Sidatih whispered into her ear as Mizuno worked her mouth down to replace her hand.

With Sidatih working between her legs and Mizuno laving at her breasts, Catherine let go, let all thoughts leave, and let her own hands slide across the bodies of the two beside her. Her eager fingers burrowed under Mizuno's loose trousers and sought the warmth between her legs, wet and dripping, probing digits finding the spot that made Mizuno moan loudly and buck her hips. With her other hand, Catherine clumsily pushed her hand inside Sidatih's joggers, wrapped it around his thick, hard shaft, and began to pump in an even tempo. His own groan was loud in her ear, hot breath tickling the side of her face as his cock jumped in her hand.

They worked each other for several long minutes, the room filled with breathy moans as the three of them climbed ever higher toward completion. Catherine's legs began to shake uncontrollably as Sidatih's magic hands kept a relentless pace, thrusting inside her while his thumb circled her most sensitive spot. The hand she had on Sidatih's cock was already slick with precum and wetness dripped down her wrist of the hand between Mizuno's legs.

Catherine felt ready to burst, the buildup between her legs almost too much to withstand. Her body was covered in the remnants of kisses and bruises sucked into her skin. Nobody spoke a word; they didn't need to say anything to tip her over the edge.

Vision whiting out, a scream ripped from her lips as Catherine climaxed, hips thrusting in the air to drag Sidatih's hand deeper. Her hands stalled for a moment on her companions, too dazed to remember how to make her hands function. But even as she shook with aftershocks, she found her rhythm again, and once more began thrusting her fingers into Mizuno, the other hand pumping Sidatih's cock faster.

His cries filled the room next as he coated Catherine's hand. She swallowed his moan with a kiss, her tongue pushing in to tangle with his. Dragging her finger tips down his length, eliciting shivers from Sidatih's body, she removed her hand from his pants and wiped the mess there on her thigh, rubbing the cooling fluid into her skin.

She kept kissing him as her hand continued to stroke Mizuno toward orgasm. Mizuno gave up focusing on Catherine's breast, instead panting heavily into Catherine's neck. She gripped Catherine's thigh tightly, like she was trying to ground herself, nails digging into her skin, leaving crescent indents.

A moment later, Mizuno let out a soft whimper, her whole body contracting around Catherine before she rolled back, limp against the bed. Slowly, Catherine slid her hand out of Mizuno but left her hand to linger on Mizuno's thigh.

The three of them rested against the headboard, breathing heavily. They didn't speak; instead, almost at the same time, Sidatih and Mizuno cuddled closer into Catherine's side and rested their heads against hers. Catherine closed her eyes and tried to settle her breathing, refusing to let any other thought enter her brain and spoil the moment.

The three of them stayed curled together in Catherine's bed for a long time before Sidatih finally stretched and got up to retrieve two warm washcloths for the women. He insisted on cleaning up Catherine, and he did so with delicate swipes between her thighs. Catherine offered to help Mizuno, but the other woman waved her off and attended to herself.

Once they had cleaned themselves, Mizuno gave Catherine a long deep kiss before slipping out of the room. Sidatih pulled back the quilt on the bed and helped Catherine snuggle under it, still naked. When she was settled, he pulled off his shirt and slid in next to her, pulling her close to his body.

"Sleep, Mir," he said gently, his breath against her hair. Catherine didn't even think to argue. She relaxed into the warmth of his body pressed against her entire back and drifted off to sleep, feeling more at ease than she had in weeks. Maybe longer.

CHAPTER 15

"What if Mizuno infiltrates in her spider form to mark all of the cameras?" Nachem asked as they set a tray of food on the coffee table and took a seat in an open wingback chair.

Catherine kept her attention on her laptop, scanning the interior blueprints, which admittedly were lacking in camera placements. "I don't know if the wards would keep her out. I'm not sure if the warehouse is spelled to keep out insects or critters that might find their way in," Catherine said.

"And even if he didn't, that doesn't mean the spells wouldn't pick up on Mizuno's magical nature. Where a normal spider might be able to get in, a magical one could be repelled or alert them that someone was attempting to trespass. And if that's the case, the whole job is blown because the minotaur will be on high alert." Sidatih grabbed a few olives from the tray and popped them into his mouth as he spoke.

"I am not thrilled at the idea of being bespelled, though it would not be the first time," Mizuno said, and her voice sounded a little sullen. Setting off a ward or two happened to every thief as some point in their career, usually at the beginning when they were clumsy, bumbling idiots playing at thievery. Catherine had her fair share of scars from offensive wardship spells and pointy physical security measures. But she knew that the risk of getting hit by a ward spell would not deter Mizuno.

Catherine stared at the computer screen for a long moment, contemplating. "There are risks if we send Mizuno in now. If we set off the alarm, all of our work so far will be lost, and who knows how long we would have to wait to try again? I'm not sure what kind of deadline we are operating on, but I know Titania, and she doesn't handle waiting well."

"What happens if you do not fulfill her terms in a timely fashion?" Mizuno asked, likely because she wasn't as familiar with fae bargaining as the rest of them were.

"That's up to the fairy. As it is the queen of the fae, likely either death or a very painful existence for an extended time." Nachem spoke matter-of-factly, like they weren't discussing the possibility of Catherine falling over dead at Titania's whim.

While Catherine had made peace with her impending death, she wasn't ready to go out at that very moment. Better to error on the side of caution than ruin weeks of effort and risk the fae queen's rash temper. "I'll call Ezra to see if he can give me some details. It's possible that a ward was placed for infestations, and he didn't think it important enough to add to the list or it slipped his mind." She made sure to check over the list of spells and wards Ezra had provided and didn't see any on the document she had typed up from Ezra's handwritten list.

She excused herself from the room, taking her phone into her bedroom to make the call. It took several rings before Ezra answered, and it dawned on Catherine that while it was late morning in Greece, it was the middle of the night in Connecticut. Not that Ezra slept, but he would still undoubtedly be in bed with his wife who still needed to sleep.

"Aunt Catherine, is everything alright?" His deep voice floated through with concern. It never failed to make her smile when he called her that, especially considering he was much, much older than she was, and until recently, their relationship was rocky. He was the only one from her old life who called her by her chosen name, but then again, Ezra knew all about what it meant to take on a new name, to take on a new life. He had done the same after a tragic event in his past, and he had been Ezra ever since.

Catherine cleared her throat. "Yes, everything is fine. For now, anyway. I have a question about the warehouse wards. Is there one in place that would keep out insects or any kind of bug infestation? We're considering the option of sending in Mizuno in her spider form to locate the interior security, but I won't put her in harm's way for fear of setting off the alarm."

Ezra made a thoughtful noise on the other end, thinking it over. "I keep one on the shop here, but I'm trying to remember if there was one I placed on the Greece shop. My wards have evolved over the years. I would say yes, there would be one for any number of creatures that posed a risk to the collection, especially with one as old as the Greece location since it was before the time of Terminix."

Catherine laughed a little at his joke. The marvels of modern exterminators certainly were better than centuries past where infuriating insects ran amuck. "Very well. We might have to go in partially blind. We didn't get to see all the cameras at the party, but I don't think it's anything Mizuno can't handle."

"Even without a ward against insects, the magic would be able to detect a jorgumo easily. Her magical signature would trip the alarms and probably trigger a nasty spell. I can't imagine she could withstand a more offensive spell in that form," Ezra said, cutting to the quick of the fear Catherine harbored at the idea of sending Mizuno in at all.

She thanked him and apologized for drawing him out of bed to answer what should have been an obvious thing. "Be careful, Aunt Catherine. I know you can handle yourself, but you're mortal now, and I'm not sure Mother will intervene if you need her," Ezra said, and the concern in his voice worried her at little.

"She won't only because I asked her not to. I'll be careful, Ezra. I promise." They said their goodbyes after that, and Catherine took a moment to herself. He was right, his mother wouldn't intervene, and maybe that had been a foolhardy thing to ask for from the goddess. Despite the fact the goddess had originally cursed her, they had become friends over the time of her guardianship, and even though the goddess didn't interfere most of the time, she always made sure Catherine made it out alive.

But when Catherine gave up her mortality and asked the goddess to not involve herself if Catherine was in danger, instead opting to let life decide for her, she didn't think she would be running a heist for a powerful fae against an ancient minotaur with a treasure trove of enchanted objects that he guarded with every magic at his disposal. Catherine had always prided herself on her intelligence and cunning, but now she wondered if she hadn't been completely foolhardy.

When she returned to the common area, she found Sidatih hard at work stitching video footage; Nachem, without their glamour, refilling water glasses; and Mizuno with a sketchpad on her lap drawing what looked like a new design for an outfit. Sunshine filled the room, painting them all with a buttery light.

The scene was so domestic that Catherine's breath caught in her chest, and a longing tugged at her heart. She knew it wouldn't stay like that; their peace would end as the job ramped up. Then afterward, they would split up again. Sidatih had talked about wanting more, a life together, and maybe she could see that happening. But Mizuno would want to return to Japan where she had her own underground and reputation, not to mention her fashion career. A part of her ached at the thought of being parted from the woman. Over the course of the last weeks, they had gotten closer, and that said nothing of their physical intimacy the other day.

Then there was Nachem to consider. Catherine was unsure what they would choose to do. She supposed that would be a question for the golem once the job was completed. It was possible Nachem would want to return to the life they had been leading since the last of her family had been killed. Maybe they would want to stick with Catherine, continue to serve the last of the Kokush line. It would be their choice, and Catherine wouldn't begrudge Nachem if they chose to return to Italy or wherever they decided to go next.

With a shake of her head, Catherine cleared the thoughts from her mind. No use thinking about that now. Her attention needed to be on the task as hand. They would be conducting the heist in a day, and she needed to be completely focused on that, not her own feelings.

"Sida, have you been able to get a copy of the guest list?" she asked. If she knew some of the attendees, she had a better chance of steering conversation with enough people to keep Arruk occupied.

"I did! The minotaur has a solid firewall for his operation, so I went back to basics. Classic phishing attack and that was all it took. Babytown frolics really. It was nothing to spoof an email from Arruk, and his PA opened the link. I planted what I needed and was out before their security could detect anything." Sidatih puffed out his chest a little, causing the laptop on his thighs to wobble. He was very proud of himself, indeed.

"I understood about half of that, but I got the important part at least. Can you send me a copy?" Catherine smiled brightly at him.

"Already done. Check your phone," Sidatih responded. Catherine pulled the phone from her pocket and saw the message on the encrypted app they used to communicate. She opened the document and scanned the contents. She found many familiar names, enough that Arruk would be shaking hands and conversing all night.

She scanned the list a second time before coming to a conclusion on their timeframe while at the gala.

A grunt came from Nachem, drawing Catherine's gaze upward. "If I may, Miriam, Saturday is the thirteenth of the month," their gruff voice said gravely.

Catherine raised an eyebrow. "Is that a problem?" She wracked her brain for anything significant about the day, but nothing came to mind.

"The thirteenth is considered a bad luck day, and bad luck comes in threes. Perhaps we should pick a better day," Nachem continued.

Catherine considered for only a moment. The gala was the perfect opportunity to pull off the job. Trying to retrieve the trumpet after the warehouse was locked up for the night would present a whole host of other problems and hurtles to work through. "I'm sure it will be okay, Nachem. Plenty of cultures dislike the number thirteen, but I don't think it's cursed or anything. We should be alright." Nachem's face remained neutral, and they didn't argue. Instead, they crossed their arms and headed back into the kitchen, which since their arrival had become something of a refuge for Nachem.

It wasn't that Catherine thought Nachem's fears were unfounded. Superstitions didn't exist for no reason. But Catherine had found in her long life that she couldn't let superstitions hold her back, or she would never get anything done. They would press on and hope for the best, which was the only thing anyone could do in a heist job. Still, she took the golem's words to heart and planned to prepare for every contingency just in case.

CHAPTER 16

The dawn was still an hour away, but Catherine couldn't sleep anymore. Not that she had slept much that night anyway. They had spent all of Friday going over every last detail of the plan, doing checks over maps and blueprints, and who would be where at any given time. Each of them knew what to do and, if anything went wrong, what measures they needed to take to get themselves out. Still, that did nothing to ease her worry or the niggling feeling in her gut that something horrible was going to happen.

She quashed the feeling as best she could. It was stealing a magical trumpet; it wasn't that dire or high profile. Catherine suspected the tension only felt so heightened because it wasn't a nameless collector she was stealing from but Arruk, her old friend. Even if their lunch had gone well, they had been estranged for so long, and she wasn't sure what Arruk would do to her or her team if they were caught. He could be utterly ruthless when provoked.

It was probably guilt.

Still, she had to push the guilt and anxiety aside for the sake of the job. As much as she respected Arruk and loathed the idea of stealing from him, she had a debt to pay, and her failure to deliver could mean any number of horrible things for her. Catherine would put her well-being over her guilt any day, and she didn't care how selfish that made her.

"Unable to sleep, Miriam?" Nachem's voice came from behind her where she sat in one of the chairs staring out the window, her knees tucked up to her chest. There was a dull ache in one of her knees that hadn't been there before, but the burn of it kept of her grounded.

She let out a soft chuckle. "No, I don't see how I could." Nachem came around to stand beside her, placing a heavy solid hand on her shoulder. It was comforting, despite being made of rock and earth, and Catherine let herself breathe easily for a moment.

"No, I do not suppose you could. Allow me to make you some coffee and some nosh," Nachem said, squeezing her shoulder gently before heading off to the kitchen before she could respond. Catherine resumed her thoughtless stare out the window, trying, perhaps in vain, to keep her mind clear.

Nachem returned a few minutes later carrying a steaming cup of black coffee in one hand and a plate of fruit and toast on the other. They set the plate on the table and handed her the mug. "I know you prefer it sweet, but I assumed the extra sugar would not be welcome on a day such as this. Hence also why I kept the breakfast fare simple. You should keep up your energy without weighing yourself down." Nachem knew exactly what she needed today, and their thoughtfulness touched her. Sure, the whole reason for the golem's existence was to take care of the Kokush family, but that didn't mean it felt any less special when they anticipated her needs.

"Thank you," she said softly, giving them a wan smile. "For everything, not just this. You have done so much for my family over the centuries, and I don't know if anyone has thanked you properly. Even now I don't think I'm doing a great job of it, but I want you to know how much I appreciate you, Nachem, and everything you do for me."

It wasn't possible for golems to blush, but Catherine noted that Nachem looked a little sheepish, if stone could look that way, like no one had ever paid them that much attention. "It is my purpose to serve, and I can only do my best, Miriam." Since they didn't have expressive eyes, there was no real emotion to see, but Catherine could tell her words touched them.

Unused to such a tender moment, at least from what Catherine gathered, Nachem left her again to return to the kitchen, likely to start more coffee and assemble more plates for Sidatih and Mizuno.

Not long after Nachem disappeared into the kitchen, first Mizuno and then Sidatih emerged from their rooms looking refreshed and composed, the opposite of how Catherine felt. They sat around the coffee table flanking Catherine, and Nachem returned with a tray of drinks and food before taking their own seat.

"Looks like I'm the only one who gets nervous before a job," Catherine said lightly as her stomach rolled with anxiety, even the toast and fruit almost too much for her stomach.

"Hardly, but then again, I'm the one who gets to sit in a box truck on my computer and away from any danger. My only concern is your safety," Sidatih said between sips of coffee. While he lounged in the chair looking completely at ease, once Catherine looked closer, she could see the tight lines around his eyes, and his shoulders were tense.

Mizuno, however, was as poised as ever, her spine straight as she sat, her movements deliberate as she ate breakfast. Then again, she had been a thief for a long time and was still actively thieving. It wasn't like the woman felt out of practice like Catherine did. "I spent the morning meditating. I must clear my mind before any operation and make sure nothing else matters but the task at hand. If I let doubt or concern enter my mind, I will not perform to my best." Mizuno smoothed away a non-existent wrinkle on her black leggings.

For once she was not in one of her high fashion outfits, instead opting for an informal robe over a simple shift dress and leggings that ended mid-calf. Her elegant dark hair hung loose around her shoulders, making a shiny dark curtain around her. The two of them would dress later for the party, so dressing for comfort while they prepared for the day was smart.

It was still early, far too early to do much other than to look over plans again, so that was what Catherine did. Sidatih spent the time going over his programs, looking over the copied loop of the warehouse he would swap out with the live feed just in case. Mizuno opted to return to her room, insisting that she needed to get her mind and body ready. It was a ritual that her master had taught her. The two of them had developed their own pre-job rituals outside of what Catherine taught them, and she knew the importance of Mizuno having that time to herself. Aritoki had been the same way. He had taught Mizuno well, and the woman was now an even better thief than Catherine had been in her prime.

Nachem remained in their kitchen domain, fixing drinks and snacks whenever they felt the team needed to eat. They didn't feel nerves or anxiousness like the rest of them were able to; they would simply do their assigned tasks, exactly as they were created for.

Maybe it would have been better to sleep the day away, Catherine thought as she shifted through the layouts and escape routes for the hundredth time. Anything would have been preferable to the hours of waiting.

"Is there anything I can do to help you, albi?" Sidatih's gentle voice cut through the swirl of thoughts in her brain. Catherine lifted her head and looked into crimson eyes wide with concern.

She shook her head. "I just want to get this over with. Once we have the trumpet and are out of Greece, then I can relax. Maybe find a nice cabin in some remote woods and forget people for a while," she said with a forced laugh. The concern didn't leave Sidatih's eyes even as he gave her a small grin in return.

"Not all people, I hope. I would very much like to spend time in that cabin with you, albi. As much time as you would like, though I am partial to forever." His grin turned into a full-blown smile, and the sight caused the tight knot in Catherine's stomach to loosen just a little.

It went without question that Catherine planned to spend time with Sidatih after their job was done. But after the day the three of them had spent after her lunch with Arruk, Catherine couldn't help imagining what it would be like to have that cabin in the woods with both Sidatih and Mizuno. An impossibility, probably, but still a nice thought and one that took her out of her own head for a moment.

"No, Sida, not all people. Once we get back to the States, let's do it." She reached over toward his chair. He met her hand halfway, and they laced their fingers together. They looked at each other for several long moments, Catherine loving the look of adoration in Sidatih's eyes. She hoped her gaze conveyed the same meaning.

Soon they settled back in their chairs, hands still linked for a time while they focused on their tasks. Having Sida's hand in hers grounded Catherine; it was something solid to cling to and minutely settled her nerves. With Sidatih around, she felt she could accomplish anything. And slowly, she was starting to feel that way with Mizuno. The woman was so capable and tender when she wanted to be that Catherine couldn't help wanting to spend more time with her.

Maybe, in another life, she could have had the both of them for as long as she had left. But she wouldn't bring that up with Mizuno. Catherine accepted that the thief would return to her life in Japan, continuing with her successful fashion line by day and her lucrative thieving career by night. She couldn't ask anyone to give up their legacy for a dalliance.

But Sidatih would be there. Their connection went back far longer than any of her other connections, centuries in fact, and it would be wonderful to have a companion even if their time would be brief in the grand scheme of things. Still, all of that should be thought of on another day. Not today. Not when so much rested on completing the job efficiently.

A cup of tea was pushed into her hands without her noticing at first. "Drink, Miriam. And get out of your own head for a spell," Nachem said and stood there waiting until she took a hearty sip from the cup.

They were right, of course. She needed to get out of her own head and stop thinking about what could be and start thinking about what was. The warm liquid filled her throat and soothed her belly. From what she remembered from her childhood, Nachem always made the best tea blends. They always knew what herbs were needed to fix whatever problem you were having, be it an ailment or a mood.

"Thank you. I'll try." Catherine took another generous sip to appease the golem and then set the cup down once they had walked away. She would finish the tea, knowing Nachem would chastise her later if she didn't.

"Better listen to the golem. They are right. You need to relax, albi. You could spend all day worrying, and it won't make it any easier." Sidatih gave her hand a gentle squeeze before finally unlacing their fingers and returning to his computer screen. Catherine wasn't entirely sure he was working on the plan anymore. No doubt he knew the ins and outs of his part of the job.

It seemed that everyone else was able to relax and not fixate except her.

But then, what did she have outside of this job? There wasn't much to go back to since she had gone on sabbatical from her job. The longer she thought about, the more convinced she was that she would retire from teaching altogether. After that, though? She had no idea. She could keep wandering, but how long until that lost its luster or until another incident like Thailand happened?

Too much was going through her mind, and it wasn't doing her any favors. "I'm going for a walk. It might do me some good," she announced to Sidatih as she stood from the chair.

He looked up from his computer and gave her a long stare. "Want me to come with you?" Catherine shook her head, finding she craved the need to be alone for a while.

"I'll be alright. Just want to clear my head," she responded, hoping that Sidatih understood her desire for the time to herself. He nodded and turned his attention back to the screen. Catherine left without another word, quickly making her way out of the apartment and onto the street.

The morning was cooler but not cold, and Catherine was grateful for the slight breeze, the chill cutting through her thoughts. She breathed in the sweet air mixed with that city smell that was always a bit sour. It was grounding in a way only a city could be. Even at that early hour, the streets were bustling, mostly with tourists, of course, but busy all the same. She let her gaze roam around the buildings and scanned the faces of those she passed, wondering where they were going and what they were hoping to do that day.

She hadn't been to Athens in so long, and it had changed so much. Maybe one day, she would return to simply sightsee. Though the chances of that after they stole the trumpet from Arruk were slim. He had connections all over the city; surely he would find out quickly if she returned to Athens, and Arruk never forgot a slight—and stealing from him was a huge slight.

Not for the first time that morning, Catherine cursed Titania's name and herself for even entering a bargain with the fae queen to begin with. One day, she would find a way to get back at Titania, though the how was still a mystery. Or better yet, at least for her mental health, she wouldn't see Titania again for as long as she lived.

The mechanics of the plan went through her mind again. The gala really was the best way in. The amount of people mingling about would give them camouflage to complete the job. Still, that posed its own risks as well. Someone could still see them. The warehouse was incalculably large, and the trumpet was housed out of the way, not one of Arruk's more prominent pieces. But with so many people there, once it was discovered the trumpet on display was not the original, there should be no definitive way to pin the theft on Catherine.

She would stick around in Greece for a few days after while the rest of them headed to London to reconvene. If she left Greece right after the theft, that would be a dead giveaway she was the culprit. Mizuno would take care of getting the trumpet out of Athens, and

Catherine would spend just enough time to keep suspicion off her.

Now that they were on the precipice of completing the job, Catherine couldn't help but think of some many different ways she could have planned it better instead of what they were about to implement. What if she had been too lax in the plan, or there was some flaw she was not yet seeing? What if the gala was overly crowded or an amorous couple snuck off near the trumpet in the middle of the job and blocked Mizuno from making the switch?

"I'm so stupid for doing this," she mumbled as she finally made the decision to turn around and head back to the apartment.

"Still talking to yourself, Miriam?" A voice came from behind Catherine, a note of amusement in the tone.

Arruk.

How in all the world did he cross her path right at this second? Athens was a huge city, and she wasn't anywhere near his home or the warehouse. Or so she thought. Catherine hadn't been paying much attention to the direction she was heading, and she realized now that she was only within a few blocks of the magical warehouse Arruk owned.

She did her best to plaster on an easy smile, though her swirling insides made it a struggle. "Of course. Sometimes the best person to talk to is myself," she said airily. Arruk chuckled and smiled brightly at her. Though he wore the glamour of a human male, his teeth were much too sharp to be totally normal.

"Where are you heading this fine morning?" he asked, taking a step forward, and Catherine instinctively fell into step with him, though she knew she shouldn't.

"Just taking a walk. I felt a little cooped up this morning and thought I would stretch my legs and see the city before the gala tonight. I always did love Athens as it was waking up for the day." The wistfulness of her tone was not exaggerated. There had been many mornings during her time in Athens in the past where she wandered aimlessly for hours just to observe the people.

Arruk nodded. He walked close enough to her that she could feel the heat from his arm next to hers, but they did not touch. "Many things haven't changed with you, Miriam. That's good to know. I like to do the same. It doesn't matter how long I have lived here; each morning feels like it's brand new. The wonders of antiquity and modernity colliding together is truly breathtaking." The minotaur kept his focus straight ahead, eyes roving over the city he loved as they walked.

"Is that what you're doing right now—enjoying the city? Or do you have somewhere you are heading off to?" Catherine decided being conversational would be best. She was a practiced liar; she had been doing it all her life. This occasion with Arruk should be no different than any other time. And it was especially important that she keep herself collected since in only a few short hours she would be robbing him of one of his treasures.

Arruk was silent for a moment, like he was contemplating how to answer. "A little bit of both, I would say. I'm heading to my collection to ensure everything is on schedule for tonight, but I am certainly taking my time getting there," he said after a few beats. There was a faint tug upward of his lips, and Catherine felt a wave of guilt wash over her. Arruk loved his collection. Procured every piece with care and precision. He would quickly notice one missing, even if it held little value in reality.

Not to mention she was being pleasant to someone she once considered a close friend all while preparing to rob him. If it had been almost anyone else there would have been no guilt, but now, especially as she walked beside him, the guilt and shame ate away at her, contracting her stomach into knots. She felt sick.

"There's definitely no rush, knowing it will all be there once you arrive. And there is something truly magical about Athens. I can understand completely why you choose not to leave it," Catherine said, also keeping her eyes fixed ahead. She was concerned that if she were to look Arruk's way, she would confess all, and then where would she be? Her time in Connecticut had made her rusty and unreliable in her former profession.

"They will be, or else I paid a fortune for security for nothing." The minotaur chuckled, sending another wave of anxiety through Catherine. They had scouted all they could about the security system in place at the warehouse, including the physical security. And yet, she still wasn't sure if it was enough.

"Let's hope then that your money doesn't go to waste, and you can enjoy your time without worrying." She forced herself to keep her tone light and casual, but Catherine knew the longer she spent with Arruk, the worse she would feel. It was time for her to get away and back to the safety of the apartment.

"Hm, yes, let's hope. Well," Arruk responded as he brought his wrist up to check the time, "I should get going. I have a meeting in twenty minutes and have yet to have my morning tea. It was lovely bumping into you, Miriam. Enjoy the rest of your stroll through my city. I will see you and your lovely wife tonight."

With a quick goodbye, he was gone, walking down the street at a leisurely pace heading for his warehouse of treasures. And Catherine was left standing there alone as she watched the minotaur fade into the distance, her head full and her guts roiling.

CHAPTER 17

"This is easily the tiniest van I have ever seen in my life," Sidatih complained, staring at the white van which wasn't much bigger than a normal sized sedan. In his hands, he carried a box that held a monitor, his laptop, and a few cables.

Catherine held back the laugh she so wanted to let out. "You're just used to overpriced ostentatious cars in San Francisco," she said, opening the back doors for him to enter. Sidatih stepped up into the van and set down his stuff on a built-in table before he turned and headed back out of the vehicle.

"Most of my business associates drive cars that are barely street legal with how low to the ground they are. I drive a 1967 Shelby GT350, and she is a beautiful beastly machine. I'm terrified of driving her around the city, which is why I use the Tesla," Sidatih said so matter-of-factly that Catherine wasn't sure if he was joking.

She followed him back inside where he was collecting more of his equipment, passing Nachem on the sidewalk where they stood watching over the van. "Why do you even bother with a car when you can transport yourself with magic?" Catherine had noted over their time together the last few weeks that Sidatih rarely used his ifrit magic, only using it for small things like starting fires and disappearing objects. She said nothing to him, of course, choosing instead to note it only, and if there was a time to bring it up, she might do so.

He kept walking and said nothing until a second box was in his arms, and they were heading back down to the van again. "The funny thing about working with technology is that soon you become reliant on it. I have to keep up appearances for my business, and so it's simply become second nature for me to do everything the human way." Sidatih's tone was nonchalant, but he wouldn't look at Catherine while he spoke, even as he moved away from the van again. There was more to it that he wasn't telling her, and maybe she should have pried or at least tried to get him to tell her more, but their focus needed to be on getting everything ready for the evening.

It wasn't like Sidatih to withhold from her. Even at the onset of their acquaintance, he had been candid about everything, maybe almost too candid. She knew more intimate details about Sidatih than just about anyone else. The ifrit had a way of seeing the shade of one's soul and deciding if he was going to allow himself to try and trust. And his trust had to be earned. And until that moment, Catherine believed she had his trust completely. She brushed off the slight sting and cleared it from her mind. Sidatih would tell her when and if he wanted; she needed to stop letting every little worry cloud her mind when she needed complete focus.

"Let us hope we will not need to escape in this vehicle. I doubt we could all fit," Mizuno said coolly as she came to stand on the sidewalk near the van. "Miriam, we should get ready for the gala. It is already 5 o'clock." Catherine nodded, looped her arm through Mizuno's, and let the other woman lead her back inside.

As Catherine entered her room, she noticed a box sitting on her bed. On top of the box was a note.

For the diamond of my heart. May you sparkle even brighter tonight.

Your Sida

P.S. It's not just a pretty jewel. It's also a Second Sight gem. You'll need it tonight.

Lifting the lid from the box, Catherine's eyes widened on the drop silver necklace with a large diamond pendant on the end and matching drop earrings. Simple but elegant, exactly Catherine's style. And a Second Sight gem would give her the ability to not only watch her surroundings but keep an eye on Mizuno as well. It was perfect. She would have to thank Sida properly later.

Catherine made quick work of getting ready, her hair curled around her face, gray streaks tucked against brown in elegant waves. Her makeup was dramatic enough to compliment the dress without being overly sultry. Last, she placed the diamond necklace from Sida around her neck, letting it drape between her exposed cleavage, and slipped the earrings through her lobes. Taking in her image in the full-length mirror in her room, Catherine hardly recognized herself. There had been few occasions in recent years to dress up, and even then, it was attending boring university events under her rather frumpy glamour.

A knock came on her door followed by Nachem's voice. "Miriam, the car is here."

"Coming," she responded with a last look in the mirror. She stepped out of the room and back into the communal space where the other three were already waiting. Mizuno had finished dressing before her.

The thief was clad in one of her own elegant designs featuring a royal blue cropped kimono top with sleeves that fell almost to her knees. The skirt hung just below the top, revealing only a small sliver of pale skin, and was a full tulled affair, much like a princess gown in shades of deep purples, blues, and black. Several rings adorned her fingers, the only jewelry she wore. Her silky dark hair was pulled up in an elaborate braided bun atop her head, a few carefully selected tendrils hanging down to frame her face. Mizuno was the picture of sophistication and loveliness.

But it was Sidatih's face that drew Catherine's attention the most. His jaw dropped, and his eyes roamed up and down her body like he didn't know where to settle his gaze. Catherine felt a level of nakedness under his scrutiny. True, it didn't help that the crimson dress she wore was entirely backless, exposed to nearly the top of her bottom, while the draped front hung low, dipping down to rest just below her breasts. Singa had been right that a bra could not possibly go with the dress. The silky material hugged every curve and brushed the floor with a single slit up the left leg stopping high up on her thigh. It was more skin than she had displayed in public in a long time, and it make her feel both powerful and exposed.

Sidatih's heated gaze made her feel the latter much more than the former. "I don't know whether to grovel at your feet or put a coat over your shoulders so that none can see your gorgeous body," he said in awe.

"You should do the groveling; under no circumstances will I allow you to wrinkle that dress. Miriam deserves to be admired and shown off like a prized gem," Mizuno said sharply to Sidatih.

Catherine snorted, ruining the illusion a bit. "I am not a prized anything, but I will accept the groveling at my feet." She laughed, letting herself enjoy the moment for now as the rest of the evening would undoubtedly be quite tense.

"You look stunning, Miriam. A bit immodest perhaps but stunning nonetheless," Nachem said, though there was no actual judgement in their words. The golem said only what was factual, not meaning to hurt her feelings at all; they simply didn't take feelings into account when speaking. And they definitely weren't wrong about the modesty factor.

"I'm sure I am scandalizing my ancestors, but I feel pretty and not the least bit embarrassed." She did a slow spin and let the edges of the dress flare out slightly. "Now, let's go break hearts and steal some shit!" Catherine announced, suddenly feeling giddy and full of adrenaline. The dread at seeing Arruk again would come later, at her moment of betrayal, she was sure. Right now, though, she felt stunning and godlike.

"One more thing, Miriam," Nachem said. They walked over to her and held out their hand palm up, inviting Catherine to place her hand in theirs. She did so, giving the solid stone a squeeze. With their other hand, Nachem slipped a delicate silver ring on her left index finger. It felt warm against her skin, and she could feel the hum of magic inside her once it settled against her finger.

"This will allow you to push away the wards. Mizuno will feel where the hole is once you make it. It will be small, and it will take much energy to maintain. You will focus on the trumpet, and the magic will do the rest." Nachem held her gaze as he explained the way the magic worked. They had discussed this already, and she knew the golem had been working on the magic for several days now when not in the kitchen.

"Thank you, Nachem," she replied, squeezing their hand one more time before letting go. She and Mizuno parted from the other two minutes later, heading for an uncertain outcome.

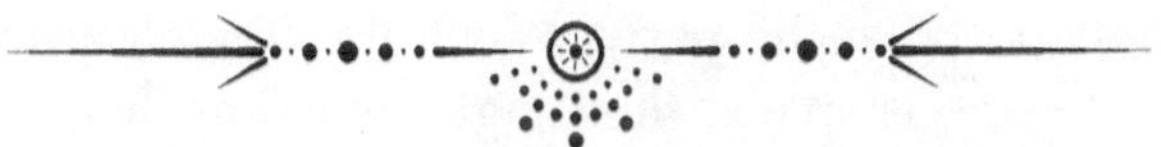

Security was tight, at least from the outside as Catherine and Mizuno approached the doors to the warehouse. This time there were two people standing outside the doors checking names against the list. Around them, people in the most elegant outfits in a variety of colors glided up to the doors.

"Sidatih, Nachem, can you hear me?" Catherine spoke aloud, though only Mizuno stood next to her.

Before leaving the apartment, she had handed out sets of recently acquired earwigs. They looked remarkably like a modern ear bud and operated as a two-way communication device but were spelled to blend with the ear. They were virtually undetectable and could not be jammed in the usual ways. It would allow them to communicate once she and the thief were inside. Hopefully, they wouldn't need to use them often.

"We got you, albi. Be careful in there. I'd hate to crash the party and burn the place down to get you out. Arruk already hates me enough, or so you say. But that won't stop me from destroying his entire collection to get you out safely." Sidatih's laugh sounded forced at the end. Catherine responded by promising they would be safe, and the chatter ceased.

With a fortifying breath, Catherine linked her arm with Mizuno's, and the two of them headed toward the entrance. Their passage through the doors was unencumbered, and for a moment, they were blinded by the brilliant light of the interior.

The space was completely transformed from what it looked like at the party. Witch fire floated around the cavernous space, the magic twinkling like stars. The floor was obscured by a cloud layer, giving the illusion that they were walking on puffy white clouds high in the heavens. People swept around the room like they glided, their finery completing the image that they were gods lounging about Mount Olympus. An unseen orchestra played somewhere from within the clouds, and already a few couples danced in an open space that had been cleared away for the dance floor.

A waiter in a knee-length white chiton walked up to them with a tray of champagne and they both grabbed a glass. Mingling between the patrons were a variety of waiters, men in chitons and women in peplos down to their ankles, carrying trays of food and drink. Catherine was thankful Nachem had fed them before they left the apartment, or she would have spent all her time focused on the food circulating around the room. Though she couldn't help herself when a waiter offered a tray of dolmades, rolled vine leaves stuff full of grain and vegetables. The flavors exploded on her tongue as she chewed, and Catherine had to stop herself from reaching for another one.

"You are allowed to eat, Miriam," Mizuno whispered to her as the waiter walked away. But Catherine shook her head.

"We have a job to do. I need to focus on that rather than the delicious food," she responded, still staring at the tray as it disappeared into the crowd. When it was out of sight, she turned her attention back to her companion. "Right. Let's do some mingling first. Get ourselves seen. Then we'll start the operation. We stay together for now, and I'll let myself be distracted and drawn away while you meander..." Catherine started, but Mizuno interrupted her.

"Miriam, I know the plan. Breathe for me. This will all be alright," she said, her voice gentle and even. Mizuno was right. Catherine had already gone over the plan with them twice that day alone. They were prepared. She was prepared.

Letting her arm fall down along Mizuno's, Catherine linked hands with the other woman and tugged her along through the room, glasses of untouched champagne in each of their hands. Catherine scanned the crowd for Arruk. There were far more people at the gala than had been at the party, and most were of the magical variety.

Events like this were a place for the magical community to gather in their natural forms. No one needed to use a glamour when they were with their own kind. The two women walked past a group of nymphs admiring a harp that had once belonged to the god Apollo, a highly valuable item leftover from Ezra's time.

A few centaurs mingled among a group with a lamia, and a satyr that Catherine recognized standing next to his wife, who was a harpy. She waved to them as she passed, reminding herself to find them later when she joined up with Arruk. The harpy gave a cursory nod at first before recognition set in, and she waved back enthusiastically. She nudged her husband with a wing, and he looked over and gave a wave and a smile of his own. There was a warm feeling in her chest. She had left so much behind; it was a shame this was how she returned to Greece. She would very much have liked to reconnect with many from her past.

"I imagine there are a few old friends in attendance tonight." Mizuno's voice cut through her reverie. Catherine nodded. "More like acquaintances, but yes. Makes me wish that I had visited sooner and under better circumstances."

Mizuno made a humming noise that Catherine just barely heard over the noise of the room. "We cannot change the past or regret what we did not do. There is now and what is to come. Maybe one day you'll return under those better circumstances." Catherine doubted she would see Greece again, but she gave Mizuno's hand an appreciative squeeze.

Keeping up appearances, Catherine took a small sip from her glass. There was no way she was going to drink the whole thing since she needed to keep her head clear, but the taste was delightful, and she liked the way the bubbles tickled at her lips.

"We should find Arruk soon. Sida, can you locate him?" She lowered her voice so that only Mizuno and Sida on the earwig would hear.

Sidatih's voice filtered through as clear as if he were standing right next to her whispering in her ear. "Greeting guests near the Sible's Bowl from Delphi. Your left about a hundred paces. He's talking to a manticore in a tux. Can't miss either of them."

"Great. Tiza's here. Now I have to deal with both of them. I should have thought of that," Catherine muttered. She chastised herself for not thinking of Arruk's longtime business partner, Tizazma Kashkouli. After all these decades, she didn't think they would still be working together. Theirs had always been a love/hate relationship. Mostly hate but begrudgingly working together. Tiza was gruff on a good day, and he couldn't stand Arruk's good humor.

"Didn't Tiza try to get you thrown out of Athens for some dumb reason?" Sida's voice filtered through her ear.

Tiza had, in fact, succeeded in getting her thrown out of Athens for all of two days for as he called it "being an ungodly heathen," and a "corruption to vulnerable young women," all because he had caught Catherine in bed with his eldest daughter.

His *married* eldest daughter.

Catherine had done some questionable things in her youth. She just hoped that wouldn't come back to bite her in this instance. Not like it did in Thailand.

"That's the one," she responded as nonchalantly as possible. Sida chuckled a "Good luck," and then the line went quiet again.

Mizuno placed a calming hand on Catherine's forearm. "Is that going to be a problem?" Her tone held more concern than Catherine expected. Not the kind of concern about the job, but more personal, said with a soft voice and eyes that looked into her soul.

Catherine shrugged. Truly, she didn't know. Manticores were a fickle lot. They would either easily forget or hold a grudge forever. It wasn't like Catherine knew Tiza well enough to know which camp he fell into, though she had a sneaking suspicion it was the latter. There was nothing to do about it now. She would just have to make due.

"It'll be fine, I'm sure. I'll have Arruk there if needed. And besides, I can probably talk him into letting bygones be bygones. Enough time has passed." Catherine tried to keep her voice even, tried to find the calm to match her words. It was all going to be okay. There was a small chance that Tiza didn't even remember her.

With a fortifying breath, she moved out of Mizuno's grip and turned toward the direction Sidatih indicated. A tug on her wrist drew her back toward Mizuno. "Miriam, be careful. Be vigilant," she said, her eyes unblinking. Then she pulled her close and pressed her lips against Catherine's. In a second, Catherine's hand rose to cradle Mizuno's jaw, and she sighed into the kiss before pulling away. With one last glance over her shoulder, Catherine walked away, registering that Mizuno turned toward the direction of the trumpet, ready to complete her part.

The kiss left Catherine dizzy for a moment, but then common sense kicked back in, and she focused her attention back where it belonged. At this point, Sidatih and Mizuno both would be the death of her if she wasn't careful.

It was relatively easy to find Arruk once Sida had given her directions. It was hard to miss an elegantly clothed minotaur standing next to an equally well-dressed manticore. The two of them were positively massive compared to the majority of the guests around them. She touched her hand to the gem around her neck, activating the spell. It was like a split screen happened before her eyes. She could see the two men before her while also seeing Mizuno make her way casually through the crowd.

Arruk was laughing into his narrow glass of ouzo. Tiza didn't so much as crack a smile, let alone share in Arruk's mirth. His eyes caught the sight of Catherine's approach first, and by the way they narrowed, she knew right away that he had not forgotten about her.

It took a moment more for Arruk to notice her, and when he did, his arms opened wide, and he stepped close to embrace her. Catherine allowed herself to be swallowed up in his arms. It was safe and familiar, his warm soft fur surrounding her in a cocoon of comfort. The knot in her stomach tightened. She didn't deserve this.

"Miriam! Look at you, you are positively radiant!" Arruk exclaimed loudly as he pulled away, holding her out at arm's length to take in her figure. Catherine could tell right away that Arruk was well lubricated with the ouzo by that point, which meant it should be fairly easy to keep him distracted.

"You clean up well, Arruk," she said, letting her gaze travel down his form. He had swapped out the plain gold horn caps for ones that were more rose gold and inlaid with precious gems. The witchfire lights made the colors gleam brightly, marking Arruk as a beacon for all the room to see.

Arruk knew very well that he looked impressive, and he didn't shy away from the compliment. "Well, I can't host a gala and look like a bum, can I? And where's the wife? Or did you leave that charming creature at home and deny us her presence?" He laughed, a booming sound that reverberated. Attention focused on Arruk by those around them.

This was good. Arruk was just inebriated enough to be loud, which would draw more attention to him anyway. More eyes on the minotaur meant fewer that could be on Mizuno. The crowd cover would do the rest. Catherine thanked whatever gods were listening for the turn of luck.

Now all she could do was trust in her team and do her job of keeping the area cleared. Mizuno had everything she needed to swap the trumpet, including the magic from Ezra that would shrink it. Once she gave Catherine the signal, Catherine would find her, and they would make a polite but speedy exit. There was no chatter on the earwigs, so she had to trust in the Second Sight spell and that Sidatih had his eyes on the rest of the room.

"I would never deny a chance to show her off. As it is, she ran into an acquaintance, and I believe they are off perusing your warehouse. Your collection seems to have exploded over the last few centuries," Catherine said, her gaze fixed on Arruk's face, the better to draw him in and keep his focus on her.

The minotaur smiled brightly, snatching a drink offered to him on a tray before setting down his finished glass. "Exploded is exactly the correct word! Yes! I daresay this place has really filled out in the time I've owned it. Of course, the last time you were here, Ezra had really cleaned the place out, but he left me several wonderful things, many of which I still have. And Athens will always be a place of trade. You wouldn't believe the things that pass through. Let me tell you—"

Arruk was cut off mid-sentence by Tiza's bored grating voice. "I would like for you to tell us more about how you ended up here in Athens, Miriam. Last I checked, you had skipped town never to return, leaving nothing but a trail of broken hearts and bad decisions."

He wasn't wrong. That was exactly what Catherine had done, and she only felt guilt about a small part of that. What she had done to Arruk, cutting him out of her life like that, had left her with a hole in her heart. She had felt it necessary since Arruk would never leave Athens, and she was bound by a duty for all time. But for others, like Tiza's daughter, well, she couldn't even remember the woman's face. Which led her to believe it was a mostly unremarkable time, as the woman was half manticore.

Catherine took a sip of her champagne to recalibrate. "I'm sure Arruk has told you. I'm revisiting some of my old haunts, saying goodbye to old friends, and such. Mortality really makes you think of the people who have been important in your life."

Tiza scoffed at the word "mortality." Most of the beings in the room would never know what it was like to face their impending demise. They would go on long after she was dust. And most had a low view of mortals anyway, Tiza was very much being in the camp of dislike.

"How sad and pathetic. Mortality, really, Miriam? As if you could sink no lower." Tiza's words were meant to cut. And perhaps they would have on a lesser person. But Catherine didn't give a shit about what Tiza thought. She hadn't back then, and she definitely didn't now.

"How are your children, Tiza? Lenuia doing well?" she asked with a saccharine smile. She knew she was playing with fire, getting Tiza riled up, but she couldn't help herself. She had forgotten how it brought her endless joy when she needled him.

Catherine wasn't aware that manticores could turn that shade of red, but Tiza's whole face turned a dark crimson, bordering on purple like he couldn't get enough air. The tension was thick between them, but even in his intoxicated state, Arruk could read a situation well enough. He slapped a large paw against Tiza's back and laughed raucously. "The two of you look ready to fight right here. I would advise against it, though, as I would have to throw you out. Come on, Tiza, you can't hold a grudge forever. Let's let bygones be bygones, and Miriam, let's all agree not to sleep with each other's offspring."

"You don't have any offspring, as far as I know," Catherine said with a smile as she took another fortifying sip of her drink. She really should slow down on the champagne, but this was turning out to be more nerve-wracking than she originally thought.

Another boisterous laugh boomed out of Arruk. "Thank the gods for that! Could you imagine me as a father? The last thing I need is a bunch of children running around claiming my treasures for themselves before I'm even cold in the ground."

Tiza said nothing to this, and instead, he tersely excused himself and slunk off into the crowd. Catherine sighed in relief. Without the manticore around, it was easier to breathe and think clearly.

"I can't believe you're still working with that ass. His demeanor certainly hasn't changed at all over the years." Catherine kept her tone light, adding a little laugh into her voice. She wished she could find Mizuno in the crowd. The Second Sight was a bit of a distraction, so as much as she wanted to focus on Mizuno's actions more, she had to keep her attention on Arruk rather than on Mizuno. It wasn't an easy task to accomplish, and a part of her wished Sidatih had warned her beforehand about the gem so she could practice with it. She didn't have much experience with Second Sight.

Arruk let out a laughing sort of snort, enough air passing through his snout to move the ring between his nostrils a little. "That old ass has the best contacts and too much money. He's a necessary attachment despite his personality."

"Miriam, I'm at the trumpet. Area is clear. Awaiting your signal for the wards." Mizuno's voice filtered through her mind via the earwig, drowning out Arruk's voracious laugh. Outwardly, Catherine kept her focus on Arruk, falling back on old practices of looking engaged when her attention was elsewhere. Instead, she twirled the silver ring on her finger three times as Nachem had instructed, and immediately she felt the surge of magic. Her mind filled with an image of the trumpet, and it was as if some invisible thread sprung from her in search of the item. Not even a second later, she felt the pull. The wards had been identified, and the magic was beginning its work.

She laughed along with Arruk as she lifted her glass to her lips. "Do it," she said into her glass before taking a drink. There was no reply, but then, she didn't need one. She could see Mizuno's transformation into her spider form, see her crawling toward the case where the hole in the wards was located.

"Where are you headed next, Miriam?" Arruk's voice cut in. Catherine hadn't been aware she had slipped from the conversation. The magic was working, but already she felt a little more tired than she had only moments before.

"Hm? Oh, I thought I would take some time away from everything and stay at my cabin in Lake Tahoe. I've been globetrotting for a while, and I think I could use a recharge." She smiled breezily, making it sound like she was taking a brief rest rather than a retreat from the world.

"Forgive me. I am not entirely familiar with North American locales. Is that in Canada?" Arruk already had a new drink in his hand, but he was still grinning.

Catherine tried a smile of her own, giving Arruk's arm a playful swipe. "You're too Athens-centric. No, it's in the States. California to be precise. It's beautiful there, serene and wonderful. I've kept a cabin up there for decades, though I've not used it as often as I would have liked."

"Blame Ezra for that. Boy never wanted to leave his shop, I bet. I hope his wife is getting him out and about," Arruk bellowed, waving his hand around wildly. The more the minotaur drank, the wilder his gesticulating became.

Catherine tried for a laugh, but it suddenly felt like a monumental effort, and instead it was a little harder to breathe. The magic took a monumental amount of energy already. Nachem had warned her it would. She just somehow didn't expect it to be quite so sudden. Not to mention she had an additional spell running that she hadn't planned for. She felt like she radiated magic.

"Miriam? Are you alright?" Arruk said with concern. He placed one heavy hand on her shoulder. The warm fur against her skin was calming, familiar, but it did nothing to stop her from feeling weaker by the minute.

She waved him off. "I'm fine. Too much champagne on an empty stomach, I think. You just had to break out the good stuff right away." Her tone was convincing enough for Arruk to pat her shoulder affectionately and withdraw with a chuckle.

He waved over a waiter, who scurried over with a laden tray. "There's more than enough food floating around. Please eat! I should see to the other guests now. After all, they all paid exuberant amounts to be here tonight."

Arruk turned to go, and Catherine had to decide quickly if she should call him back, distract him for longer or let him go. There had been no word from Mizuno yet, and Catherine wasn't sure how much longer she could keep the connection with the ward breaking spell before she eventually passed out. Her sight was already a little fuzzy, and she couldn't see Mizuno clearly with the Second Sight. The thief was too small. Then she saw the trumpet disappear for only a second and then reappear, only it was the false trumpet in its place.

"I have it." Mizuno's voice filtered through the earwig, now back in her human form. Arruk had only moved a few yards away, still well away from where the trumpet had sat. Catherine immediately focused on the ward spell, severing the connection. She fell forward half a step, catching herself before she completely fell over. A headache was beginning to form at the front of her head, and she felt slightly dizzy, like she really had drunk too much on an empty stomach.

Catherine slowly made her way toward Mizuno, attempting to keep upright with each step. She brushed her fingers over the gem again to deactivate the spell, and her vision cleared only a little. With some food and sleep, she would feel better, but first she had to find the thief and get them both out quickly. At least now she didn't have to feign an excuse to leave should Arruk spot their exit. She felt horrible and undoubtedly looked it.

Cool hands caught her forearm as she stumbled forward again. Mizuno's hold was strong yet gentle, and she kept Catherine upright with little effort. Mizuno moved her arm so it wrapped around Catherine's waist, and a small weight fell against Catherine's palm. Mizuno had handed over the miniaturized trumpet, and Catherine unnoticeably slipped it into the secret warded pocket in her dress.

"Come along, Miriam. Let me get you home," Mizuno said, loud enough to be heard from the few around them, her tone filled with concern.

"Mir, albi, are you okay? You look like you're about to be sick. Did they slip you something in your drink? I didn't see anything from my view, but that doesn't mean it wasn't possible." Sidatih's voice sounded frantic in her ear.

She shook her head, knowing full well that Sidatih could see her on the security cameras. "No, nothing like that. The warding magic took a monumental amount of energy, just as Nachem said. It's been a while since I've experienced magical burnout." Catherine kept her voice low and her held tilted toward Mizuno, giving the illusion she was talking to the other woman.

"You have a clear exit. Nachem is holding the wards. The minotaur is across the room and out of sight of the doors. Security has been slacking off since everyone got inside, so they won't notice you leaving.

I'm having the car brought up now. It will be there to meet you outside." Sidatih continued to talk through the earwig, giving Catherine the peace of mind she needed. All that was left was to get out of the building, and they would be free.

"Just a few more steps, Miriam," Mizuno said, giving Catherine's hip a squeeze. It felt like her head was heavy and her heart was beating out of her chest. This was the one part where everything could go to shit and all their work would have been for nothing. With the exit in sight, this was the most dangerous part of the job. When she could see the end but wasn't there yet, that's when mistake happened.

A few more steps and they would be outside, and then Nachem would whisk them away in the car, and they would be gone with the trumpet. Then Catherine could sleep for a day and replenish her strength. Once the trumpet was out of Greece, then she could breathe easy again.

"Leaving so soon, Miriam?" The voice behind them was cold and grating and belonged to the last person Catherine hoped to run into on their way out.

Tizazma Kashkouli stood at the doorway leading into the warehouse proper, triumph in his dark eyes.

CHAPTER 18

Tiza's scorpion-like tail whipped behind him like he was an excited dog, finally catching the car it had been chasing. There was no way for him to know if they had taken anything, no reason to suspect them of anything. All Tiza had was his old grudges, and he would use any excuse to find a way to punish Catherine for past transgressions.

Catherine was still too weak to do much, but she straightened her spine and leaned a little more into Mizuno. "I'm afraid the drinks are not sitting well with me. My wife is taking me home. Enjoy the rest of the party, Tiza. I would say it was wonderful to see you again, but we're beyond lies at this point." Mizuno took her cue and started to turn them back toward the exit.

"No, I don't imagine they are. I find it funny that you disappear from Athens for years only to turn up now when the gallery is fully open to anyone, and suddenly you want to spend a little time with Arruk. Strange after all these years, don't you think?" He was gloating; of course he was, the bastard. He didn't have any evidence of them doing anything, and yet he was going to find a way to have her arrested or worse.

"Good timing, I suppose. I didn't know about this little party until after I had arrived, thanks to Arruk sharing the knowledge. But if you have something you want to accuse me of, Tiza, by all means, go ahead." She felt so heavy; it would be hours yet before her strength returned, and still she kept her tone light, bored even. The last thing she should do was get defensive or confrontational. For centuries, Catherine had dealt with men like Tiza, who thought they held all the power in the room. She wouldn't be bested by this one.

Tiza didn't respond right away. Instead, he lifted his sleeve and tapped the face of his watch. In seconds, two centaur security guards appeared, wearing dark shirts on their human half and regular earpieces. "Search them," Tiza commanded.

"Is this really necessary, Tiza? Where exactly would we put anything in these outfits? Even our bags are too small to fit anything of value," Catherine responded, trying to sound both bored and affronted when all she wanted to do was close her eyes and not say anything to anyone for a long while. She wasn't worried about the security guards finding the trumpet. The pocket created in her dress could not be found by anyone except by her. They could move their hands right over the trumpet and not feel it. And unless they used some high-level magic, they shouldn't be able to even detect the ward in her dress.

The centaurs moved toward them, their hooves clip-clopping against the elegant marble floors. Catherine and Mizuno made no move toward the door, standing stock still at their approach. Both of the women were seasoned thieves; they knew better than to run. They would submit to what Tiza thought was necessary, play along until he was satisfied. Maybe Catherine was relying a little too heavily on magic to conceal the theft, but she had to trust in it to see her through. It wasn't like she had enough energy to do anything else.

She had to hand it to the security guards. They were thorough but not lewd in their search, keeping their touches professional. They found nothing, of course, not from a simple pat down. When they gave Tiza the all clear, the manticore's triumphant gaze turned sour. His tail swished now out of agitation, and while normally Catherine would have returned his agitation with a smirk, now even doing that was a monumental effort.

Nachem really undersold how draining that spell was.

"I don't think Arruk would take kindly to you accusing and searching his guests. Seems to be bad form to me, especially since it's not your collection anyway." It felt harder to breathe than it should. Catherine's heart was racing, her composure slipping when she should have felt in complete control. Something wasn't right. This wasn't just the spell draining her. Something else was interfering with her body. Poison maybe? But she only had one drink and who would want to poison her? Well, besides Tiza.

"Maybe not, but he will understand that I am acting only in his best interest. You always were a thief, Miriam, and we can't change who we are any more than we can change the stars." Tiza drew his eyes away from her and tapped his watch again.

Beside Catherine, Mizuno remained still, saying nothing. Catherine didn't know how she could convey that something was amiss with her body without Tiza noticing. But then, as she felt weaker by the moment, she knew that might not matter.

"Tiza, what's going on here? It's a party. Why are you all standing by the door?" Arruk strode up, another drink in his hand. He didn't seem nearly as sober as Tiza, not surprising considering he had another full drink in his hand. The minotaur certainly was having a good night without any worry that he would be robbed.

Arruk walked up to them and gave Tiza a slap on the back that would have sent a mortal man flying across the room. "Come on. Let's all get back to the party. The dancing has just started!" His voice was loud, echoing through the entry hall.

"I don't think Miriam is quite in the mood for dancing. Certainly not with the hemlock working through her system. I bet she can barely fill her lungs at the moment." Tiza's smile was full of malice as he directed his words toward Arruk while his gaze remained firmly locked on Catherine.

It took a moment for the words to sink it.

Hemlock.

Tiza had poisoned her. There was no way of knowing how much he had dosed her with, though clearly it was not so much to kill her, at least not yet, otherwise she would have been dead already. But she could feel the effects the poison was having on her. The labored breathing and racing heart made more sense now. The ward spell may have sapped her strength, but the hemlock would slowly kill her.

"You son of a bitch!" Mizuno made to step toward Tiza, a flash of one of her knives glinting in her hand. But she stopped just as quickly when Catherine slumped toward the ground, Mizuno no longer holding her upright. The knife slipped back into place and Mizuno's arm once again wove around Catherine's side, keeping her from falling again. Catherine could feel Mizuno's body vibrate against hers, anger shaking every inch of the other woman's body.

Sidatih and Nachem had to be hearing this. In the growing haze of her thoughts, Catherine thought of Sida and how he must be losing his mind watching everything happening. She wished she could reassure him, but she wasn't even sure she could convince herself everything would work out.

Tiza shrugged, causing the suit jacket to stretch across his shoulders. "It was a precaution. You don't think I would allow Arruk to keep such a large collection unguarded. It was only logical for me to want to protect the assets of my partner, especially where my money is also involved, and the timing was rather too convenient."

"Tiza, you can't honestly think Miriam would ever steal from me. And to poison one of my guests on a hunch and a grudge, that's low even for you. Come, Miriam. Let us get you to my healer. She keeps plenty of potions on hand for such things." Arruk reached out a hand to beckon her forward. If only Catherine could force her legs to move. She would feel more guilt if she could focus on that emotion, but her body shutting down was taking over the bulk of her attention.

Tiza put out a paw to stop Arruk. "Not until we know for certain they haven't taken anything from your collection."

"Then what do you suggest, Tiza? That we take the time to search them while poor Miriam slowly fades? She looks ready to collapse in a moment. I would like to have my healer take care of things for her, and then we can all get back to the party." Arruk's attitude was clear; he wanted to have fun, not deal with what he assumed were Tiza's bad faith antics.

"I propose a locator spell, and from there she can be dealt with as you see fit, be it arrest or restoration. Personally, I'm hoping for the former rather than the latter. If she lasts that long." This he directed squarely at Catherine.

The feeling is mutual, she managed to think as she stared at the two men.

"Quick spell, then healer, and then it's back to the party," Arruk said, taking a long pull from his drink. The minotaur was having a great time, unaffected by the fact that she had been poisoned with hemlock, of all things, just to make sure she wasn't stealing anything because Tiza thought she might.

"Sidatih, what are you going to do to get us out of this situation fast?" Mizuno spoke to the earpiece, but she had turned her face to speak the words for Sidatih into the side of Catherine's head.

"Nachem is eager to come inside. We don't want to give them any justification for holding you longer than necessary." Sidatih's response sounded like he was trying to keep the panicking at bay, but only just. "The escape route is still open, but unless you can get away from the guards, I don't see it being much help."

"Is Nachem still holding the wards?" Catherine said, breathing into the side of Mizuno's neck, struggling to get air into her lungs.

"I am, Miriam." Nachem's gravelly voice came through the earwig. As much as she wanted to sigh with relief at having her golem close, they were not out of trouble yet. Far from it.

Tiza took a step toward her. "If you want to live a full human life span, Miriam, I suggest you subject yourself to the spell. Though we all know you are not innocent. Once a thief, always a thief; you can't help yourself." His eyes narrowed on her, a fire burning behind his dark orbs.

"Lead on, Tiza. I have nothing to hide." Catherine took a step, faltered, and leaned on Mizuno for support. Tiza gave one more parting triumphant sneer and turned on his heel. Mizuno gracefully walked them forward, following behind Tiza and the guards. Arruk came up on Catherine's other side, wrapping his free arm around her for additional support.

"Don't worry, Miriam. Tiza has always been paranoid, and clearly, he can't let ancient history go. I'll have my healer sent for and then rest assured Tiza and I will be having a discussion about his methods. Not that it's much comfort at the moment," Arruk said, giving her body a comforting squeeze.

He was right; it wasn't much comfort. Not when her body felt like it was shutting down, which is probably was. The sooner she was seen to by the healer, the better. It was unlikely Tiza's spell would be able to detect the trumpet in her pocket, so the search shouldn't take long. At least, she hoped it wouldn't.

Tiza led the group off to the other end of the entry hall where a second, much smaller door than the main entrance, stood. He pressed a button on a control panel by the door, designed in a similar fashion to Ezra's shop back in New Britain, and a little ping announced the door had switched to the room he wanted.

Going through the door revealed a large office space. Everything was dark paneled wood, imported no doubt, and altogether it looked like a very uninviting place. Cold and humorless, with only the fireplace and a few dim lamps to give the space any light. Tiza's office was not used to visitors.

"Stand there, both of you." Tiza directed them to the center of the room. "Search them again," Tiza ordered the guards. The two of them trotted over to the women, and with firm hands, they began to search their persons. The centaurs were purely professional, no lingering touches or advances, but this time they were more thorough, letting no inch of their body go uncatalogued. A hum of magic passed over Catherine's skin, the warmth of magic searching every inch of her. She prayed the warded pocket kept its secret.

When the thorough magical pat down had been completed, both guards trotted back. "Nothing, sirs," one of the centaurs said in a high voice.

"Nothing we could detect using the search spell either, sirs," the other centaur added, his voice a rumbling bass. Catherine wanted to sigh with relief, but that would give away too much, alerting Tiza that there was something she was hiding. The manticore missed very little.

"There! See, Tiza? Nothing to worry about. Now let's get Miriam to my healer, and we'll go enjoy the rest of the night. Unless, you don't feel up to it, of course, Miriam. Poison is nasty business, and Tiza will be making up for this whole incident." He directed the last toward Catherine, though she was only vaguely aware of his words, her mind too preoccupied with not panicking as she gulped for air. She felt so stupid. After enough years of getting into a plethora of troubles, there were a few essentials she always kept with her—one of which was a potion to reverse poisons— which she had left back at the apartment thinking she wouldn't need anything else.

She was an absolute fool. And if she didn't survive this, she planned to haunt Titania to the end of her days for causing the whole mess over some dumb magical item.

Catherine took a wobbly step forward, supported by Mizuno. But again, Tiza halted them. Rather than a disgruntled look on his face, he had that same triumphant smug smirk back, like he knew he won even when the evidence so far had pointed to the opposite. "How naïve you are, Arruk. You are far too trusting, which is why I had an extra layer of wards added to your collection last evening before the staff started setting up. A precaution really, but it seems to have paid off."

"I know you stole Pheme's Trumpet. The moment your friend here turned into a spider form to infiltrate the display, my wards went off. You're not nearly as clever as you think you are, Miriam," Tiza pronounced proudly, like some detective who had unmasked the culprit.

Arruk's gaze turned to her, boring into her soul as if trying to detect the answer in her eyes. "Miriam, is this true?" He sounded more sober, like he was finally taking the situation seriously, and even through her weakness, Catherine felt the gnawing teeth of guilt.

"Fuck it, I'm sending in Nachem," Sidatih's voice came over the earwig. Catherine wanted to tell him no, but she had no voice left.

"They also have some kind of communication devices, Arruk, no doubt to collaborate with others outside. A whole thieving operation has taken place right under nose, and you let your affection cloud your judgement. I suggest we call our police and let them handle her. I doubt this time she will see the light of day again." Tiza puffed up his wide chest, his pride filling the whole room.

The whole time Mizuno had stayed silent, giving nothing away. She didn't break now, her focus completely on Tiza. Only now the manticore squirmed a little under the scrutiny as he looked at the women. Catherine might not be able to do much other than lean against the other woman, but Mizuno could be intimidating even with her glamorous appearance.

Behind them, the door to the office suddenly burst open with enough force to splinter the wood from its hinges. Nachem entered the room, a hulking mass filling the space more than they should. Catherine had never felt such relief in her life at seeing her golem standing there. They were the embodiment of familial magic, and they would care for and defend her to the very end with magics the men before her couldn't hope to achieve. Nachem was solid and comforting and they would get her and Mizuno out.

"What is that?" Tiza yelled, the noise echoing around the room.

"My golem. And now gentlemen, if you don't mind, Nachem has come to escort us out," Catherine said in a weak voice, mustering what little strength she had to speak. Nachem stepped up to the two of them, and Mizuno passed Catherine off to the golem, probably knowing that they could more easily take her weight.

They turned to go, leaving the stunned minotaur and manticore behind them. "Don't just stand there, you idiots. Stop them!" Tiza growled at the centaur guards. Arruk said nothing; he had stood there the whole time as if stunned. Catherine couldn't look back at him. She could only move forward.

They were nearly to the door before any one reacted. But then the hum of magic filled the room, and Catherine was pushed behind Nachem's body while they turned to face their attackers. A silvery arrow flew from a conjured silver bow held by one of the centaurs and pierced Nachem's chest.

There should have been no cause for worry. That kind of magic or weapon couldn't hurt a golem; they could take nearly any kind of attack. But then Nachem half turned around, and if they could display emotions, Catherine was sure they would have looked stunned. Because the arrow had hit its mark and the *aleph* on Nachem's *shem* was pierced. The only way to destroy a golem was to destroy its *shem*.

She screamed.

Nachem's hand raised only a little toward her, and then they crumpled into dust at her feet.

Catherine fell, too weak now to even stand, whether from the poison or from her heart breaking into dust like her golem on the floor. Mizuno kept her from bashing her knees on the hardwood floor, instead gently lowering her down.

In her ear, she could hear Sidatih yelling, but Catherine couldn't make out anything he was saying. If there was any talking going on around her, she had no idea. All she could do was stare at the dust that was once Nachem and hear the blood whooshing in her ears, knowing the sound was bringing her closer to death with each passing minute.

"Miriam, we need to leave." Mizuno's voice filtered through the haze. She looked up into the other woman's face and then toward the other men in the room. Arruk was advancing on her, and Catherine felt fear then. This was worse than anything else she had ever faced, and she knew with absolute certainty that she would die soon, either by Arruk's hands or from the poison.

"Go, Mizuno. Get out now. I'll find my own way," she said, voice too airy, barely there.

"Mir—" Mizuno started, but then stopped. She saw everything on Catherine's face and nodded. She touched Catherine's chin and placed a soft kiss to her lips. When she stood, she gave one last look at the minotaur who stood only steps away, then her gaze flicked over his shoulder to Tiza who still stood across the room. In a movement too fast to even see, Mizuno let loose one of her knives, waiting only long enough to ensure it embedded itself in Tiza's chest.

After that, she changed rapidly. First an inky blackness covered her form to reveal an oversized pure black spider in her place. With the same graceful movement she had in human form, Mizuno sprang onto the walls while Tiza's burbling shouts toward the guards reverberated around the room. The knife had pierced his lung. He must have been in pain as blood filled the organ. But Catherine kept her eyes trained on Mizuno, who easily dodged arrows aimed at her despite her large size. In a blink, the large spider shrank down to the size of a normal spider and disappeared into the darkness of the ceiling.

That left only Catherine, crumbled on the floor without the strength to even stand, let alone ward off any attacks. Arruk's rough hand grabbed her around her forearms and tugged her none too gently to her feet.

"I knew you were a thief. But I thought you were better than to steal from your friends. You've betrayed me once, and here you are breaking my heart again." There was no kindness in his tone, no sympathetic eyes. There was only cold hard ice, and Catherine deserved it all.

He seemed completely unperturbed that his business partner was behind him choking on his own blood. He barely noticed as the centaurs carted the manticore off between them with some difficulty through another doorway Catherine hadn't noticed until now, likely to find the healer quickly. The chances they would find them in time to save Tiza were low, for that at least Catherine was grateful.

"I would have given you the trumpet, you know. If you had only asked," Arruk said, his voice now a whisper. And oh, how that hurt even worse. It was like a knife to the chest, and Catherine prayed for the poison to take her now, but it was being stubborn and not killing her quickly enough. Fucking Tiza probably screwed up the dose and now she would only suffer but live.

She hung her head in shame. "I know that now. Too late." Words came even harder. She only had one last chance before she could do nothing else. "I'm sorry, Arruk." And then she used the last of her strength to tap her wrist three times. A symbol in black ink appeared on her skin, one that looked like a crooked *R*, *raidho* or journey in the Norse runes. She tapped it again and blinked out of Arruk's arms and the warehouse entirely.

CHAPTER 19

Even as a small child of six, Miriam always wanted adventure. Staying still was her biggest struggle. The idea that she would spend the rest of her life stuck in the village, eventually married off to one of her playmates, tending house, and raising babies seemed so dull, so boring. Miriam wanted more from her life. She wanted to see the world beyond her village, beyond the borders of Crimea.

She wanted to go to university one day, maybe in London or France, or even the university at the heart of the empire in Istanbul. Why shouldn't she get an education like the boys? It was a question she posed to her parents on a regular basis, and every time, they gave her the same answer: it was her role to learn how to manage a house, to raise her children with the Torah, and to keep an observant household. They said it was her duty as a woman.

With so many children and grandchildren, though, her parents couldn't spare much time on Miriam's desires. She was left mostly on her own to do as she wished when she had finished her chores. Nobody seemed to notice when she disappeared for hours to wander the rocky hills by herself.

When she sat in temple on Saturdays, her gaze always drifted to the open windows, her mind traversing the streets when her body could not while her father, the rabbi, read from the Nusah Kaffa. The other women would shoot her disapproving looks until either her mother or one of her sisters would nudge her sharply to get her to focus.

There was no one Miriam could really connect with. Her parents were loving but far too busy to give her enough attention. Her siblings were off starting their own families or had their own friends. Family members tried to look out for each other, and she had plenty of aunts and uncles and cousins, but they could only give so much time and attention to one little girl.

One particular day during Shavuot, Miriam waited until after the reading of the Book of Ruth before slipping away from the village to explore the hills once again. There was plenty of feasting that would be happening throughout the day, but Miriam craved a moment of quiet away from the bustling hearth of her home. At least she made sure to do the milking before leaving, else her mother would have accused her of deliberately sabotaging the festivities.

The wind was little more than a gentle breeze, and Miriam thought if she concentrated hard enough, she could smell the faint tinge of salty sea air coming from the coasts. Despite living on a land almost completely surrounded by water, Miriam had never been to the sea. Her family almost never traveled outside of their village. She wondered, not for the first time, if it was as blue as so many had claimed. The ships were said to be gigantic, like floating cities on the water.

What if one day she boarded one of those giant ships and sailed to Istanbul? She would have to learn the language, of course, which meant she would have to convince her father to let her have schooling outside of religious study. Sure, she had already learned her letters, but the Hebrew Aleph Bet didn't even use the same form as the one in Istanbul. Already she was behind in her education.

Miriam settled under a gnarled-looking tree set atop a particularly craggy hill, placing the small sack of food she had filched from the kitchen next to her on the grass. She looked down on the village below, imagining she could see her neighbors bustling about for the holiday. She couldn't; her eyesight, while sharp, wasn't nearly that good.

From the sack, she pulled a canteen and a heel of bread one of her older sisters had slipped her before Miriam took off. She chewed slowly, savoring the warm yeasty taste of the bread her mother had made that morning. It was comforting in a way only a mother's cooking could be.

Once she finished, she brushed the crumbs from her fingers and stood, ridding her skirt of the mess as well. Her attention then turned away from the village and up toward the tree instead. She had the burning need to be higher still, and so slipped off her shoes and stockings and began to climb.

Halfway up the tree, which turned out to be much taller than Miriam expected, or at least seemed to be much higher than she thought, she realized climbing that particular tree had been a bad idea. The branches weren't nearly thick enough to hold her weight, despite her small stature. On top of that, it was clearly half dead, if the creaking of each branch was any indication.

But Miriam was a persistent child who didn't know when to quit, so she kept climbing even against her better judgement. Finally, she managed to reach the top, though her perch was more than a little precarious. With one hand anchoring her to the tree, she stared at the horizon, thinking maybe she could see a line of blue indicating the ocean.

She couldn't; they were too far inland for her to see even a hint of it. Her attention turned once more to the village below. Indeed, she felt so much higher above it. She raised a hand high in the air like she could touch a cloud if she just reached far enough. Below her feet, the branch groaned, and a second later, a loud snap split the air and Miriam was falling.

Her own scream rang out across the hills before it was cut short by her body hitting the ground, knocking all the air from her lungs. For several minutes, she lay at the bottom of the tree, stunned. An ache formed at the back of her skull, but it was dulled in comparison to her arm. The one she had stretched out to the sky felt like it was on fire. With a monumental effort, she attempted to raise the arm from the ground, but the appendage refused to move; instead, lightning bolts of pain shot all the way up her arm into her shoulder. She screamed again. When she finally turned her head to look at the useless arm, she saw that it was bent at an unnatural angle.

Broken, then.

Miriam had never broken a bone before, though she had seen enough men with splints after a farm accident. She had also seen plenty who had to have limbs amputated because they festered and turned poisonous to the body. Her mind was in a panic now. What if that happened to her? What if they removed her arm? No one would marry her with only one arm. She would never be the great scholar she yearned to be with only one arm. People would only pity her, and she would be left destitute, or worse, a burden to her parents and then siblings.

Tears ran down her cheeks, but it was the only thing she could do. Her body felt too heavy, and there was too much pain for her to do anything else. Nobody knew where she was, so no help would be coming anytime soon. Maybe they would find her in a few hours, or worse, a few days. They would only find what was left of her by then.

Miriam started to spiral, her young mind thinking of only the worst possibilities. A noise coming from her right startled her. It sounded like footsteps, very heavy lumbering footsteps. Her eyes focused on the figure approaching over the hill, and she nearly cried again in relief.

Just a few paces from where she lay on the ground, Nachem, the family golem appeared. The pupilless eyes fixed on her, and they seemed to speed up to reach her.

"Little one, what has happened?" Nachem's gravelly voice was accompanied by a gentle caress across her brow.

Miriam sniffled. "I was climbing the tree and then I fell. My arm hurts really bad."

Nachem tutted softly. "Do not move, little bird. I am going to heal you. Then I will take you home where you will stay." They placed one hand on the top of her head, and Miriam tried to stop her tears. "I am going to touch your injured arm. Scream if you must."

And scream she did when the golem placed their stone hand softly on her arm. There was no pressure, but even the slightest touch sent more pain shooting through her. The warmth of magic came quickly, though, and Miriam could feel the tingles of it in her fingers. A loud popping noise broke the stillness and Miriam screamed again as her bone snapped back into place. To her young mind, the healing was almost worse than the actual injury.

But in less than a minute, the pain was gone. All that was left was the tingling in her fingers and arm and the residual warmth of the magic. "There. That should do it," Nachem said, removing their hands from her arm, though the other remained on her head. "Do you think you are ready to sit up?" Their concern was palpable, even if their voice had no inflection.

Catherine nodded, and slowly allowed Nachem to assist her into a sitting position. "I should not have climbed the tree; it couldn't hold me, and I knew it."

Nachem actually chuckled. "No, you should not have. Keep your feet on the ground for now, little bird. One day when you are older, then you will be ready to fly." The golem patted her head. Then, grabbing her little body up in their arms, Nachem began to carry Miriam down the hill and back to their home.

"You have always taken care of our family, Nachem. Thank you," she said softly.

"And I always will. It is what I was made for," Nachem replied, face tilted down at the girl in their arms.

"Promise?" she asked in the innocent way only a child was able.

"Yes, little bird, I promise," came their gravelly reply.

CHAPTER 20

Catherine's body made a loud *thump* as she appeared on the floor of the apartment. The room was silent; everyone was still near the warehouse. Well, most of them anyway. She had to push the pain of Nachem's destruction aside and get to the potion in her room.

She tried to stand, but her knees gave out half way up, and she flopped back down on the floor. With shallow and shaky gasps of air, she started to crawl across the room, too slowly, but she kept pushing forward despite her arms starting to quake.

Hours or maybe only minutes later, she reached the door to her room.

The closed door.

She cursed herself for shutting it. She leaned against the door for support and reached up with monumental effort. Her fingers slipped on the knob, and her hand fell heavily down by her side. Again, she reached up, her arm shaking the whole time, but she managed a firmer grip and the door swung open. Without the door holding her up, she fell forward onto the rug covering the hard wooden floor. Pushing herself back up enough to crawl again, she scanned the room for her bag.

There, next to the nightstand. Breathing was so hard now that she felt her lungs strain even as she drew in air. Her head felt fuzzy or hazy—she wasn't even sure what word applied—all she knew was that her brain was starved of oxygen.

Without looking, she started rooting through the dark brown leather bag, shuffling things around without care. Her fingers grazed a small bottle, and she latched onto it, willing her fingers to grasp the glass.

The potion was clear with only the faintest glow around it. It contained a sample of the sacred waters of Black Mesa, blessed by a Hopi holy woman. It was a precious gift now that the waters of Black Mesa were disappearing. And at that moment, it was the only thing that would save Catherine.

She thanked every god she knew that the bottle was a twist off. The idea of trying to pull a cork out now seemed a gargantuan effort, using strength she didn't have. It took only seconds to drain the bottle, and all Catherine could do was collapse on the rug and hope the magic would do its work. Her eyes fluttered closed, and she let the darkness, whether from death or sleep, take her.

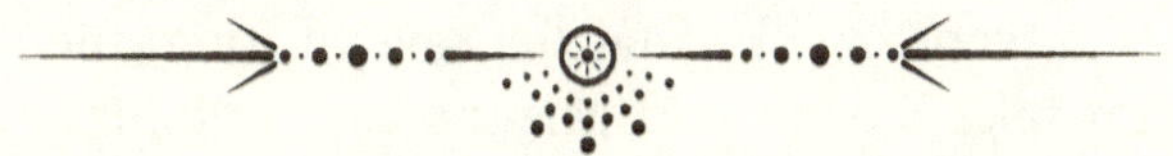

Catherine awoke in her bed, her body heavy and her face wet from tears she had shed while asleep. She lay in the center of the bed cushioned by two warm bodies wrapped around her. Sidatih had her head tucked under his chin with one arm slung low across her stomach. On the other side, Mizuno was nestled into Catherine's neck, clutching Catherine with an arm banded around her just under her breasts. They both held her close as if protecting her.

Neither of them was asleep judging by the way both of their fingers traced soothing shapes on her skin. There was no way to know how long she had slept. Her body was bone tired, her emotions wrung out, and her head felt heavy. The press of bodies on both sides was the only thing keeping her held together. A choked gasp escaped her as the memories came flooding back.

"Let it all go, albi." Sida gripped her hip and planted a soft kiss on her temple. From her other side, Mizuno moved her nose gently against Catherine's neck, a comfort more than anything more.

And then Catherine cried. No, she sobbed great heaving breaths as tears poured from her face in rivers. Her chest rose and fell quickly, and it felt like her whole body contracted, squeezing itself. Pain quickly bloomed in her head and cramps tightened her stomach. Mucus dribbled out of her nose; everything was so raw inside her. Her eyes stayed firmly shut as she let everything out, every single drop of grief and guilt, heartbreak, and failure.

She went on like that for several long minutes. Meanwhile, Sidatih and Mizuno said nothing, only held her tightly and gave her their warmth and comfort. Finally, her tears lessened, and her breathing turned deeper. There was still the pounding in her head, but the cramping in her stomach started to dissipate. A whole-body weariness was all she was left with, and even the thought of lifting her head seemed too great an effort to even try.

"I'll go make tea," Mizuno whispered against her skin. But as she began to pull away, Catherine finally found some strength to move and pulled on Mizuno's arm before she could get too far.

"Please don't leave me," she said, sounding scared and small. She couldn't be alone; she couldn't be without both of them by her side. Mizuno and Sidatih were the only things holding her pieces together. Without a word, Mizuno resumed her spot, tucking herself closer to Catherine.

For a long time, no one said anything. Catherine drifted in and out of sleep, too bone weary and heart heavy to stay conscious for long. When she was awake, all she could think about were her failures, even as Sidatih and Mizuno held her close. And she had failed in so many ways.

The job was supposed to be easy. They had the advantage of knowing many of the wards ahead of time. Catherine gained the trust of Arruk enough that they could walk right in and survey everything from within the warehouse. If only Tiza hadn't put those additional wards right before the event, she and Mizuno would have walked right out the front door with no one the wiser as to what they had done. It should have gone on without a hitch.

But her downfall was the one thing Catherine hadn't thought of: the manticore. The worst part was that Catherine should have factored Tiza in from the beginning. Arruk and Tiza had been business partners for longer than Catherine had been alive. There had been no reason to believe they would have severed that connection in the centuries since she was last in Athens. The truth was, she hadn't even thought about Tiza at all, had completely forgotten his existence until the gala. All her planning was for nothing because she had forgotten one major piece.

She had gotten careless in her years away from thieving. The old Catherine, no, Miriam, would never have overlooked something so glaringly obvious as a business partner who had very good reason to hate her until the end of his days, especially since manticores were not the forgiving type.

And now...

Now, because of her stupidity, Nachem was gone. They had survived for centuries, growing stronger as they were reinforced by generations of new magic. Countless plagues and war the golem had seen, the near decimation of her people, and because of her, they were destroyed. Not even all that familial power could prevent what happened. Once a golem's shem was destroyed, the magic was broken. Nachem had served her family for so long, they deserved better than to be dust on Tiza's office floor. They deserved more than to serve her as the last descendant.

But that couldn't be helped now. It wasn't like she had time to sweep up the dust before she succumbed to the hemlock. Arruk would have hauled her away quickly if she hadn't acted as quickly as she did.

"It wasn't your fault, albi," Sida whispered against her hair, warm breath fluttering the strands. On her other side, Mizuno placed small comforting kisses against Catherine's neck.

"Yes, it was." Catherine's voice was barely there as tears began to slowly leak out again. She couldn't lay down anymore. If she did, there was a good chance she would never get back up again. With more effort than she wanted to admit, Catherine sat up, scooted herself so her back rested against the headboard, and pulled her knees up so she could wrap her arms around them. Settling her chin on her knees, she stared at the opposite wall, unblinking.

Beside her, Mizuno and Sidatih mirrored her movements, each shifting so they were pressed against her sides once again. Sidatih reached for one of her hands, and she let his warm hand engulf her frozen one. Mizuno massaged the back of Catherine's head, easing the tension that had gathered just a little.

As much as she wanted to sink into their soothing gestures, Catherine wouldn't allow herself to relax. "Nachem deserved better. I shouldn't have left them. Arruk will just have his staff sweep them up like they are dirt. I let them down. I let all of my ancestors down." She wanted to wail, to pull at her hair, to scream, but instead, Catherine let her tears fall silently, not bothering to wipe them away.

"Maybe we could try to get back in and collect them," Sidatih said.

Mizuno leveled him with a sharp look. "Are you an idiot? You do not hit the same mark twice, especially since we barely made it out. And Miriam is correct: what was left of the golem is long gone by now."

Sidatih turned his head away. "It was just a thought. I hate the idea of Nachem being left in a dust bin somewhere."

"Yes, well we all do, but there isn't anything we can do about it," Mizuno replied stiffly. She kept her emotions in check, though there was more bite in her tone than usual. Mizuno may not look affected, but she was.

If only it were feasible, Catherine would have found a way to get Nachem's remains. But it wasn't. They couldn't risk going back to the warehouse on the distant hope there was anything left to collect. No, what they needed to do next was get out of Athens, out of Greece, as quickly as possible.

"How long was I asleep?" Catherine first needed to determine how much time had actually passed. The longer they stayed, the likeliness of Arruk finding them increased.

"A day, well, nearly," Sidatih said, wrapping an arm around her shoulders.

Too much time already, Catherine thought. She pulled away from Sidatih and Mizuno, crawled to the end of the bed, and placed her feet on the floor. Her legs felt wobbly for a moment, and she gave herself a few seconds to adjust to her weight before moving again.

"We don't have time to waste. We need to leave. The airport is out, as well as any major highways. If I know Arruk, he's already started looking for us. It's one thing if he willingly gave us the trumpet, but we stole from him, and that won't go unpunished." She had already pulled out her suitcase and was emptying the drawers of the armoire.

"How are we to get out? Assuming the minotaur has eyes around the city, which I take it he does," Mizuno asked, standing from the bed.

"He does. Arruk has always been well connected. We need to get to Egina. It's an island not far from Athens. There's an ancient olive grove there. We'll have to tree-walk. The process is imprecise, and it'll take a while to find another grove that's old enough to house portals, but we'll make it work until we're far enough away." Catherine threw everything she could find without care into the suitcase until it was full.

From the bed, Sidatih sighed deeply and closed his eyes. "I have another way. It's quicker, and we won't have to risk leaving the apartment."

"You don't sound particularly enthused about taking this route, Sida," Catherine said, plopping down on her suitcase to keep it closed while she zipped it up.

He didn't open his eyes while he responded. "I'm not. It's been a while since I've journeyed through Jahannam, and I was hoping to keep avoiding it for a while longer."

"What's Jahannam?" Mizuno asked, tripping a little on the word.

Sidatih flopped back, resting his head against the pillows. His eyes opened, but he only stared at the ceiling. "One of the underworlds. There's a bridge we can take that spans the whole of the underworld that'll make the trip easy. Well easier. It's not the one the souls take or anything; it's how ifrit travel around."

"Did something happen in Jahannam the last time you were there?" Catherine asked, standing up again now that her luggage was closed.

Another sigh from Sidatih. "Sorta. Not everyone likes the fact that I spend most of my time in the mortal realm, and they like to make their displeasure known in ... physical ways. So, it'll be quicker, but there's a chance we'll get hassled on the way. If that's not a problem for the two of you—I know we've all been through a lot in the last twenty-four hours."

Catherine sat down on the bed next to Sidatih's feet. "We just need to get out of here. It doesn't really matter how we do it at this point. And if we can avoid going out into Athens, that seems like the better way to go."

Beside them, Mizuno nodded. "I agree with Miriam. We did not make friends in our time here. It's best we leave without being noticed."

"Good. Let's get going. Go grab your things." Catherine hopped off the bed and grabbed her luggage.

"Uh, albi, are you going to really trapse through Jahannam in a party dress? Not that I'm complaining. I just wonder at the practicality of it," Sidatih said, a sparkle in his eye, though his smile was a little wan.

Catherine looked down at her body. She was still in the red dress from the gala. Even her jewelry was still on. The only thing missing was the weight of the trumpet, but one of them must have taken it out so the magic didn't wear off in her pocket.

"I probably shouldn't have packed all my things before changing. Where is the trumpet?" She dropped down to open up the suitcase she just finished shutting.

"I have it with my things," Sidatih said, rising from the bed. "I'll bring it to you while you change. Mizuno, let's be ready in five." Then he left the room. Mizuno gave Catherine a last look and followed him out.

Popping open the case, Catherine pulled out the first thing she could reach and quickly put on the high-waisted jeans and white V-neck t-shirt. The red dress was shoved haphazardly into the suitcase. She felt bad for treating such a work of art so carelessly, but she was in a hurry, and the sight of the red fabric already made her heart clench with despair.

Once they were safely out of Athens and the trumpet was handed over to Titania, then Catherine could properly mourn Nachem. But until then, she had to push her grief aside and focus on making it out alive and getting the whole deal done. Her focus now was making sure the rest of her team stayed safe. Catherine wouldn't survive losing another of her cherished people.

In what felt like seconds, the three of them assembled in the living room. Though Catherine felt a little hungry, she couldn't even look in the direction of the kitchen, not at Nachem's domain where they had cooked and cared for them all. Pushing the thoughts of her golem aside for now, her attention went to Sidatih.

The three of them held their bags, and Catherine wondered for the first time if it was a good idea to bring anything with them through the underworld. But they still needed a way to transport the trumpet, so the luggage would go.

"Can we shrink the trumpet again? Might be easier in case we need to ditch the stuff," Sidatih asked, shouldering his backpack.

Catherine shook her head. "The charm only had a one-time spell, small charge item. So, no matter what, we have to make sure the trumpet makes it out."

If she wasn't mistaken, Sidatih looked a little nervous. Mizuno, of course, looked unphased, her expression neutral yet focused.

Sidatih's shoulders slumped for a moment, then he straightened his spine. "Well, let's do this. Keep close to me and keep your eyes forward. Don't look down and don't listen to anything you might hear. It's going to be a little warm, but it'll go quickly. If anybody stops us, don't engage. I'll handle it. Now, join hands, and we'll get on our way."

The three of them clasped hands with whichever one was free. With one last fortifying breath, Sidatih concentrated hard, and the Athens apartment around them disappeared.

CHAPTER 21

The first thing Catherine noticed when they materialized in Jahannam was the heat. It was more than a little warm, despite what Sidatih said. Within seconds, she could already feel beads of sweat forming on her skin.

The three of them stood on a rough stone platform. Ahead of them was a narrow bridge with pits of fire on either side. All around them were the sounds of screams of agony echoing throughout. It was more than a little unsettling.

Catherine couldn't imagine kind, easy tempered Sidatih ever living in a place like this, let alone manifesting from it. "Keep your eyes on me no matter what," Sidatih reminded them, and Catherine didn't think that would be much of a hardship. She had no desire to see more of Jahannam than she already had. Both she and Mizuno nodded, and Catherine noted that Mizuno likewise looked unnerved. It was a rare sight, which did nothing to calm Catherine's own trepidation about their shortcut.

Sidatih's shoulders heaved with a sigh before turning toward the bridge. The two women followed single file behind him, Catherine in the middle and Mizuno taking up the rear.

It was harder than Catherine thought to not look down. It felt like the flames were licking at their ankles, and the sounds of anguish did not diminish the farther they went. From what Catherine knew of Jahannam, which admittedly wasn't much, there were layers to it, with the lesser offenders on the top layer and getting progressively worse the deeper it went, much like Dante's circles of Hell.

She would ask Sidatih about it once they were top side again. She didn't feel up for talking while walking, or really, jogging at that point through the underworld. And she suspected Sida felt the same way. Ahead of her, she could see his whole body was tense, his hands gripping the straps of his bag. He looked ready to start running any moment, Catherine thought.

As much as she wanted to spare a glance back at Mizuno, Catherine didn't dare take her eyes off Sidatih, didn't even want to risk seeing something she didn't want to see if she turned her head back.

The bridge was narrow, barely enough for two feet side by side, but Catherine couldn't concentrate on that. She was confident in her balance; she had to be. The heat was weighing her down quickly though, and her luggage started to feel heavier than it had before they left.

When Sidatih said this route was quicker, he didn't exactly specify how much quicker it would be. They could be traveling for hours for all Catherine knew. The grove hopping would have taken half a day, and then they would have to find a way to England since no old groves existed. But then, so could the bridge through Jahannam.

"We're nearly there," Sidatih shouted over the noise. He was practically running now, his large bag bouncing behind him. They were going make it through without being accosted, and Catherine thanked the gods for that.

The relief, however, was short lived. Sidatih stopped abruptly in front of her, and Catherine barely stopped in time to not run into his back, likely sending them both toppling over the side. She stretched a hand out and placed it on his shoulder, wishing she had a free hand to reach back for Mizuno's.

His muscles were tense under her touch, a clear sign something was wrong. A booming voice ahead of them broke through the noise. "Sidatih, home at last." The voice was teasing, but it was not a playful tease.

Catherine wanted to crane her neck, to see around Sidatih's head and the thing ahead of them, but she didn't. Instead, she kept her focus on the back of Sidatih's head, following his instructions. Whoever it was, Sidatih would handle this.

"Just passing through for now, Ghaibo." Sidatih's tone was level with a hint of annoyance. Catherine vaguely heard the sounds of loud sniffing.

"I smell a mortal, Sidatih. You wouldn't be smuggling souls of the damned out again, would you?" Ghaibo asked, his voice amused and accusing.

Again?

Catherine had to wonder if this was the reason Sidatih had been avoiding returning to his home. It sounded exactly like something he would do, stealing souls away from the underworld. But she found herself wondering who he would risk punishment for.

"This one is not one of our souls. She still has her mortal body, and we're just passing through. We have business together," Sidatih responded, giving away nothing more than the bare minimum.

There was the sound of laughter, but it sounded more like chains rattling than true mirth. "And you mean to use our bridges for your own amusement? I think not, Sidatih. You bring live mortal flesh through our level; you must pay the toll." A lead ball sank to the bottom of Catherine's stomach. She hadn't had much contact with other demons and ifrit from Jahannam, so she didn't know what kind of toll they would extract. And would it be from her or Sidatih, or maybe both? The only safe one, she assumed, was Mizuno, who wasn't mortal and didn't seem to be a concern.

"I don't answer to you, Ghaibo. You will not touch my human." Sidatih's tone was forceful, his shoulders straightening. Catherine could feel the muscles bunch below her hand, and she squeezed him gently.

"Give me a taste, and I'll let you pass," Ghaibo responded, his tone leaving no room for negotiation.

A taste? What did he mean by a taste? Would he try to eat her? Or something worse? Catherine shuddered, unwilling to even think of the possibilities. Sidatih would keep her safe; she had to trust in that fact, trust in him.

"Find your own mortal. You don't get to touch mine." This time Sidatih took a step forward, and Catherine's hand dropped from his shoulder. He advanced on Ghaibo, and now Catherine could see the demon before them.

The demon wasn't nearly as grotesque as she imagined he would be. Instead, he looked very human himself, though he was much taller and broader than any human she knew. His russet skin glowed from the fires below, and his simple shirt and loose pants were stark white. Wild dark curls covered one eye, where the end of a scar peaked out just below the strands. No, he was far from horrifying. He was beautiful. He looked more angelic than demonic, but looks could be deceiving, as was clearly the case here.

Ghaibo's eye, the only one she could see, locked with hers. His eye gleamed red, mirroring the fires below. "Ah, I think I know this one. Yes, you've made a lot of enemies in the mortal plane. I'm sure you taste delicious." Catherine was sure if Ghaibo could see more of her, his eye would be roaming over her body. She couldn't repress the shudder that went through her as his blazing gaze held hers.

"You'll not touch her, Ghaibo. If you do, I will end you!" Sidatih's hands slammed into the other ifrit's chest, and he stumbled backward a few steps. Catherine held her breath, hoping Ghaibo would slip off the side, but the ifrit regained his footing quickly. He stood tall and then he laughed, mocking and cruel.

"You? Ha, Sidatih, you have become so tainted by the mortal plane that I doubt you could even harm an imp. It's quite revolting." Ghaibo's mocking laugh rang out over the cacophony around them.

"You underestimate me, Ghaibo. You always have—" Sidatih began, but Ghaibo cut him off.

"I underestimate nothing. You have so little power here, Sidatih. Stripped of your duties is what I heard. Your magic might be strong on the mortal plane, but here, you are hardly better than a mortal soul." Sidatih's hands balled into fists at Ghaibo's gloating. Catherine wanted to reach out and take his hand in hers, but she held back, unsure if Sidatih would appreciate the gesture or if it was only for her own comfort.

As if sensing her needs, Catherine felt Mizuno's fingers thread through hers and squeeze. Catherine clung to the touch like a lifeline. This wasn't what she expected her first trip through the underworld would be like. Well, she had hoped there would have been only one trip to the underworld, and if they didn't get past Ghaibo, there very likely would be only this one.

Her pulse beat furiously, and it felt like her veins were bulging from the blood flow. Ghaibo's eye seemed to fixate on a point on her neck, maybe even seeing the pounding of her pulse against her skin. He licked his lips salaciously, and Catherine cringed.

"I could simply toss you all over the side. At least, that's what I would do with you, Sidatih. The ladies I could use as some form of ... entertainment. But if you give me just one small taste, there won't be any trouble." Ghaibo addressed the patch of skin he was fixated on.

Blood. He meant a taste of her blood. An ifrit could learn a lot about a person from a taste of their blood. Not that he would have control over her or anything, but it could open her up to Ghaibo's machinations when he was on the mortal plane.

"I accept. One drop, and you let us pass safely without any further interference," Catherine said loudly over

Sidatih's shoulder, a challenge in her voice as she stared the ifrit down. Sidatih's head whipped around, and he stared at her with mouth agape. She must have really surprised him if he willingly took his eyes of Ghaibo.

"Mir, don't," Sidatih whispered, though it was hardly a whisper at all since he had to speak loudly to be heard over the constant screaming.

Catherine returned his pleading stare with a shake of her head. "We've been through enough, Sida. Let's get out of here without a fight. Pick our battles." She was simply too wrung out to even attempt to fight. Sometimes it was better to give in, do what must be done, and live another day.

Ghaibo's smile was both victorious and menacing, forcing a shudder down Catherine's spine. There wasn't space on the bridge for either of them to pass around Sidatih, so she wasn't sure how they were going to make the exchange from where they stood now.

The ifrit, however, solved that problem a moment later. He turned, tipped over the side of the bridge and began to walk normally upside down as if he were standing right side up. With another turn and another step, he righted himself back up on the bridge to stand directly in front of Catherine. She took a step back on instinct to allow him space, bumping into Mizuno who steadied her with a hand on each arm.

Ghaibo might have been extremely handsome if he didn't look like he was about to suck the soul from her body. She wasn't entirely certain he wouldn't try to do such a thing. But Catherine had to trust in the tenuous bargain. Though why she would continue to trust in bargains after everything lately, she didn't know. But she was so tired; fighting and bravery had left her, and she only wanted to continue on as quickly as possible.

"Don't look, Sidatih. Please," Catherine called over Ghaibo's shoulder. Without a doubt in her mind, she knew that if Sidatih watched, he would likely do something altogether stupid.

He actually listened to her and kept his gaze forward toward the exit. Mizuno's hands dropped from her arms, and while she missed their weight and the chill Mizuno's touch left that she could feel even through her leather jacket, Catherine knew the space was needed.

With a long-fingered hand, Ghaibo reached out and tilted Catherine's head to the side, pushing back her bobbed hair to expose the unblemished span of peach skin. "Don't worry. I promise this will hurt," he said, leaning in toward her neck.

"Yeah," she breathed, "it will." With a quick movement, she dropped out of his grip, making sure to keep one foot planted while she cast out her leg and slammed against Ghaibo's legs below the knee, sweeping him off his feet. He shot her a look of surprised horror as he lost his footing and fell, toppling over the side of the narrow bridge, and plummeted into the flames below.

"Move! Quickly!" she yelled, and Sidatih didn't even turn before he started to sprint across the bridge. Catherine's suitcase banged heavily against her leg as she ran behind him. Though she couldn't hear Mizuno's rapid footsteps, she knew the other woman was easily keeping pace as they made a mad dash toward the end.

From behind them, Catherine heard an enraged bellow and knew that the fall hadn't gotten rid of Ghaibo for long. She pushed herself to run faster, though the heat still made her feel heavy, and sweat was pouring in buckets down her body.

"We're almost there. Don't look back!" Sidatih yelled over his shoulder. It took a considerable amount of control to not immediately turn her head, but Catherine charged ahead, seeing, finally, the bridge widen out into another platform and what looked to be a circular hole with stairs leading upward.

Just as they stepped onto the rocky platform, Mizuno slammed into Catherine, lifting both women off their feet to crash headlong into Sidatih. The three of them sprawled on the ground as pain spread through Catherine's palms. Her hands took the brunt of the fall, and she could already feel blood dripping down her palms as the three of them scrambled to their feet to face Ghaibo.

The ifrit's hands were still outstretched from the magic of the blast he sent after them. "I am going to drain every last drop of blood from your pathetic mortal body, and then I am going to make your soul watch as I tear your husk to shreds," Ghaibo seethed. There were flames in his crimson eyes to match the ones below.

"Hey, Ghaibo! Get fucked!" Sidatih yelled, flipping off the other ifrit before grabbing ahold of Catherine and Mizuno's hands. As Ghaibo lunged forward, the three of them disappeared from Jahannam, leaving the heat and fire behind them.

CHAPTER 22

When they reappeared, it was dusk, later than Catherine expected it to be. The three of them faced the back of a bronze statue, wet cobblestones beneath their feet and cool night air breezing past them.

"Where are we?" Catherine asked, blinking into the sudden gloom.

"London. Kensington Gardens by the looks of it," Sidatih replied, shifting the bag on his back.

"How can you tell?" Mizuno asked, clearly unfamiliar with their surroundings.

Catherine's eyes slowly adjusted, and she could better make out their location, including the statue in front of them. "Peter Pan," she said. Mizuno threw her a questioning look. Catherine pointed to the bronze statue in front of them. Even though they faced the back, it was recognizably the statue of Peter Pan in Kensington Gardens.

"Let's get out of here. We can go to my flat." Catherine led the way out of the park, and they took a taxi back to her home.

The flat was dark when they arrived, seeing as Catherine didn't have a chance to ring her housekeeper to alert her of their impending arrival. It was also quite chilly inside, but Sidatih made quick work of that, a snap of his fingers causing a cheery fire to burst into life in the fireplace.

Their bags were dropped around the living room haphazardly, and Catherine was the first to crash down heavily on a chair. The other two followed suit, and for a long time, nobody said anything. What they all needed was a chance to breathe, to think, and most of all, decompress from the whirlwind of the last day.

Catherine felt as if she had aged ten years, an unnerving feeling since she hadn't done much aging for centuries. But she was so tired, stretched thin, and ready to break. She needed food and her bed. And tomorrow she would face Titania and be done with the whole ordeal.

"Let's order in and then sleep. I don't think I can do much more," she mumbled. The other two made sounds of agreement. Food was ordered and dinner was a solemn affair, none of them saying much, instead each just staring into their containers and eating quickly.

Catherine made sure that Sidatih and Mizuno were comfortable in her spare rooms before retiring to her own. While she loved their company, and they were a comfort to her, she needed to be alone now. They wouldn't allow her to spiral and obsess over everything that had happened in Athens. She didn't want to be distracted or forget. Catherine wanted to wallow and think about everything that went wrong. She needed to examine her failures and what she had lost.

What she needed was to drive herself a little crazy before she could let it all go.

For hours, she lay in bed, staring at the ceiling without really seeing it. Every single detail was analyzed, from the moment Titania sat down at her table, to the confrontation with Tiza. The memory of Nachem in that instant before their destruction—she couldn't think about that. She couldn't think about that last look as her golem crumbled. But she could focus on Arruk's face of betrayal right before she disappeared.

How many more people would she disappoint before the end of her life? How many more friends would she betray for something selfish before she expired? Catherine thought she had gone out into the world to see old friends and make amends with people she had wronged in her past. Instead, she was making enemies of friends, and making things worse with the enemies she already had. And that would be her legacy: a thief who would throw away anyone if it meant she could keep going on for another day.

Her family would be ashamed if they saw her now.

But they were long gone. They lived out their mortal lives, content with what they had. All her sisters and brothers, nieces and nephews, all gone now that their normal lifespans ceased. And while Catherine didn't ask for immortality, she had enjoyed it all the same, even with having to play nanny to a brooding angel on his mother's behalf for the entirety of it.

There was no one left but her. Not even the family golem remained. Catherine felt like a fuck up in every way. She had botched an easy job. Betrayed a friend. Sacrificed a part of her family. Put the people she cared about in a dire situation. Even Tiza, though she disliked him immensely, but that didn't mean she wanted him dead. Didn't matter now because he was. And even if he had intended to kill Catherine and she wasn't even the one to deal the killing blow, she felt responsible. His blood was on her hands.

She rolled to her side and looked out into the night through the crack in her curtains. Sleep was not coming for her tonight, not that she felt like she deserved it anyway. Nothing would alleviate her guilt. A pounding started behind her eyes, and she closed them, focusing on the pain in her skull. No tears were left, only the pain and guilt remained, and eventually she let that carry her off into oblivion.

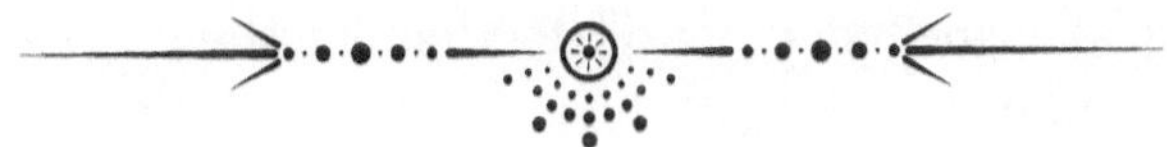

The next day, Catherine returned to the same grubby pub where she met Titiania at the start of her whole misadventure. The fairy queen would find her soon enough, probably alerted to Catherine's arrival the minute they appeared in Kensington Gardens.

This time, Catherine didn't bother with tea. A large glass of whisky sat in front of her, already half gone, though she couldn't have been sitting for more than a few minutes.

By the time Titiana arrived, sliding into the seat in front of Catherine at her table in a forest green dress that hugged every curve, Catherine was already well into her second drink. "Starting a little early, Miriam. How unlike you." Her sultry voice dripped with amusement, and Catherine felt the gnawing impulse to throw the rest of the drink in the fae's face.

"Not early enough," she muttered, taking another swallow. The burn felt good and lit a fire in her belly. She would need that if she was going to get through the meeting with Titania without throttling the woman. "I suppose you heard all about what happened in Athens."

Titania pouted her lips. "I did. How horrible." Her voice was all mock pity, and Catherine felt the rage within her swell. Grief and guilt took a backseat now that Titania sat in front of her, looking at ease and triumphant at the same time. Of course she did. It wasn't like she had to get her hands dirty, lose so much, and run for her life.

Catherine hated her. Hated her like she had never hated in her life.

"Do you have my trumpet?" Guess that was the end of pleasantries. Titania no doubt had managed to acquire all the details of the botched job. She was probably delighting in Catherine's failures and sorrow.

"Not sure why you need the thing since you have ears everywhere and are more than capable of spreading your own gossip like the wind," Catherine said, pulling the trumpet from her satchel and slamming it down on the table between them.

The table rattled and the whisky sloshed in her glass. The owner, the same woman from last time, shot her a glare from across the pub. "Take it. Our bargain is complete. Consider us done." Catherine stood from her chair, more shakily than she would have liked. She threw a few quid on the table and picked up her satchel to leave.

"It doesn't have to end this way. We can still be close friends. Why don't I take you over to my house, and I can make you forget all about Athens? It'll be like old times." Titania also stood. She grabbed the horn from the table, seemingly uninterested in it all that much, and stepped close into Catherine's space.

Catherine didn't move, staying rooted to the spot. She leaned in just a little toward Titania. She dropped her voice into a whisper, sounding almost seductive. "If I ever see you again, I *will* kill you." She left Titiana standing alone in the pub with a disgruntled look that marred her beautiful features, and a magical trumpet dangling from her fingers. There was nothing more to say. Catherine was done with the fairy queen forever.

CHAPTER 23

Mizuno's bags were in the hall when Catherine arrived back at the flat. It wasn't a surprise that she would be leaving, Catherine knew the thief had to return home to Kyoto eventually. She just didn't think it would be on the same day she turned over the trumpet.

"Sidatih said you would be home soon," Mizuno said evenly. Catherine looked up from where she had been staring at the bags to take in Mizuno's appearance. The woman was standing at the other end of the hallway nearest to the living room. She was impeccably dressed, as always, with an open kimono-style jacket in deep blue over high-waisted black trousers and black cropped shirt. Her long black hair cascaded down her back with a bright sheen.

"So, you're leaving, then?" It was posed as a question, though it wasn't one. There was no mistaking the bags. There was a pang in her chest, right in her heart. The two women had grown close over the course of the job, had shared something special. Catherine had held onto the naïve hope they would have more time together.

"The job is complete. My debt has been paid," Mizuno said, her tone flat.

Catherine nodded. Of course, it was only a job to Mizuno. She had her master's debt to repay, and that's all there was to it. Only Catherine had seemed to feel like it was something more, and she cursed herself for being so blind.

"Right. Do you need a ride to the airport? I can a get you a car." She didn't really know what to say; she wasn't ready for Mizuno to go.

"There is no need. I can manage. Besides, I wanted time to say a proper farewell to you. The ifrit has left for a few hours to give us some time ... alone." Mizuno paused before the last word, and it took Catherine a moment too long for her to understand the meaning. Sidatih was giving them a chance to have a proper goodbye without his interference.

"Well then, we wouldn't want to waste the time we have left," Catherine said, her voice huskier than she intended. Knowing they would have a few hours to spend together made her glad they wouldn't have to rush and could enjoy this last moment.

Mizuno's dark eyes grew wide, and she crossed the distance to Catherine in a few measured strides. One cool hand slid against Catherine's jaw before she brought their faces together. The kiss started off gentle, two pairs of soft lips pressed together in a tender gesture.

It quickly turned more heated as Catherine swiped her tongue across Mizuno's mouth, begging for entrance. The other woman didn't hesitate to do so, and Catherine wasted no time in twining their tongues together, tasting every inch of Mizuno's mouth.

Hands started to pull at clothing, both too impatient to care where things landed or in what state. They may have plenty of time before Mizuno's departure, but Catherine was far too eager to get started to take the undressing part slowly. As articles of clothing flew, Catherine edged Mizuno backward down the hall. The stairs were going to be a problem, so without taking her mouth away from Mizuno's, she steered them into her living room. A couch would work just as well as a bed for now.

Once they were both standing naked in front of the living room fire, Catherine maneuvered a hand between their bodies to cup one of Mizuno's small breasts. The nipple hardened under her touch, and she rolled it between her thumb and forefinger. Mizuno moaned loudly into Catherine's mouth, and she pushed her chest forward, urging Catherine to touch her more.

Cool fingers grabbed Catherine's ass, pulling their bodies close until there was no space left between their naked bodies. The hand on Mizuno's breast could barely move, yet she still had the ability to pinch and twist the nipple, eliciting more moans and gasps from the other woman.

Mizuno was light enough for Catherine to pick up without breaking the kiss. Catherine was by no means a strong woman; she relied on agility and her slim stature to be quick rather than rely on strength, but it was as if Mizuno weighed nothing. Lowering the other woman gently onto the couch, Catherine pulled away and fell to her knees on the plush rug.

Hands on each of Mizuno's knees, she pushed them apart until Mizuno's pussy was on full display for her. Catherine licked her lips, suddenly ravenous to have a taste. "Be as loud as you want," she said, her voice full of desire before she dove into Mizuno's hot, dripping center.

The moan that filled the room was loud, reverberating, and primal, and it didn't come from Mizuno. Catherine's eyes rolled back as she tasted, overcome with lust and all the sensation flooding her as the other woman's juices started to coat her face. There was no sweeter taste that she had experienced. She could get drunk feasting on Mizuno's exquisite pussy.

Now that she had Mizuno where she wanted her, Catherine started with slow swipes of her tongue interspersed with soft sucks on the other woman's clit. Mizuno's breathing picked up, and she squirmed a little under Catherine's mouth. But mostly she was silent; Mizuno's eyes were shut tight, her head thrown back in a silent scream. Sliding a finger into her slick channel, Catherine began a slow pumping in and out, her gaze locked onto Mizuno's face, taking in every movement from her.

There on her knees, knowing this was their last time together, Catherine felt powerful, like everything between the two of them had been building toward this one moment, and Catherine wasn't about to waste it feeling sad that Mizuno was leaving.

Once she added another finger, only then did Mizuno make a noise. It was a small moan as Catherine pumped her fingers and pulled hard on her clit. The sound spurred Catherine on, and she couldn't hold back anymore. Going slow was agony, and she was far too impatient as she felt the slickness gather between her own thighs. What she craved most was Mizuno's orgasm, and she was going to get her there quickly.

No longer were her licks and sucks gentle and light. Instead, she went hard, fingers pushing in at a punishing pace while her tongue flicked over that small bundle of nerves in furious circles. As Catherine pulled her lips away, Mizuno let out a needy whine at the loss, and Catherine quickly replaced her lips with her thumb, circling Mizuno's clit with pressure that was surely on the border of pain.

The walls of Mizuno's channel clamped down on her fingers, and Catherine knew she was close. Moving her thumb away, she once again used her mouth to suck hard, wanting to feel Mizuno cum on her face, needing those juices coating her mouth as she orgasmed.

It didn't take long for Mizuno's thighs to start shaking, and she clamped them tightly around Catherine's head. She couldn't pull away even if she wanted to. And Catherine didn't want to. For the entire time she had been on her knees, Mizuno had kept her hands fisted in the couch, but now her fingers slid into Catherine's hair and pulled on the brown-gray strands tightly. Catherine relished the sting on her scalp, and her fingers moved faster still, in and out of Mizuno, meeting the other woman's bucking hips.

It was like a dam bursting when Mizuno orgasmed. She didn't make a noise, but her head was thrown back with an almost pained expression on her face. Catherine felt the gush against her lips, and the juices ran down her mouth and chin. She licked up every last drop as her fingers began to slow.

Mizuno panted above her, and Catherine pulled away, taking in the sight before her. Fingers stilled, and she slowly pulled them from Mizuno who shuddered at their loss. Bringing her two digits up, Catherine placed them in her mouth and sucked the taste of Mizuno off her fingers, moaning loudly as she did so.

When Mizuno's breathing started to even out again, Catherine stood from the floor and climbed into the other woman's lap, straddling her. Her lips slammed against Mizuno's, hoping she could taste herself on Catherine's tongue. Mizuno wrapped her arms around Catherine's waist while Catherine's hands held the back of Mizuno's skull, keeping their mouths pressed together.

Her hips began to rock against Mizuno as they kissed, seeking friction to quell her own heated desire. In return, Mizuno's hips lifted, pushing back against Catherine. But it wasn't enough, even as Mizuno's hands began to knead her breast, pinching and flicking her nipples. Catherine still needed more. She whined greedily into Mizuno's mouth, and the other woman understood her meaning.

Mizuno shifted their bodies, encouraging Catherine to stand. "By the fire now, Miriam, and sit down," she said, her voice barely audible. Catherine did as she was told, sitting down with legs out on the rug placed in front of the fireplace. The flames only intensified the heat in her body further.

In seconds, Mizuno was kneeling over her, hands on either side as she lowered herself to place another deep kiss on Catherine's lips. With cool fingers, not at all influenced by the fire, Mizuno positioned Catherine's body so that one leg was slipped between Mizuno's outstretched legs. They moved their bodies close together and wrapped their arms around each other.

Catherine moaned loudly as her pussy rubbed against Mizuno's. They were both soaked. For a moment, neither moved, just relished the sensation of their two heated centers coalesced together. Then Mizuno rolled her hips, and the friction was enough to send Catherine moaning again.

Their hands roamed each other's bodies as they writhed against each other. Nipples were teased into hard peaks, and kisses moved from lips to throats to breasts. Fingers snaked between their bodies so they could thrum them against each other's clits. Catherine could no longer tell where her body ended and Mizuno's began.

Her body heated still further from their movements and the fire; Catherine felt she would combust any second. Then, like the wave of a tsunami breaking on the shore, Catherine's orgasm was on her, and she screamed until her throat was hoarse and her vision whited out. Moments later, Mizuno followed her over the edge.

Catherine fell back against the rug, pulling Mizuno down with her. Mizuno settled herself so that her head rested between Catherine's breasts, her ear pressed against her chest where her heart beat wildly.

Catherine placed a small kiss against Mizuno's hair, and she held her close, letting the chillness of Mizuno's body cool her off.

As they lay there, wrapped around each other, Catherine wished they could stay like that forever. "I want to ask you to stay, but I won't. But I don't want this to be the last time we see each other," she whispered against Mizuno's dark silky hair.

"It won't be, Miriam. It won't be," Mizuno breathed against her skin. They said nothing for a long while. Eventually, they made their way up to Catherine's bed, where they spent the next several hours with their naked bodies twined together as they said their good-byes with lips and hands.

CHAPTER 24

Miriam had been to Kyoto only once before. She was younger then, only a handful of decades into her immortal life. Ezra had decided to travel, so she went too. But that was just after the capital of Japan moved from Kyoto to Tokyo. From what Ezra had told her then, the city was a shadow of itself, fallen in power and influence.

Now Ezra was moving the shop for a bit into the new modern city. It was growing now that a new canal had been built a few years previous, and with the approaching twentieth century only five years away, it was, according to Ezra, the perfect time to help the magical community looking to settle in Kyoto.

There were far more westerners in Kyoto than the last time she had been. Centuries before, she had been nearly the only one in the city. Japan had entered a new world in the last few decades, and she no longer stood out among the crowd so much.

"I think I preferred the fashion the last time we were here," she complained to Ezra, who was doing his best to ignore her. The air was warm and muggy, and her layers of clothing had long become stifling. Even a day dress wasn't light enough to stave off the sweat that had accumulated along her neck and back.

"You could always find somewhere else in the world that doesn't put women in such restrictive clothing. In fact, I insist you find one of those places as soon as possible and leave me be." Ezra said something of that nature constantly over the centuries Miriam had watched over him. So far it had done nothing to drive her away. In the beginning, he had meant it with an abundance of conviction, but now it was simple part of their repartee, a script they followed. Their relationship was a begrudging tolerance.

She signed wistfully, knowing it would annoy him. "If only I could. Alas, I am forever tied to the most unrepentant arse to grace the world. One would think I have suffered enough, but my curse continues."

Ezra said nothing as they entered the newest building to hold his shop. It was quaint, more of an old world look than what was becoming popular now in Kyoto, but she suspected that would draw the magical community even more as many creatures would flock to the familiar. Ezra didn't plan to keep the shop there long, no more than a few years before moving it to London; at least, that was the plan.

Miriam had already acquired her own house. Over their long time together, she and Ezra had developed a routine for their entwined lives. She would check on him once in a while, never staying far away, and he would keep her updated on shop moves or anything big happening the magical community. As per the agreement from their first meeting, Miriam gave the goddess the bare minimum of information concerning her son. If the Lady was unimpressed by Miriam's less than thorough reports, she never said, so Miriam never provided more. Ezra never said as much, but she knew he was grateful.

"What do you plan to do while we're here?" Ezra asked, closing the door to the new shop behind her. The space was already filled with odd trinkets, shelves lined with most of the same stuff as he had back when the shop was in India.

Miriam inspected the shop briefly before turning her attention back to Ezra. "I have an old friend I wanted to visit. He has a new apprentice I wanted to meet. He says she is exceptionally talented."

"Ah, so crime," Ezra deadpanned, heading toward the back of the shop where a single door stood with a half curtain in front of it.

"You make it sound so pedestrian. Besides, it's been an age, and I don't want my skills to get rusty. More than that, this friend was once a pupil of mine. So, you could see it as meeting my granddaughter of a sorts." She had no living relations, so the people she mentored had become like a family to her, as well as Ezra in his own way.

"Well, go meet your crime granddaughter and try to stay out of trouble," Ezra said, ending the conversation.

Miriam laughed, turning back toward the door from which they entered. "Ezra, darling, I've been in trouble for three hundred years. I'm not about to stop now."

"Good bye, Aunt Miriam," Ezra ground out before disappearing through the back door just as she stepped back out onto the street.

If Miriam cared about scandal, she would have considered having Ezra escort her to her next location. Being an unchaperoned woman, seemingly unmarried, though that was far from the truth, she should not be walking the streets alone even in the daytime. As it were, Miriam had stopped caring about social conventions long before she became immortal. Besides, she looked matronly enough with her few gray strands of hair; she could easily pass for a widow or a spinster.

The streets weren't all that crowded due to the heat, and she met no one as she made the trek on foot toward her new home. It was modest enough. She had never cared for large elaborate dwellings, though she had the money for them. Instead, she preferred the small cozy setting of her little house. It, too, was an older structure, boasting none of the western inspiration that was now all the rage.

She slipped through the gate and shut it behind her. Without being able to tell exactly how, she knew that she needed to be cautious when entering her home. The set of throwing knives she had in her custom sewn pocket sheaths brushed against her thigh as she slipped a hand inside and grasped the handle of the first knife. She was going in, and she was doing it prepared.

The door was locked, as she expected, but that didn't mean she would be alone once she was inside. She removed her shoes after entering, setting them off to the side as she listened closely. There was complete silence through her house, which didn't mean much to Miriam. Silence could betray a lot.

With a hand still gripped on the knife, she ventured farther into the house, the slippers she put on to enter slipping against the floor. But it wasn't loud enough to cover the sound of something or someone moving. She continued to make her way through the house as if she didn't hear the sound, but she kept her ears pricked for continued movement.

It didn't take long for her vigilance to be rewarded. Another quiet slide of a footstep, and Miriam knew the location of the intruder. She turned abruptly, and the knife she had been clutching sailed across the room, imbedding itself in the wood a hair's breath from a body dressed in black. A small squeak of surprise came from the figure.

"Your master has told me what a promising young student you are, but that was sloppy. You put too much weight on your toes. You need to roll through the step," Miriam said loudly in Japanese for the other person to hear.

From the shadows, the intruder stepped out and removed the dark mask that had covered their face. A beautiful, if stoic face was revealed, long hair tied up in a functional bun. Her eyes were piercing, and she looked on the line of leaving girlhood behind and embracing womanhood. Her form was slender, meant for moving gracefully. Miriam couldn't help but feel a little struck by the woman's appearance.

Miriam gave her an appraising look for a second, before directing her attention away. "You have to learn to make a better entrance. Using my house for your practice is not in our deal," she said, addressing the ceiling now.

A low chuckle filtered into the room, and seconds later, a diminutive man with a waxed mustache appeared next to his pupil. One eye was milky white while the other was a brilliant cinnamon. "You have not lost your edge, Master Miriam. One would think after all these years you would have grown soft, but I can see that is not the case."

"I should hope not. I taught you better than to let your skills go rusty. I had hoped you were an attentive pupil," she said with a laugh. In a few quick strides, she crossed the room again and hugged the man. "It's good to see you again, Aritoki. It's been far too long. But I suppose the fault for that is my own."

He held her close, arms wrapped around her middle. "It is good to see you again, Master." Pulling away from each other, he stretched out an arm to indicate the young woman who had stepped farther into the kitchen. "May I present my student, Yuwa Mizuno? In her years under my tutelage, she has done very well. You would be proud of her progress, Master." He beamed at Mizuno, clearly quite proud himself to show off his student. Miriam couldn't blame him; she also loved to praise the successes of her own mentees.

"You are a jorgumo, Aritoki tells me. I can imagine it is useful to have the second shape in our line of work," Miriam said, giving the woman an appraising look. Mizuno was beautiful in a quiet, if deadly way. Her beauty would be an asset to her.

Mizuno's gaze darted to her master, asking with her eyes only for permission to speak. *She's well trained, indeed,* thought Miriam. Aritoki gave her a small nod, and Mizuno turned her attention back to Miriam. "I am, Master. It has served me well since I began my training with Master Aritoki."

"Excellent. Would you like some tea? It would be rude of me not to offer refreshment, despite the fact you broke into my home." She got to work preparing the kettle while the two thieves took a seat at the low table in the next room. The rice paper doors were left wide open so that conversation could continue.

As Miriam set the tea service in the European style on the table, she took note of her two guests. Aritoki sat serenely, completely at ease in Miriam's home. But Mizuno looked uneasy, unsure of herself. Miriam had to remind herself that the woman was still young. She didn't have the centuries of experience that she and Aritoki had, but soon she would come into her own, and her confidence would grow.

"I would tell you to relax, Miss Yuwo, but I remember when I was first starting out. I was a nervous mess almost constantly. However, you are in good hands, and you will learn to control that anxious nature." Miriam gave Mizuno a sympathetic look as she sipped her tea.

While Mizuno didn't exactly relax, her shoulders eased away from her ears, and she finally drank from the tea she had clutched tightly between her hands.

"This one is a perfectionist. She puts too much pressure on herself to be correct the first time. Such dedication I have rarely seen in anyone, let alone in one so young," Aritoki said, giving his attention first to Miriam before directing his words toward his student with a smile.

"There's nothing wrong with striving for perfection, so long as you know that it is a process. I think we can expect great things from you, Miss Yuwa. I look forward to seeing how you thrive." Miriam felt the compulsion to encourage the young woman. Despite the outward nervousness Mizuno exhibited, there was a quiet confidence under the surface that Miriam hoped could be coaxed out in the time she was in Kyoto.

Mizuno shot another look at her master for his permission to address Miriam. Once again, he gave her a small nod. Bowing her head low over the table, she said, "Thank you, Master." She straightened in her seat and continued, "I have followed your career for many years, and I must admit, I was very excited to meet you when my master told me you would be staying in Kyoto."

Miriam let out an amused chuckle. "I don't know what your master has told you about my exploits, but I can assure you most of them are exaggerated." Aritoki laughed along with her, his good eye shining with mirth.

"Do not let her lie to you, Mizuno. Everything I have told you is absolutely true. I would not be half the thief I am today without her guidance. She found me pickpocketing, poorly, I might add, in Siam when I was still a young man many centuries ago. That was when the shop I told you about was still in the kingdom there. I believe you left in somewhat of a hurry after causing quite the scandal there." He gave her a knowing grin as he was familiar with her antics in that country. Probably in most places she went.

"I'm sure I have no idea what you're talking about. I've always had a pleasant time in Siam." She feigned an air of innocence and sipped her tea demurely. Her attention turned back to Mizuno, who continued to sit quietly unless addressed directly. "Now, Miss Yuwa, I would like to know if you would be interested in a lesson. The Ninomaru Palace here in the city boosts these wonderful nightingale floors, meant to alert residents of thieves. They are a brilliant challenge for any thief working to be nimble on their feet. Would you care to try it with me?"

Mizuno looked at Miriam for a long moment, but this time spoke without looking for her master's permission. "That castle is not open to the public; it is where the imperial cabinet holds congress, and it belongs to the emperor. The punishment for being caught there would be most severe."

Miriam smirked behind her teacup. "Well then, don't get caught, my dear, and you should be fine. I want to see what you're made of." The smile that slowly spread across Mizuno's plush lips made something inside Miriam trill with excitement.

CHAPTER 25

When Sidatih returned hours later as darkness fell, Catherine was curled in an armchair by the fire, sipping from a cup of strong tea. She had been like that since Mizuno left, climbing into a cab without a backward glance after a passionate goodbye.

"Mizuno's gone, I take it," he said, taking a seat on the couch where not that long ago Catherine had brought Mizuno to completion. "You okay?"

Catherine nodded. She was okay, but that didn't mean it wasn't bittersweet. In one day, she had lost two lovers: one with whom she had centuries of history and one she had started to care deeply for. Though the pain of losing Titania didn't sting as much as Mizuno's departure.

"I know I'm a simple consolation prize, but I'm here for you, albi," he said with a small smile on his lips.

"You are many things, Sidatih, but a consolation prize is not one of them. I'm sorry if I made you feel that way." Catherine felt a pang of guilt. She cared for Sidatih deeply, maybe even loved him, and she didn't want him to feel less than simply because she was despondent over Mizuno's leaving.

Sidatih made a humming noise in acknowledgement. "You didn't make me feel that way. I was only teasing. I know you have grown attached to Mizuno. And who wouldn't? Once you get past that stony exterior, she is a lovely person. Mostly. Even with our disagreements, I'm sad to see her go. She really cares about you, too, you know."

"I know, just like I know you care about me. I'm lucky to have you both in my life, even if only for a moment." Catherine couldn't look at him, so instead she stared into the fire for comfort. But all that did was sting her eyes after a few moments.

"I more than care about you, Miriam. I love you; I have for a long time. I've never said that to anyone in my long life, but I thought you should know. While I was out, it gave me a lot of time to think, and I realized I want you in my life, for as long as you'll have me, and for as long as you have left in your mortal life. And when the time comes, I want to be the one to escort you to the underworld, just as I once escorted you into an immortal life." He stopped then, and Catherine heard him sigh deeply.

She turned to look at him now, compelled to look into his earnest eyes. "I want that, Sida. I do. There's just something I have to do first."

Sidatih nodded. He knew exactly what she meant. "Want me to go with you?"

Catherine didn't hesitate in her response. She had thought long and hard on it, debating if she was strong enough to do it on her own. But she was, and she needed to face her past and her failures. "No, this is something I have to do alone. There are things I need to put to rest before I can move on with my life."

Sidatih only nodded, then stood and held out his hand. Catherine contemplated for a moment, then placed her hand in his and let him lead her upstairs to her room.

It wasn't an easy trip to get to Crimea, even flying. The village Catherine had grown up in was long gone as most Jewish villages had been destroyed during the war. In the end, she rented a car from the airport in Simferopol and drove north. The landscape had changed since she had left, but few places in the world could remain unchanged for over five hundred years.

Leaving the highway, she headed off onto narrow paved roads that soon gave way to dirt paths, clearly only used by locals and not for any commercial traffic. There was no way for Catherine to know for sure where she needed to be. The GPS didn't list the names of long forgotten villages and hardly any structures existed anymore now that she was away from the cities and towns.

But there, she recognized the ridge ahead. It was one she spent countless hours running over when she wanted to get away from the hustle and bustle of the house and ignore her chores.

She stopped the car in the middle of a field. The landscape was bare for the most part. Patches of long grass sprang up around rocks hills, but there wasn't anything to suggest a village once stood there. Catherine wasn't even sure how long the village had been abandoned. For all she knew, it had been centuries or only a few decades. But it was enough time that nothing remained of the human life that had once called this place home.

Her eyes scanned the grass, and her gaze snagged on a cropping of rocks that looked more intentional. Atop each rock was a collection of small stones.

Grave markers.

As Catherine approached, she saw that the rocks were half covered by the grass and moss; even the stones on top had started to be covered in the green film. It had been a long time since new rocks were added. There wasn't anyone left to visit and remember. Nobody except her.

Not all of the stones had names; in fact, many had no markings at all, only the mementos on top. But a few stones had names she recognized. Not all were family members, just neighbors, people she had known in her youth.

But then she saw them: the stones with the names of her mother and father. There were no dates, just the names Tovi and Ya'ara Kokush. A wave of grief crashed into her, and Catherine fell to her knees in front of the stone. Tears began immediately to pour down her cheeks as she stared at those names. She leaned forward and rested her head against the unforgiving slab. It was the closest she would ever be to her parents again.

"I'm sorry. I shouldn't have left home. All you wanted was a happy life for me here, and that should have been enough. I should be resting here beside you after living my one lifetime. But I was greedy. I wanted more and I got too much." She paused, not sure how to continue, not sure why she was speaking at all. The dead couldn't absolve her of the guilt she felt. "Nachem is gone, and it was my fault. It feels like I destroyed our family. All things end, I know that, but they saved me without a thought to their own well-being. And it feels like I lost the last connection I had to you."

That was why she felt so horrible, so wrong. While yes, she was devastated by losing Nachem, the golem was also the last tie to her family. And without them, it felt like her family was lost to her all over again. Nachem may have only been a construct, but they were also family. She had heard enough stories from her mother about how Nachem had cared for her when she was young, and her mother before her. Now all Catherine had were stories and nothing left to show that her family had once existed.

There was no one there to give her comfort or compassion. Just her and some old cold stones. For several minutes, she sat on the ground, head leaning against her parents' names. She stayed until her tears dried and salty crust tightened her cheeks. Then she sat back and pulled a rock from her pocket and placed it atop her parents' stone marker. She found a small stone farther away from the plot and placed it next to her parents' marker. On top of that one, she placed another rock and thought of Nachem.

She stood and stared at the names on her parents' marker a little longer.

"What are you doing out here?" a male voice asked in Ukrainian from behind her. Catherine turned to see a young man in coveralls with a mop of brown gold hair and brown eyes similar to her own. Behind him sat a work truck with bits of tools sticking out.

"Just visiting. I wasn't aware this was private property," she responded, looking away from the stranger toward her car. She must have been so absorbed that she didn't hear him pull up in his truck.

"Well, it is. You from around here? I've never seen you before," he asked, his tone wary.

Catherine shook her head. "No, I'm just passing through. Sorry for the trouble. I'll just leave." She took a tentative step toward her car, going slowly as she knew she would have to pass the man and didn't know how he would react.

"Are you a relation?" he asked, nodding his head toward the stones.

She stopped and nodded. "I was."

The man's wariness melted away and instead was replaced by a smile, wide and toothy. "Guess that makes us cousins. I'm Oded Kokush."

He held out a hand, and Catherine could only look at it in surprise. She regained her composure after a moment and shook his hand in return. As far as she knew, her whole family had been wiped out, yet here this young man stood bearing the same name as her own, the same eyes.

"Of a sort, I suppose. I'm Miriam Kokush." She wasn't sure what exactly compelled her to use her given name, but it felt right. "Do you tend to them? The stones, I mean." The idea that someone was still remembering, someone still remembered enough to care for the resting places of her family warmed Catherine to her bones.

Oded shrugged. "When I can. I don't get out here as often as I would like. I don't live nearby, but I'm the one with the extra time since my siblings all have children. So, it's me and my rake when I have some time."

Siblings. Children. There were more of them, more of her family, even distant, and she didn't exactly know. Someone had survived all the terrors brought down on her people and created a family, rebuilt what was almost lost. If she wasn't completely wrung out of tears, Catherine would have started crying all over again just from that thought alone.

"I wouldn't mind the help. It's been a while, so things are a little overgrown. Or is that too presumptive? You said you were just visiting, and my siblings always say I'm pretty oblivious to people. Sorry. That was rude of me," he started to babble, his ears turning a dark shade of red.

Catherine needed to put him out of his misery quickly. "I would love to help. I feel like I owe them that, at the very least." She received another broad smile from Oded.

"Ah, I don't think the dead need you to owe them anything. But maybe they appreciate the gesture all the same." He walked back to his truck and began to pull out a pair of rakes, spades, and hedge trimmers. When he returned to Catherine, he handed over a spare set of gloves before pulling on his own pair.

"Sometimes my nieces and nephews come with me to help, so these might be a little small. Should still work for you." Catherine pulled the gloves on, and he was right—they were a bit snug, but she could still flex her fingers.

The two of them got to work raking up dead things around the stones and pulling weeds. Oded used the side of a spade to remove the moss from the sides of the stones, tossing the green springy balls several yards away. Catherine used the hedge trimmers to clip away the tall grass around the stones, making them more visible. They didn't speak while they worked, something Catherine was grateful for. Though she wanted to know more about Oded and his family, this was not the place for chatter.

The plot was not large, so the two of them finished up in under two hours. It was in far better shape than it had been when she arrived. "I'm heading into town for a drink, maybe some food. Care to join me?" Oded asked, wiping sweat from his brow. The sun was now at its peak; the morning had passed quickly with the work.

For a moment, Catherine considered taking Oded up on his offer. But she had come here to find closure. To lay her family to rest in her mind. There was nothing to be gained by learning about strangers. Though he might be related by blood, it was a distant blood, and he would have no knowledge of the people she left behind because they were ancient history to him, names he saw only on faded gravestones. She was content enough to know there was still family out there in the world, that they had endured.

"I should be going. I finished what I needed to do, and now I need to start heading back," she tried to say it gently so as not to offend.

Oded didn't seem to be phased though. Instead, he shrugged. "Suit yourself. Thanks again for the help. It was nice to have the extra set of hands. Made the work go faster." They didn't shake or hug or say goodbye other than to give each other a curt head nod, and then Oded headed for his truck.

He stopped and turned to her as he opened his truck door. "They're gone, aren't they?"

Catherine looked up at him. "Who?"

"Nachem. The golem. They're gone?" Oded's voice was solemn, his eyes a little sad.

It was an effort for Catherine to hold back her tears. She turned away from Oded and looked at the stone she had placed for Nachem. There were two stones sitting atop it now. Oded must have placed one while they worked. "Yes, they are. They saved my life and did their duty until the end."

From the corner of her eye, she saw Oded give another nod, wiping a tear from his eye. Without another word, he got in his truck and drove away.

Catherine stood in the field for a while longer, letting the breeze whip her hair around. As a child, she had tried to imagine she could smell the sea from the hills, but she knew better now, knew she was far too inland for that. But Catherine had seen seas and oceans now. She had seen them all. And soon, she would join the rest of her family in the ground, to sleep eternally.

It had been right to come to Crimea, to see where so many of her people had once lived, and now they were long gone. Catherine placed her hand on her parents' stone one last time, and for the first time, she began to recite the Mourner's Kaddish.

CHAPTER 26

A bell tinkled above her head as Catherine entered Spirit Antiques. It felt likes years since she had stepped into the shop, though it had only been a few weeks. Her heart was heavier than it had been before.

At the counter stood Brie, always the stalwart pillar of the place since she first came to work there years before. "Dr. Fry!" she exclaimed happily once she spotted Catherine.

With some extra effort, Catherine managed to conjure up a smile for her former student and crossed the room to embrace the younger woman. She had given Brie her immortality, hoping that she would live a long happy life with the man she loved. If only Catherine had done the same, found someone to settle into a life with and be happy with her immortality. Now, maybe she did have someone she could spend her mortal life with, if she only took the chance.

"Brie, dear, you can call me Catherine. I'm not your professor anymore," she said. She received a laugh from Brie for this.

"No matter how hard I try, it still sounds weird. Teachers aren't people, even to college students. You here to see Ezra? How did everything go with the... you know, heist?" Brie seemed excited to hear about all that had happened, but Catherine thought it better to tell them both together, rather than explain twice.

"Why don't you go find your husband and then we can talk?" Catherine responded. Brie agreed, and she followed the young woman into the Storage Room, the back of the shop that housed everything Ezra had in stock, which made for a much larger space than was physically possible given the location of the building.

"Can you find Ezra?" Brie directed her question out into the open space of the Storage Room. It only took a few minutes before a flying carpet with a tall man sitting up on top of it came around the corner and stopped before the small platform the women were standing on.

He unfolded himself and stretched out his black jean clad legs. "Aunt Catherine, you're back. Why don't we head to the apartment so you can tell us how it went?" After weeks of hearing her old name, it was nice to hear the name she had chosen to use for so many years. That was the nice thing about Ezra. He respected and understood the desire to start anew.

He led them out of the Storage Room and shut the door behind them before punching a new number on the key panel beside the door. A snicking sound filled the air, and he opened the door again to reveal a lit hallway lined with picture frames. The few times Catherine had been in Ezra's place before he met Brie, the hallway was always dark, the walls bare. There had hardly been any warmth there; it was like he didn't even live there. The only part that had life then was the living room.

Now the hallway was well lit. The pictures covering nearly every inch of space showed Brie and Ezra with their friends, on vacation, around the shop, and their wedding photos. One photo stood in a place of honor on the wall at the end of the hall. It was a picture of a younger Brie with her brother Wes and adopted mother, Maddy. In her short life, Brie had lost not one, but two mothers. Catherine's heart ached as she paused for a moment on that photo before following Ezra and Brie into the living room.

That space had remained mostly unchanged. There were more doors leading out of the room than Catherine remembered, but the wooden furniture was the same, plush and inviting. A few more bookshelves adorned the walls. But what truly made it a magical room were the walls themselves. The space was magicked to be like a forest at dusk. Trees went off into the distance, though when she placed her hand on the walls, they were flat. A woodsy breeze ruffled her hair, just as if she were in a real forest.

Catherine recognized this forest. It was where Ezra first started his cart that would one day span into an actual shopfront that would move across continents. But this forest, the real one long gone now, cut down in the name of progress, was where Ezra's life changed. It made sense he would fashion his home after it.

"Make yourself comfortable. I'll get us some wine," Brie said, heading away from the living room to the open kitchen.

Catherine settled in one of the chairs, crossing one knee over the other while Ezra took a seat on the couch. "That look tells me things didn't go well," he said, giving her a piercing look.

"You could say that," she said with a dismissive wave. Brie moved into the living room with a tray with a bottle of red wine and three glasses.

There was silence between the three while Brie poured out the wine and dispensed the glasses. "Okay, tell us everything," she said, taking a seat next to her husband.

So, Catherine did. Her wine remained untouched between her fingers as she told Ezra and Brie about everything that happened in Greece. Ezra sat stoically, saying nothing as she spoke. Brie was more reactionary. She gasped and commiserated at all the right points. Her wine was chugged, and her husband handed over his untouched glass, and she continued to listen with rapt attention.

When she got to the confrontation with Arruk, Catherine's voice hitched in her throat, and she had to stop and take a deep breath. After she finished, Brie moved from her spot and knelt on the floor to throw her arms around Catherine in a tight, if slightly awkward, hug. Neither Catherine nor Brie were particularly huggy people, but in the moment, it was exactly what Catherine needed.

"I'm sorry you had to go through that, Aunt Catherine. Is there anything we can do? Anything you need?" Ezra asked when his wife rejoined him on the couch. He didn't offer to hug her, which would have been completely against his character anyway, but she was thankful for his words and concern.

She shook her head. "I think it's best for me to take some time away from the world. Sidatih and I are meeting in Tahoe, and I think I'll stay awhile to regroup and figure out what I want to do next."

It was the best thing for her, she had decided on the way back to the States. All the plans she had to travel the world to see old friends for the last time now seemed like a bad idea. In the last few years, it seemed like she experienced more trouble than she did good times. There were only so many times she could face down death in one year and hope to survive. Sometimes, it was best to let the past stay where it was.

No, it was time to find a quiet place and rest for a while. Maybe stay out of trouble. And hope that no one else would call in old debts.

"By mortal standards, you don't really look old. You still have a lot of time to live. Decades may not be centuries, but you can still do a whole lot of living in that time," Brie said with a smile. She smiled more now that she had Ezra; they both did.

Catherine had to laugh. "You've become very wise over the last few years, Brie. You were always clever, but wisdom takes work. I'd like to think I influenced that just a little."

"You definitely did. I couldn't have asked for a better advisor, Dr. Fry." Her smile was luminous. Catherine hadn't thought about children in a long time, but if she had ever had a daughter, she would have wanted her to be like Bridget St. James.

"I think it's time to put Dr. Fry to bed. I think it's time I took back my family name, Kokush." Catherine didn't know why she said it, but it felt right. Catherine Fry was a persona, someone she took on to blend in. But now it was time to live for herself.

Not wanting to overstay her welcome, and generally wanting to be alone, she soon after said her goodbyes to Ezra and Brie. The pair of them walked her out of their home and back into the antique shop.

"Take care, Aunt Catherine. If you ever need us, we're always here," Ezra said. And in an uncharacteristic move, he reached out to her and pulled her into an embrace. His wife followed next, her hug tighter and lingered longer. Catherine felt an overwhelming tide of love, and not wanting to cry in front of them, she made a quick exit.

The autumn night air filled her lungs, and she pushed the tears back down. People walked leisurely down the street around her as she headed back toward campus. Even on a weekday, students still braved the chilly air to fill the town's bars. There would be snow soon, undoubtedly. New Britain was always beautiful in the snow, that magical time before it all turned to miserable slush.

While she walked, she kept her mind clear. There would be time to ruminate alone in her house, but for the moment, she wanted peace and quiet in her brain. Only decades of meditation kept her thoughts from drifting, but she focused instead on her surroundings: the campus buildings as she passed, the students bundled up, the cars cruising down the street carrying those unwilling to travel by foot.

Catherine had spent several years in New Britain, safe in her academic bubble and the tight-knit magical community around her. But it was time to move on. This life didn't suit her needs any longer. And besides, her colleagues at the university were starting to be more and more suspicious of her lack of aging. Glamours were annoying to keep up and large glasses and bad fashion only went so far when other tenured professors she started with were beginning to retire.

When she got home, she would write her intent to retire letter. It was past time she did so. The sabbatical had been an excuse, but she knew deep down her time at the university was over. Hundreds of students had learned from her, and she hoped many of them went off to do some good in the world. Brie was definitely one of them. But it was long past due for Dr. Catherine Fry to retire and disappear.

Her house came into view, the streets no longer full of students. Living around professors meant most were either in for the night or drove out of town to get away from the student scene for dinner. The lights were off as she approached her door, the house shuttered until her return.

The lock opened with a click, and she slipped inside. Without turning on the lights, she hung up her coat and bag next to the door, and toed off her shoes before venturing farther into the house. She made her way to the kitchen in the dark, suddenly ravenous and in need of comfort food. This time she had called her housekeeper to stop by and stock the place.

As she entered the room, a light clicked on. Her kitchen was suddenly brightly illuminated. Catherine stifled a scream, knowing it would do nothing to help her. As she scanned the room for what was obviously an intruder, her eyes landed on a hulking frame standing at the island.

Arruk.

"Still predicable enough, Miriam. The minute you get home, you head for the kitchen." Though his words were teasing, he just sounded weary.

Unsure of what Arruk would do, Catherine determined to keep the kitchen island between them. There was no use trying to look for a weapon. All the knives were on his side of the room, and she wouldn't be much of a challenge to a minotaur.

She must have looked like she was about to run because Arruk held up one massive hand. "Relax, Miriam. I'm not here to hurt you. I just want to talk."

"The trumpet is gone," she said, keeping her eyes locked on Arruk and trying to breathe normally. Relaxing was out of the question.

Arruk nodded his head, eyes weary. "Yes, I know. Titania has made that very clear. Like she needed the trumpet when she was already the loudest gossip in the world. What I want to know is why."

Catherine squirmed where she stood. She wanted to turn her head, to look away from the object of her guilt. But she couldn't. "She called in a debt..." She trailed off, not sure how she could justify her actions.

Still, Arruk nodded his head in understanding. "I understand, Miriam. A debt to a fae does not have an easy out, more likely it would kill you to refuse, especially a debt to the queen of the fae. And yet all you had to do was ask me, let me know what was happening, and I would have gladly helped and given you the trumpet. We may have parted ways long ago, but I have always considered you a dear friend despite the distance. If you had come to me and told me of your debt to the faerie queen, I would have helped you without question. So, tell me why, Miriam."

The *why* seemed nonsensical now that Arruk stood before her. "Because I left you, and I never bothered to come back. Didn't even keep in touch. I didn't think your generosity would extend to me after that. I know now it was stupid to think that way. It sounds so pathetic, but I thought you would hate me. I thought you already hated me for leaving. And it was my own ego. How would it look to come back to you after all those years with my hands out asking for something?" It was more honestly than she had intended to give him. Catherine didn't want to admit her faults and especially didn't want to admit that her own ego got in her way and cost her so much. But there was no denying that was what it was.

"You wanted the last thrill. You were a thief for a long time, and then you weren't. You needed it, didn't you?" Arruk said it with no accusation in his voice; it was more matter-of-fact. Because despite the years between them, he knew her.

It wasn't something she had admitted to herself. Catherine wanted to believe she was above chasing cheap thrills. But she wasn't. She had wanted that last hurrah, that last thrill of a stolen item in her hand and a job well done.

"Yes," she breathed out, her voice barely above a whisper. It felt as if her soul had been laid bare before

Arruk, and she could not stem the flow of its contents to him. He saw it all, read her innermost thoughts, and called her out.

Arruk shook his head, and Catherine finally looked away in shame. She couldn't stand to look at him anymore. Guilt and shame warred in her belly, and she wanted to go to her room and hide from this conversation. And yet, it had to happen. Her sins had to be exposed, and while she didn't expect forgiveness from Arruk, the two of them needed closure. Or maybe it was only she who needed the closure.

"Miriam, giving up your immortality, while it's not something I agree with, is clearly taking a toll on your heart. You are making mistakes you never would have before. I worry that you have not fully come to terms with the fact that your life will end sooner than you planned." His words were harsh, but they were true.

"You think I made the decision lightly? That I didn't agonize over it? Because I did. I had the opportunity to give my immortality to someone more deserving of it, someone who will live a long happy life with someone who loves her. I made the right decision in offering it to her." Catherine felt suddenly defensive, and her gaze shot to Arruk, her eyes hardened into a glare.

Arruk was not intimated by her, however. Instead, he waved her off. "Bah, nobody questions your morals. I'm sure the girl does deserve it. However, I am not convinced that you really took the time to think about yourself. Though not as old as I, you have lived centuries, Miriam. You have seen the rise and fall of empires. You have seen a world change beyond recognition. You have changed lives just by letting people know you. Are you truly ready to give that all up to rot in the ground forever?"

She wanted to retort that yes, she was. The words were there, but she could not force them from her throat. Because she wasn't. Not really. Yes, she had thought over what giving up immortality would be like. The decision had seemed so easy at the time because she felt stuck in her life.

Now?

Now she wished, maybe, she had thought it all through once more. She didn't regret bestowing her immortality on Brie. Not even for a second. But it was possible she could have petitioned the goddess to allow her to continue on. True, it had once been a curse, had been meant to be a curse anyway, but it had become so much more than that. A blessing in the end. And she had given it up without really processing what that would mean.

The last few years, she finally started to do the things she had wanted for decades. Leaving New Britain, seeing the world she once had was intoxicating, exciting, and she found herself wishing she hadn't given it up so easily, especially since she wasn't tethered to Ezra any longer. She was free.

With a deep sigh, she focused on Arruk. "You're right. I didn't think it all the way through. I got too comfortable here and thought this was it."

"And now?" he prompted.

Another sigh. "Now? I'm not so sure if I'm ready. You're right. I've been making poor decisions lately, things I never would have done before because I had the time to think them through. What do I do, Arruk?"

She couldn't keep the pleading from her voice. What she wanted more than anything was for someone to tell her what to do next with her life.

No, what she wanted was her mother and father there to tell her their plan for her.

Miriam, it is time you found a husband. Benyamin is ready for a wife. You are of a similar age. You need your own home. For what have we been teaching you if not to have something of your own?

The words of her parents rang clear in her mind. It was something they had said to her often after her first blood. And Benyamin would have made a fine husband. They were already friends. And she nearly went through with the marriage. But at the last second, she had rejected that life, rejected what she could have had with Benyamin and her family. Maybe Nachem would still be alive if she had just lived the life she was supposed to and let the golem go on to future generations.

"There's no use wondering about maybes and what might have beens, Miriam. You are here now. You have the future ahead of you, and only you can determine what that future looks like." Arruk moved around the island and while Catherine had a thought to flee, it was passing, and she stood still.

Two large hands gripped her shoulders and spun her to face him. She looked up into his sad dark eyes and felt herself break a little more. She didn't deserve Arruk's kindness. The minotaur pulled her close and enveloped her in a hug. Her face pressed against his soft shirt, and she let herself feel the warmth and safety of his arms. "I am sorry about your golem. Nachem was loyal until the very end. I'm sorry their death is upon you." He wasn't wrong. Nachem's death was on her, and she appreciated Arruk not sugar-coating the whole thing.

After a few long moments, Arruk pulled away, leaving her bereft of his warmth. He tucked a hand under her chin and lifted her face to his. "I forgive you, Miriam. The trumpet was a trifling trinket anyway. You are lost and confused right now, but I hope you find something out there in this wide world that brings you back to yourself. And maybe puts a little reason into that head of yours."

Bending at the waist, he leaned down and placed a feather-light kiss on her forehead. Then, without a backward glance, he left the kitchen. A moment later, Catherine heard her front door open and shut, and she was alone once again.

CHAPTER 27

I should have just tree-walked, Catherine thought for at least the third time since boarding the plane three hours ago. She was so tired of flying that even the comforts of first-class seating weren't enough to make her disdain for flying easier. The flight to Tahoe was over six hours, and then she had to drive from Reno up to the mountains. Why she didn't ask Sidatih to pick her up, she didn't know. It would have made things easier.

No, tree-walking would have been easier. Then she would have come out right in front of her cabin. The flight attendant came by and refilled Catherine's empty glass of champagne. If she was stuck on a long flight, she might as well enjoy herself.

By the time the plane touched down at the Reno/Tahoe airport, Catherine was buzzed. Maybe more than a little buzzed. Either way, she felt good despite just getting off a plane.

Even in her inebriated state, she should have known better. Sidatih was one of the best hackers in the world. It was easy for him to track her movements, especially when she booked a ticket under her own name. He probably had her name pinged for any transaction. Because as she came out of baggage claim, there he was.

No sign this time. Just him. Perfect and wonderful Sidatih standing in a suit, an honest to gods suit, in black and tailored to his body perfectly. His dark curls still framed his face, and with his long black lashes, piercing chocolate eyes, Catherine's heart rate sped up, and her mouth went dry. He was so beautiful, and he was all hers.

Part of her wanted to drop her bags and run into his arms, but for the moment, she kept a steady, dignified pace. Soon, though, she abandoned all pretense, let her bags drop with a thud and flew the last few feet into Sidatih's waiting arms. His warm body pressed tightly against hers, and she didn't know if she was lightheaded from the champagne or from his heady cinnamon scent; all Catherine knew was that she was happy.

"Should have known you'd be here," she mumbled against his chest.

His laughter rumbled against her ear. "There's nowhere you can go that I don't know, albi." He loosened his arms enough to put space between their bodies only to draw her back so he could kiss her deeply. She moaned into his mouth wanting to bring him even closer, but they were still standing in a crowded airport.

When they finally broke apart, they rested their foreheads together, breathing the same air. "Let's get you home. I need to feed you and then I plan to spend the rest of the day worshipping you." While his pupils dilated at his words, there was no hint of lust in his voice. Sidatih planned to take care of her in more than one way. Catherine buzzed with excitement. She wanted to get back to her cabin and tear off Sida's clothes the minute they were inside.

Sidatih laughed. "I know that look, Mir, and nothing else happens until I have put food in your belly." He walked her out of the airport and directed her to his Tesla parked in the hourly lot.

"Did you drive from the city?" Catherine asked, sliding into the front seat after stowing her bags.

Sidatih sat down in the driver's seat and started the car. "Figured I needed to switch out my laundry and get my car. It's not a long drive from there to Tahoe. This way, we didn't have to deal with a rental."

"I don't have an electric car charger at the cabin. How long have you been here?" Catherine asked. She had left him in London over two weeks ago while she tied up loose ends in Crimea and Connecticut, including moving out of her house. Now that she had retired from her position, she needed to move out of the university owned house. She was sad to leave it. She had made it a home for so many years. Her stuff would be shipped off to one of her other houses for the time being.

"There is now. I took the liberty of having one installed. Even if you don't keep me around, it'll be good to have. I left London right after you, so I've been there for a bit. The cabin's wifi also got a boost. As much as I love you, albi, I would literally die if I had to continue using that dial-up adjacent you called wifi." They both laughed as the car pulled away from the airport and joined the flow of traffic headed off into the mountains.

Catherine's Lake Tahoe cabin was a picturesque cottage high up in the trees with a clear view of the lake. She bought it ages ago and had spent considerable money maintaining it over the decades. Despite attempts from many companies trying to get her to sell the place, or at least a few of the acres surrounding it so they could build vacation homes for tourists, Catherine had resisted all offers in order to maintain her peace and solitude on the rare chance she got to visit.

The whole back half of the cabin was dominated by windows, the better to see the sparkling blue lake and let in an abundance of light. She liked to sit back there, curled up with a book and blanket, and look over the greens and blues beyond her window.

The rest of the cabin maintained a rustic cottage feel. Her second favorite place was the kitchen. There was an open fireplace she sometimes used to cook, the walls were lined in river stone, and from the exposed beams there hung a canopy of dried herbs. All the appliances were top of the line; she still needed her creature comforts like an espresso machine and double oven. Everywhere else in the cabin was designed for maximum comfort with plush furniture and small tokens from her life.

Sidatih led her back into the kitchen, and lifting her up with ease into his arms, he placed her on the counter with a gentle kiss to her lips. But Catherine wanted anything but gentle. She nipped at his bottom lip as she threw her arms around his neck and pulled him closer. Her legs opened to bracket his hips, and he stepped between her thighs. His hands threaded through her hair and tugged lightly, tilting her head back just enough to open herself more to him.

Their kiss grew more heated, and she moaned into his mouth, hoping she would get what she wanted, and that was Sidatih behind her while he bent her over the counter and claimed her. But at her moan, Sidatih slowed their kiss and then pulled away, stepping out of her reach. "Albi, if we don't stop now, I'll never get you fed. After food, we can continue this."

Catherine pouted, but when her stomach let out a loud growl, she turned pink with embarrassment and let Sidatih cook her a meal without further distractions. She hadn't eaten on the plane, and now that she thought of it, the only thing she'd had that day was coffee at the airport and champagne during the flight. It was a good thing Sidatih put a stop to where her mind was going because she probably would have passed out from hunger if he hadn't.

Within the hour, he had set out of a spread of olives and dates to go with the kabsa, a rice dish Sida made with chicken, carrots, and peas with a handful or two of raisins on top. A plate of saj sat next to the main dish holding the kabsa. How he was able to make everything so quickly could probably be attributed to magic, but in the moment, all Catherine could think about was how hungry she was and how she couldn't wait to eat everything.

"It's been a long time since you've cooked for me, Sida," she said, reaching for the serving spoon. Sidatih knocked her hand away and, picking up her plate, began to serve her.

"You're right. It has been too long. I intend to make up for that by cooking for you as often as you like, as many meals as you can handle," he said with a wide smile. He placed the now heaping plate down in front of her and poured her a cup of tea along with it.

Catherine tilted her head down toward the food and smiled to herself before beginning to eat with gusto. The two of them didn't speak much as they ate, mostly due to the fact that Catherine rarely had a moment where she wasn't putting another spoonful of food into her mouth. Sidatih's cooking was beyond flavorful. The spices he used sang out and filled her senses with the images of busy bazaars and rolling hills of sand, images she had dreamed about as a girl in Crimea when she wished to one day study in Istanbul. And when she finally realized her dream, it was even more beautiful than she had ever imagined.

Across the table, Sidatih ate more slowly, a soft smile on his face as Catherine consumed the food he made. She loved the way he looked at her, as if she hung the moon itself and just simply eating his food was the greatest honor she could bestow on him. It was an easy thing to love Sidatih. She just hadn't told him that yet.

"I have dessert if you've got room for it," he said, once Catherine had cleared a second plateful. She didn't, though she desperately wished she did.

"I honestly can't eat anymore. But later I will absolutely devour it. Don't even need to know what it is. I know it's fantastic." She patted her stomach, wishing she had worn leggings instead of jeans, something with a little more stretch to them.

Sidatih laughed. "It seems I have fulfilled my purpose. Now, let us have some coffee and a rest before we carry on with the rest of our evening." Quickly, he prepared two strong silky coffees and they retreated to the back of the house where the windows afforded them a few of the sun dipping below the horizon in a haze of pinks, reds, and yellows.

They sipped their coffee silently, though it was comfortable. They didn't need words to feel at peace with each other. For the first time in what felt like years, Catherine felt the tension leave her body in waves. "I could definitely get used to this," she said, her voice soft as if speaking louder would break whatever spell the dusk had on them.

"We can. We could have this forever, if you wanted," Sidatih replied, barely above a whisper. His eyes concentrated on the setting sun and the way the last of the light glinted off the water. He didn't look at her, and Catherine didn't know at first what to say.

"Sida, I—"

"I know your days are much shorter than mine, Miriam. I know you made your decision to live out a mortal life. All I ask is that you let me in and let me spend the last years with you. Please." He finally looked at her. No, he looked into her, saw her soul, pleaded with her very essence, and Catherine couldn't ignore that.

"I ... I don't know if I want that anymore. A mortal life, I mean. I want you. Gods, do I want forever with you. Because something Arruk said to me has really shaken my confidence." She couldn't turn from his gaze.

"When did you speak with the minotaur?" Sidatih tilted his head in confusion.

Catherine had completely forgotten to tell him about Arruk's visit. "He was waiting for me at my house in Connecticut. He didn't threaten me or harm me." She held up her hands before Sidatih could speak, knowing he was already concerned. "We just talked. He forgave me after quite the guilt trip, which I rightfully deserved. But he also said that I made a hasty decision. That while he knows I don't regret giving my immortality to Bridget, I didn't stop to really think about what mortality meant. I haven't been mortal in so long, I had forgotten it. And maybe... maybe I made a mistake in giving that up. I don't know how to be mortal, how to live out a normal life span. I've become accustomed to my long life, to knowing I would always have a next day. It scares me that I don't have forever anymore."

Darkness began to fill the room, and Sidatih directed a hand toward the cold fireplace. In a second, a blast of magic ignited the wood in the grate, and a cheery fire started. "I understand what he meant. You've been Ezra's watcher for so long, you haven't really lived since settling in the States, not like you used to. Now that you have the freedom to go any-where, do anything, and not have to watch over him, you don't know what to do. But Miriam, the point of immortality is to live. And it's one of the hardest things to do in this world. And if you do want to give that up, I understand, and I will be by your side until the end. And when the time comes, I will lead you to the underworld myself. But if that's not what you want, I will do everything in my power to make sure you live the life you want."

"You don't think I seem, I don't know, too indecisive? I did think about it before approaching the goddess to give it up, but I now think I was keeping Brie's interest in mind without considering my own. She has been through so much in her young life, it felt like I could give her something good. Maybe that's more motherly than I've ever been, but I'm protective of her." And she had been. Catherine had rarely felt the pull toward motherhood. She had thought about it when she was growing up only because that was what was expected of her. Her students over the decades never felt like her children, though she certainly had to act like a mother to them sometimes when they needed help in class. But Brie brought out another side in her, one she never thought she had. Catherine wanted to take care of someone. Not simply in a romantic way, but in a way where someone needed her and she could be there. Maybe that was why she was closer to Brie than any other student she had ever had. Brie had already lost two mothers, and Catherine, while she would never replace them, could be a motherly figure that couldn't leave, wouldn't die.

Maybe, just maybe, there were others out there too who needed someone to look after them. Guide them into a better life like she had once been.

"I don't think you are indecisive, albi. I think that once again you put someone else before yourself. But it's not too late to change your mind. You have a friend in a goddess, and I'm pretty sure despite what you told her, she hasn't entirely left you alone." Sidatih's smile reached his eyes, which now flicked over her shoulder.

Catherine turned to follow his gaze which revealed a tall dark-skinned woman with long tightly curled white hair. She was dressed in white robes with a rainbow hem. "Hello, Miriam," she said in an ethereal voice that sounded like warm sunshine and light as the wind.

"Lady Ania, I didn't expect you here," she said in a whisper. She was too shocked to see the goddess in her house to speak any louder.

The goddess smiled serenely. "You didn't expect me at all. You said to let you go, to keep my distance. And I have, of a sort. Now, I believe you have something to ask of me." The Lady Ania, as Catherine had always called her, though the goddess had countless names, always seemed to know when she was needed, even before Catherine knew she needed her.

"I think I'll head to the kitchen. Holler if you if need anything, Mir," Sidatih said, removing himself from the room. Catherine found she was grateful for his departure, not because she didn't want him near, but because this encounter with the goddess seemed too personal.

"If I ask for it back, would that be too much?" she asked, voice shaky. A part of her was afraid of the answer, but she had to know.

"You can ask anything of me, Miriam. You know that. After all you did to watch over my son and now Bridget, your punishment went on far too long. I owe you a gift." The goddess didn't seem annoyed with Catherine or like she was in a rush to get their conversation over.

"I appreciate it, Lady. Can I have some time to think about it?" She wasn't about to jump into another hasty decision before taking the time to examine all her feelings. They were all jumbled as it was. She didn't know what she wanted or what she was feeling. It was everything, all at once, and Catherine felt a little scared and overwhelmed.

The goddess nodded, a knowing smile on her serene face. "Take all the time you need, Miriam. You may call upon me whenever you have your answer. Now." She paused, her gaze moving toward where Sida had left the room. "I believe your young man is eager to spend more time with you. Alone. Goodbye, Miriam. I hope to see you soon."

A bright light filled the room, so brilliant that Catherine had to avert her eyes. When the light dimmed, she turned back to where the goddess stood, but the room was empty. The goddess was gone.

"Is it safe to come back in?" Sidatih's head poked around the corner. He scanned her face as if he could ascertain if she had become immortal again. The answer clearly wasn't on her features because he moved farther into the room and stared at her, waiting.

Catherine nodded, unable to actually form words. Sidatih entered the room and knelt before her, one hand on her knee, and the other reached out to cup her face. One thumb swiped across her cheek, wiping away tears she hadn't even realized had formed. "Miriam, albi, what's wrong?"

She sniffed loudly and nuzzled her cheek into Sidatih's hand. "The goddess gave me the choice. I just need to figure out what that's going to be."

Sidatih leaned forward and kissed her head tenderly before resting his forehead against hers. "You don't have to make any decisions tonight. Or tomorrow. Take as much time as you need. And no matter what you decide, you'll always have me." His words made her want to cry all over again for a different reason. It had been so long since someone wanted to put her first. It was like her heart was growing, and her whole body was flushed with warmth at Sidatih's words.

"Right now, I just need you," she said, moving her head so she could kiss him.

"You have me, always, albi," Sidatih whispered as he pulled away from the kiss to lift her up from the chair. He cradled her in his arms and carried her bridal-style through the cabin to the master bedroom. The whole way through the house, she wrapped her arms tightly around his neck and her face buried in his chest, inhaling the spicy cinnamon scent that clung to him and knew he was her home.

CHAPTER 28

Sidatih laid her gently in the center of the bed but didn't join her right away. Instead, he stood at the foot of the bed and stared at her with stars in his eyes. It wasn't like she was dressed to impress him. Still in her jeans and dark t-shirt from the plane, Catherine felt entirely ordinary. She barely had on any makeup, save for a few swipes of mascara. But the way Sidatih looked at her, it was as if she were dripping in diamonds.

"You're so beautiful, Mir," he said reverently, his gaze raking over every inch of her body. The brown of his eyes was gone, his pupils blown wide enough to encompass the color. "I need you to undress now, albi. Please."

Sidatih was a generous lover, especially since it took so long to feel comfortable enough with someone to do the act. The two of them had orbited each other for centuries, and though they had come together many times, this felt different. Like she was giving up a piece of herself to him, that he was finally seeing her stripped bare: body, heart, and soul.

She let go of all her thoughts and sat up on the bed to remove her clothing. Her shirt was pulled off and thrown across the room, and she didn't care where it ended up, her bra following a second later. The jeans and underwear she still wore came off together with little grace; she was in far too much of a hurry to be naked to care how she looked doing it.

She pushed gray-streaked hair out of her face and laid back on the bed, arms wide, legs open, inviting Sidatih to look and taste. There was a long, charged pause between them as Sidatih stared at her body spread out for him, but he didn't move from his place at the end of the bed.

He stared so long that Catherine started to squirm under his gaze. She wanted to snap her legs shut and cover herself; suddenly, the heat from his look was too intense.

As if sensing it was his time to finally move, Sidatih placed one knee on the bed and crawled closer to her waiting center. He took his place between her open legs and ran his smooth hands up the insides of her thighs. Catherine whined when he stopped his hands right before reaching where she wanted him most. Sidatih chuckled and kept his hands moving up, over her hips then her waist. Exploring fingers traced circles around her breasts, and her nipples pebbled under his touch, but he didn't move his hands any closer to their peaks. Gliding up still farther, one hand rested on her clavicle while the other clasped her neck in a gentle hold and a thumb pushed under her jaw, forcing her head back. He paused his movements to stare at her, at his mercy below his body. Then he tipped forward and his mouth latched against her throat, licking and sucking at her pulse point.

Her body felt hot, like every place his fingers glided over was now on fire. The moan that escaped her was too loud in her ears, but she didn't care. All she could focus on was the feel of Sidatih's lips as they started to move down the column of her throat and farther, replacing where his hands had been.

He moved farther down, planting kisses and licking as he went. His fingers no longer teased at her breasts, instead his mouth replaced where he had been touching her, and slowly, agonizingly slow, he moved toward her hardened peaks. When his mouth finally latched onto her nipple, a scream broke out of Catherine's throat, and she arched her back, pushing her breast deeper into his mouth. She could feel him smile against her flesh; Sidatih was pleased with himself.

Not to be neglected, while his mouth worked one nipple, his fingers started to pluck at her other tip, rolling it between his thumb and forefinger, tugging on it until she thought she would explode from the pleasure of it all. His mouth made a *popping* sound as he moved from one breast to the other, his hand switching over to the kiss the bruised nipple he just released.

"Sida!" Catherine whined, wanting more, needing more of him.

But he didn't give it, not yet. He lifted his face from her breast. "Shhhh, albi, I'll give you what you need. Just be patient." With more restraint than she thought possible, Sidatih kissed his way down her body, unhurried at a leisurely pace. It was as if he had all the time in the world to work her up into a frenzy, but Catherine didn't know how long she could hold out. She thought she would die if she didn't get more.

His chuckle reverberated against her pelvic bone as he kissed still lower. She wanted to shove his face exactly where she needed him, but instead, she fisted her hands in the blanket, digging her fingers in for purchase. "Sida, please! I need—" she begged, her voice too high, too breathy.

Then she screamed as Sidatih finally made his way down to the apex of her thighs and his tongue swiped across her clit. "Gods above, Miriam, you are so wet," he breathed against her before diving back in to suck on her bundle of nerves.

Without mercy, he toyed with her clit, driving her to the edge of madness. Even as she tried to thrash and buck her hips up to his mouth, he used one hand to pin her to the bed. Rarely did Sidatih betray his ifrit strength, but as he devoured her, Catherine couldn't move from his hold even if she wanted to, and she most certainly didn't want to.

Her breathing was loud and heavy, filling the room, and the only other sounds were the obscene noises coming from Sidatih's mouth between her legs. Catherine may have stopped breathing altogether when Sida slid two fingers into her dripping opening. It was his turn to moan loudly. She felt the noise reverberate against her, sending up a new kind of spark.

"Fuck, Mir, you are so tight," he said as he lifted his mouth from her. There was a dazed look in his eye, and his mouth and chin were already glistening with her juices. His grip moved from her hip, and he used the free arm to prop himself up while his other hand occupied itself slowly thrusting in and out of her sex. As he glided his fingers inside her, he stared intensely at where they disappeared into her inviting folds, like he was mesmerized. Catherine could only look at him, watching his reaction to her pleasure. That only seemed to heighten her enjoyment.

She would have been content to just watch him enjoy himself, but then Sida added a third finger and the pressure became deliciously too much. Throwing her head back, she screamed again, and she couldn't stop the nonsensical noises coming out of her mouth as he started to thrust his fingers faster into her. And when he swiped his thumb over her clit again as he continued to fill her, her back bowed from the bed. Likely, she would feel that in the morning, but in the moment, she was too overwhelmed by sensation. Her orgasm ripped through her with abandon, coming on so fast she didn't even have time to tell Sidatih.

Not that he minded. He watched in fascination as she rode his fingers through her orgasm. As she started to come down from a mind-blowing release, Catherine could finally appreciate how simply erotic it was that she was completely naked while Sidatih brought her to her peak still fully clothed. Though the bulge in his pants looked hard enough to split the seam, and Catherine was ready to reciprocate.

"Not yet, my heart. You must be patient," he said when she sat up and started to reach for his shirt. With graceful ease, he moved from the bed, leaving her spread out naked, satiated for the moment, and an utter mess. "I could look at you like this for an eternity and never tire of the sight," he said reverently, his gaze taking in the whole tableau of her.

"Or you could join me instead and be a participant rather than an observer," Catherine said, her voice husky and a little hoarse from screaming. She wanted him to quit teasing her and remove his clothes before joining her on the bed. But Sidatih was in control of this scene, and she was determined to follow his lead.

He chuckled. "Patience," he said as he slowly, oh so slowly, started to unbutton his shirt. Catherine sat back on her heels in the center of the bed, watching him. As button after button came undone, she fought the urge to spring across the bed, rip the buttons off the shirt, and have her way with him. Instead, she placed her hands between her bottom and calves and tried not whine as Sidatih took his damn time undressing. This was its own kind of torture. All she wanted was to run her hands over his smooth, warm skin, and the bastard knew she was craving him. Which explained why he had a smug look on his face as he slid the shirt first from one arm and then the next.

Every part of her wanted to lunge forward and rip off his pants. They needed to come off, and she longed to wrap her lips around his cock and return the favor. But that would be pushing Sidatih's boundaries. It wasn't a control issue exactly, but he just needed to go at his pace, and Catherine had to learn to slow down. In the end, she would get what she wanted.

The sound of his zipper was like a Pavlovian bell to her. Immediately, her mouth watered, wanting to taste him. Still, she remained unmoved in the middle of the bed and waited for Sidatih to come to her. "I know what you're thinking, albi. But tonight, I need to be inside of you. We have all the time we need for everything else."

With a soft thump, his clothes hit the floor, and faster than she could blink, he was on her. Lips smashed against her, no longer teasing, but claiming, like he was trying to pull her very soul into him. With his weight resting on his forearms, he pressed his body against hers just enough for her to feel the solidness of him. Catherine chased his lips as he tried to move them down her throat, and he responded by nipping at her lower lip.

A hand left the bed and moved down between their bodies. Sidatih gripped his length and guided his cock along her seam, coating himself in her arousal. It was another torment, having him so close to where she needed him and yet he still wouldn't give it to her.

Still sliding and teasing, he bent down close to her ear. "Get on all fours, Miriam," he whispered. A lightning bolt ran down her spine, and she felt electricity all the way down to her toes. Without a second's hesitation, she wiggled out of his grasp and turned to present her back to him.

Sidatih moved behind her, running a smooth hand up her spine to tangle in her hair while he used his other hand to coax her legs apart. With a tug on her strands, Catherine arched her neck back right as Sidatih sheathed himself in her. It was good that he prepped her with three fingers because she felt incredibly full, like she would split apart if he started to move. But then he did, pulling out almost to the tip before slamming in again. She made a choking noise as the air whooshed from her lungs.

Now that he was seated inside her, Sidatih slowed down again, moving in and out with monumental control. He seemed unhurried as he pulled on her hair with one hand and began to strum at her clit with the other. It was clear he planned to draw the evening out for as long as possible.

Catherine, on the other hand, was a squirming mess. She writhed against his hand, wanting to both push her hips into his hand and push back against his pelvis with each thrust. The slight sting to her scalp where Sidatih pulled added another level of pleasure that was starting to make her head go fuzzy.

"Sida... ah... please..." She didn't even know what she was begging for, only that she needed more of him. Yet, he knew and responded with an increased speed to his thrusts and punishing circles on her clit. The hand in her hair dropped, and instead, he draped himself over her back, wrapping his arm around her middle so that one hand rested on her breast. His cheek pressed against her heated and sweat-slick back, holding her close to him as he pounded into her.

It didn't take long for another orgasm to build inside her, and then Catherine was pitched over the edge, screaming Sidatih's name. Behind her, Sidatih's now frantic thrusts became erratic, and he came with a loud guttural moan.

Their heavy breaths were the only sound in the room now. Soft kisses were placed along Catherine's spine as Sidatih held her close, still seated inside her. With slow, reluctant movements, they disentangled their bodies and lay down on the bed, Sidatih flat on his back with Catherine nestled against his chest.

"I love you, albi. You are my everything," Sida said, his voice so low she could barely hear him.

"I love you, too," she breathed against his chest.

CHAPTER 29

I stanbul was overwhelming. Up until recently, Miriam had never set foot in a place larger than her village. Growing up there, she had longed to travel across the sea to this city, to live amongst its people, to get an education, and to see the world beyond what she knew.

But now that she was here, standing alone in the crowded streets, she didn't know what to do. There were so many people, so many noises, and so many directions to head toward. It wasn't like she knew anyone here. The goddess hadn't given her much in terms of help. All Miriam knew was that she was to go to Istanbul and find a specific shop called Ruh. This was where her new charge was located.

The biggest problem Miriam was facing now, though, was that she had no idea where this shop was located and didn't speak any of the languages around her. Her education up to that point had seemed more extensive, but knowing only her mother tongue that wasn't spoken much outside of Crimea, Hebrew wasn't going to be much help in a city like Istanbul.

In the few times she had stopped to ask someone for help, all she could communicate was the name of the shop, Ruh, which simply earned her curious looks and the person tapping at their chest. She had no idea what it meant, but several people had already done it, so it must mean something.

"You look lost," a melodic male voice said from behind her. Miriam whirled around to face an absolutely stunning man. He was tall, his skin bronzed, and his dark hair hung in roguish waves down to his shoulders. A simple golden hoop looped through his nose. Golden eyes drew her in immediately. There were no men in her village who looked like this stranger.

She was so captivated by him that it took her a moment longer than it should have for her to register that he had spoken to her in Hebrew. The first person who she could communicate with was someone so beautiful she could barely look at him.

"You speak my language." She meant it as a statement, obvious though it was, but it came out as more of a question. The man smiled, and it was blinding, then he chuckled.

"Many people in the city do. You just have to find the right ones. May I help you find where you need to go?" He stood taller than she. Looking up into his smiling boyish face, she immediately felt the urge to trust him.

"I'm looking for a shop called Ruh, but I keep getting strange reactions from everyone I ask. Is it a real place?" She was confused when he started laughing, eyes closed in mirth.

"Oh, sweet girl, it means your spirit. You would certainly confuse anyone if that was the only thing you said to them," he said, calming his laughter. "Come. I know the way. We are not far." He grabbed her hand, and a jolt of electricity traveled up her fingers and arm. She'd had many lovers over the years since leaving home; they simply weren't the type to hold hands. But she didn't pull away, and she let the stranger lead her through the crowded streets. He matched his strides to Miriam's and strolled rather than the brisk walk of those around them.

"So, you know Ezra?" he asked.

Miriam contemplated the question for a second. She couldn't divulge her mission. Who would believe her anyway, that she had been cursed by a goddess with longevity so she could watch over her wayward angel son? It sounded ridiculous even to Miriam, and it was her life.

"No, not as of yet. I am a ... friend of his mother's. She has sent me to see to him." If there was one thing Miriam had learned in her time as a thief, it was always to keep as close to the truth as possible without completely revealing it. It meant less lies she had to keep track of later.

The stranger laughed again; he laughed so easily, and it was already becoming a sound Miriam adored. "Ah, well then you are in for a real treat meeting the likes of him. Who knew a god could create such a surly creature as Ezra?" He must have seen the worried face she made because he added, "Do not worry. His exterior is for show. Ezra is very accommodating once you get to know him."

That didn't reassure Miriam as much as the man probably hoped. The goddess didn't say much about her son, only where to find him, and that he was in need of someone to look after him. Miriam didn't have the foresight to ask questions, and she cursed herself now.

"I do not even know your name, sir," she said, wishing she could snatch her hand away from the bold stranger, but the fear of losing him in the crowd kept her from doing so.

The man stopped abruptly, nearly causing Miriam to stumble. "Gods above, how rude of me. I am Sidatih. Whom do I have the pleasure of escorting?" He looked at her expectantly, and Miriam knew she should lie, should give him one of the many aliases used for jobs.

But she found herself giving him her real name. There was something about him that made her want to trust him. "Miriam Kokush. If you know about the goddess, does that make you a god?"

Sidatih tugged on her hand, and they began walking again. He laughed lightly at her question. "I think I would make a poor god. No, I am an ifrit. Many call my kind demons, but I prefer to stay topside with the humans. There is so much we can learn from them."

A demon? Now Miriam really wished she could pull her hand away. Maybe run in the opposite direction. But she really needed to get to this shop to find Ezra. "You are not going to hurt me, are you?" Her voice came out with more trepidation than she meant. It wasn't as if she hadn't seen her fair share of evil and dealt with absolute villains, but those had been human. Until a few days ago, she had known nothing about the magical world. It felt very much as if she had been thrown into the ocean and told to swim.

"You look ready to run. I take it you have not encountered my kind before. Perhaps you have not encountered many of the ... others. What are you then, curious girl?" He gave her a sidelong glance, but it wasn't leering or suspicious, only curious.

"Is it not rude to ask that question?" Miriam didn't know the decorum in the magical world, but she didn't know yet how she fit into it, if she fit into it at all.

Sidatih actually threw his head back and laughed loudly, drawing looks from everyone around them. Miriam didn't like the attention they were getting and kept her eyes focused on the ground, watching as her feet kept moving.

"Perhaps you are right, but then I have always been too curious to always adhere to manners. So, will you tell me?" Up ahead, she could see a sign that at first glance appeared to be written in Arabic and incomprehensible to her. But in a blink, the sign was in her native Crimean Tatar, and it read "Spirit."

"I'm only human. Is that it?" she asked, quickly glossing over her answer to point at the building ahead. Sidatih looked at her for another beat, as if gauging her truthfulness, but then he faced the shop as well and nodded.

"That is the one. Let us head in, and I will make an introduction." Sidatih led them through the doorway. A bell tinkled as they entered, though Miriam couldn't see from where it sounded. "One of his wards to alert him of customers. Are you familiar with wards?" Sidatih gave her an amused look as if she were a small child.

Miriam felt indignant at his tone. "I am, thank you. My family golem is particularly adept at them. I may not know much about magic, but I am not entirely ignorant." She wanted to cross her arms and glare at the beautiful man but felt that might be too childish.

This seemed to surprise him. His eyes were wide and then he seemed to study her. "What?" she asked haughtily, feeling a little unnerved under his stare.

"Hm, it is curious—"

But he didn't get a chance to tell her what was curious because right at that moment a door situated behind a colorful curtain opened, and a rather tall, lithe man stepped through. He had long black hair and medium brown skin. Gem-like eyes scanned the two of them. "Sida, it is good to see you," he said, and Miriam found she could understand him though she was sure the words he spoke were Arabic.

"And you, my friend. Miriam, allow me to introduce Ezra, the man you've been looking for." Sidatih held his arms out toward Ezra like he was showing him off.

The man then turned his full attention on Miriam. "You I do not know. You appear human, but you are not entirely."

The look he gave her was as if he were peeling back the layers of her being, trying to uncover what was beneath. There had been plenty of instances where men had looked at her like that, usually though it was an interrogation for a crime she probably committed but somehow managed to weasel her way out of a conviction. This time it made her feel like she was guilty, and she couldn't stop herself from squirming under his scrutiny.

"I... uh, I'm not sure what I am. I don't have any magic, but I was recently cursed with immortality."

There was no other way to put it because she really didn't know what it meant to be cursed to live forever. It had only been a few days.

"Oh, well that explains a lot, then," Sidatih said brightly.

Ezra studied her for a moment longer, then his eyes narrowed in suspicion. "She sent you, didn't she?"

"Who?" Miriam asked, unsure if he meant the goddess or someone else.

"My mother. She sent you to spy on me." It was an accusation, and guilt pooled low in her belly.

Miriam shifted uncomfortably on her feet. Clasping her hands tightly together in front of her, she tried not to twist her fingers against each other. "Not spy, exactly. She said I had to look after you, to make sure you were okay and had someone if needed."

Ezra huffed and crossed his arms tightly over his chest. "Well, I do not need anyone. So, you may go back to my mother and tell her not to meddle in my life anymore. She has done enough already." There was a fleeting look of sadness across his eyes, and then it was gone, replaced by a furious scowl.

Miriam looked over to Sidatih, uncertain of what she should do. She struggled to find words, her mouth opening and closing, but nothing came out. "I think what Miriam is trying to say, Ezra, is that she does not have a choice but to be here. I do not think anyone would willingly volunteer to play your nursemaid. If I know the gods, I can bet that she is here under pain of death. Which honestly might be preferable to having to be around you." Sidatih laughed, but Ezra didn't.

Miriam felt grateful that the ifrit could find the words for her when she could not. His knowledge of the magical world must be great if he could understand her predicament after only a few words from her. *Are the gods that predicable?*

Ezra made a harumphing noise and looked unmoved by her plight. "Just stay out of my way. And any reports you make back to my mother must be as vague as possible. The less she knows, the better. That is my deal. Understand?"

Miriam was nodding before he even finished speaking. She didn't care what his terms were so long as she didn't have to worry about punishment from the goddess. "I understand."

Ezra gave her a long appraising look before turning to Sidatih. "She is your responsibility while we are here. Find her a place to stay, and for god's sake, feed her."

"Why me?" Sidatih asked, though he didn't sound at all put out.

"You brought her here," was all Ezra said before he disappeared back through the door from which he came.

Miriam and Sidatih stood side by side in silence for a few moments. Then Sidatih turned his bright smile toward her. "Well, then sweet girl, let me take you home and get you settled in my fair city."

She followed him back onto the streets of Istanbul, wondering what kind of turn her life was about to take.

EPILOGUE

"There's no reason to be nervous, Cat," Sidatih said, handing Catherine a cup of tea. He had started calling her Cat lately, after she told him she wanted to exclusively go by Catherine. Miriam came with too much baggage, too much grief. Cat was her new beginning. She liked the nickname coming from him.

"Easy for you to say. You're not the one who is telling the people you love that you realized your decision to give up your immortal life for a mortal one was, in fact, a really hasty and really stupid one." Catherine couldn't help wringing her hands together. She needed something to do with them.

Sidatih grabbed one of her hands, trapping it between both of his. He brought her fingers to his lips and kissed each one gently, knowing it would help calm her down. It worked, and she felt a knot of unease loosen, if only slightly. There really wasn't anything to be nervous about. Ezra and Brie were important people in her life, and she wanted them to know. After all, she had given up her immortality once for them, and there was little reason to think they would judge her for asking for it back. Knowing Brie, she would be happy for Catherine. Ezra too, probably, in his own Ezra way. Their relationship had been on the mend, even as had Catherine traveled the last few years.

They were meeting the couple soon at their shop in New Britain. Not just them, but a whole host of their friends and family for a dinner party. It had been some time since Catherine had seen many of them, the people who were closest to the people she loved.

Without protesting, she drank the tea Sidatih gave her and set the empty cup on the coffee table in her living room. She had moved out of the professor housing when she retired from teaching, but the bungalow-style house she bought soon after was a nice cozy space to stay when she came back east to visit.

For the last year, she and Sidatih had stayed at their cabin in Tahoe, avoiding people and simply enjoying each other's company. The made love on every surface of their home and plenty of places outside of it. They got to know each other on a much deeper level than they ever had. Catherine had left behind the ghosts of her past in that field in Crimea, and now she wanted to focus all her attention on the future with Sidatih.

After a year in isolation at the cabin, Catherine finally made the decision that she had not yet lived enough to say goodbye just yet. Not once in all that time did Sida pressure her to make a decision, and she was thankful for that. She wanted to make sure her choice for immortality was entirely because she wanted it, not because of someone else's influence. Though, without trying Sidatih may have influenced the decision a little. He was an attentive lover, and Catherine found she couldn't bear the idea of him having to watch her die. She wanted forever with him, whatever that looked like.

So, when she had contacted the goddess a year after she appeared in Catherine's sun room, she came with a knowing smile, like she knew all along Catherine would make the choice to live. The goddess had pressed her soft lips against Catherine's, and as she closed her eyes, Cat felt the magic flow into her again. It was like all the aches and pains her body had endured over the last four years of aging normally were gone, filled with renewed vigor and strength. She felt powerful. The goddess had held her face for a second, looking deeply into Catherine's eyes, and then she had blinked out of existence in a blinding light.

Now, Catherine was sure she had a made the right decision. Even as she and Sidatih stood outside the door to Spirit Antiques, she knew that no matter the reaction they got once they announced it to the people she considered family, she had made the right decision this time.

"It's time to go in, Cat. We can't stand out here all night," Sidatih said, lifting her arm to thread it through his own. She nodded up at him and let him lead her through the door he held open. Brie stood behind the counter, waiting for them it seemed, since everyone else in their little family had direct access to their magical door.

"You made it!" Brie said joyfully. She rushed around the counter and first pulled Catherine into a tight hug, then released her to do the same to Sidatih.

"Yes, I know we haven't seen much of anyone this last year, but I'm glad we're here now," Catherine said, trying to ease the tension in her gut with a smile at the young woman.

Brie led them toward the only door at the back of the shop and through to the home she shared with Ezra. In the living room, there were already several people assembled. Several Catherine already knew: the witch Lily and her vampire mate, Albert, and of course, Wesley, Brie's adoptive brother. The man sitting with Wes was new to her, though she could tell whoever he was that he and Wes were clearly together. Two others were in the room that Catherine did not know. A young woman dressed entirely in black with dramatic makeup sat on the other side of Wes. Across the room, leaning against a wall apart from the group, stood a vampire in a fitted button-down shirt with several of the top buttons undone to reveal pale skin, their features completely androgenous.

Lily stood from where she sat and walked over to hug Catherine tightly. Lily hugged everyone as if they were a long-lost friend, and they usually got a mouthful of her natural curly hair. "It's good to see you again, Catherine. It's been so long since we've had you back for longer than a second. And I'm so excited about your news, but don't worry, I didn't say anything." Lily was a powerful psychic, so it was hardly surprising that she already knew. Lily released Catherine and pulled Sidatih in for an embrace as well, despite never having met him. That was Lily's way; she made everyone feel like they belonged to her. Her mate, Albert, did not hug, but that was just Albert. He only showed affection to Lily. Instead, he gave them a curt nod from his place in the kitchen where he was preparing dinner while a put-out Ezra stood off to the side.

"That's Sam over in the shadows. They are one of Albert's siblings, and they're staying with us for a while," Lily said brightly, pointing out the vampire against the wall. Sam gave them a curt nod but didn't engage further.

Wes stood up once Lily moved away to hug Catherine and to shake hands with Sidatih as Cat made the introductions. "Nice to meet you, Sidatih. Catherine, I wanted you to meet Cameron, my partner," Wes said, indicating the very large man who had stood up from the chair to greet them.

"It's great to finally meet the infamous Dr. Fry, er, I mean, Dr. Kokush. Cameron Griswold. It's a pleasure," Cameron said, his smile big and bright. His large hand engulfed Catherine's and then Sidatih's.

"Griswold? Are you one of Christopher and Emily's kids?" she asked, wracking her brain for the names of all their children. They all started with c so it got terribly confusing sometimes.

Cameron's smile got even brighter. "I am! You might have had my sisters Charlee or Camilla in one of your classes."

Catherine laughed. "And your mom and dad. Your father liked to sleep through my classes. I think even your grandfather took a class or two of mine."

Cameron slung his arm around Wes's shoulders. "That sounds like Dad. He just wanted to bake all the time."

Wes smiled at Cameron, then indicated the woman next to him, who stood up. "And this is Candy

Thermopoli. She's my unfortunate TA in the geology department." Candy didn't smile like the others, but she did shake Catherine and Sidatih's hands with a surprisingly strong grip.

"Your mother used to teach geology, correct?" Catherine asked, vaguely recalling an extremely tall, willowy woman she would see around campus.

Candy nodded, a small sad smile on her face. "She did. Mom was one of the best geologists in the field." The grief in the young woman's eyes spoke volumes, and Catherine watched as Wes grabbed Candy's hand and gave it a squeeze.

"Aunt Catherine, Sidatih, do you want something to drink?" Ezra called from the kitchen, defusing the sudden gloominess and clearly wanting to be useful since Albert the vampire had completely taken control of dinner preparations. They both accepted the offer for a drink, but Brie stopped Ezra before he could move more than a foot.

"Nope, I'm on guest duty. You're helping Albert in the kitchen," she said, swooping in and taking the wine glasses Ezra had just picked up. Ezra stared at his wife for a second and then turned his gaze toward Albert. The vampire returned his look with a hard stare and a subtle shake of his head before turning back to the stove. Catherine suppressed a laugh when Ezra sighed, and he leaned back against the kitchen island, useless in his own kitchen.

After Brie handed over the glasses of wine, Catherine took a fortifying drink. She had decided the best time to tell everyone of her decision was right at the beginning. That way, if their reactions were not positive, they could make a hasty escape back through the hall, no need to disrupt the dinner. And if all went well, then they would sit down to a fantastic meal and enjoy the company.

Catherine looked at Sidatih out of the corner of her eye. He looked back, giving her a wide smile before reaching over and plucking the wine glass from her hand. Setting them on the coffee table, he laced his fingers with hers and gave her a reassuring squeeze. With a deep breath, Catherine got the room's attention. "So, I have some news I wanted to share with you all."

Every head turned to look at her, well, except Albert's, whose attention was completely on making dinner. Sidatih squeezed her hand again to keep her talking. "As you all know, well maybe only most of you know, years ago I gave up my immortal life so that Brie could have it. That was the agreement I made with Ezra's mother, and..." She stopped and scanned the room. The assembled people, the family Brie had found and cobbled together, looked at her with smiling faces.

"And, after taking the last four years to reevaluate my life, I... um... asked the goddess for immortality, and she gave it to me." Catherine wanted to shut her eyes, didn't want to see any of their reactions. She especially didn't want to see what Brie and Ezra's faces looked like. The others she was friendly with, but Brie and Ezra were her family. She didn't want them to be disappointed. But she kept her eyes wide and her gaze fixed straight ahead, not looking at any one person, not even Sidatih.

"Do I get to keep my immortality, or is this like a take-backsies kind of deal?" she heard Brie ask, though there was a hint of laughter in her question. Catherine's eyes landed on Brie, who was smiling wide.

"It's a separate gift, something I asked for myself. I would never take that away from you," Catherine's voice sounded desperate, though she didn't know why. Maybe because she had to make sure Brie knew she would never be someone who would let her down.

"I know. And I'm happy for you. I'm happy that you're going to be sticking around a long time, and I'm especially happy that you have Sidatih. You're good together," Brie said with a smile, and she raised her glass of wine high. "To a long life," she toasted.

The others lifted their own glasses and repeated her words. Even Albert in the kitchen raised an opaque glass probably filled with blood, though he kept his back turned to them.

"I told you, albi," Sidatih whispered into her ear.

Catherine smiled and leaned her head against his shoulder. "You did, love." She finally allowed Sidatih to lead her to a seat. As she settled against the cushions, she looked around at the group. She saw the next generation building their lives and twining them together, forging a community of love and magic, and she knew the future was bright.

For a moment, she thought of that young girl in Crimea all those centuries ago, who stood on a hill overlooking her little village and dreamed of something bigger than herself. And then she looked at Brie and Ezra, standing in their kitchen wrapped around each other while their family laughed loudly in their home, and then into the face of the man who loved her, who had been a constant in her life for over five hundred years, and Catherine realized this was her something bigger, something better.

THE END

Book Club Questions

1. Catherine chose to become mortal. If you had the choice, would you want to be immortal?

2. Throughout the book Catherine goes by Catherine and Miriam, depending on the people in her life. Did you find this confusing to keep track of?

3. Did you expect the heist to go as planned? What were the flaws in Catherine's plan?

4. There are multiple partners in Catherine's life. Did you find one to be better for her than the other? Or did they offer her something different in their own ways?

5. Was Arruk too forgiving of Catherine? Should he have forgiven her at all?

6. What did the flashbacks into Catherine's past as Miriam add to her character?

Author Bio

Kait Disney-Leugers is an author of romance books with a little magic thrown in. Originally from Ohio, she has a degree in history from Ohio University. She now lives in Maryland with her husband and two kids and uses her history degree to be insufferable while watching historical movies and shows.

When not writing in the dead of night once everyone else is asleep, she enjoys playing D&D, trying in vain to get through her giant pile of books, and baking bread to 90s hip hop.

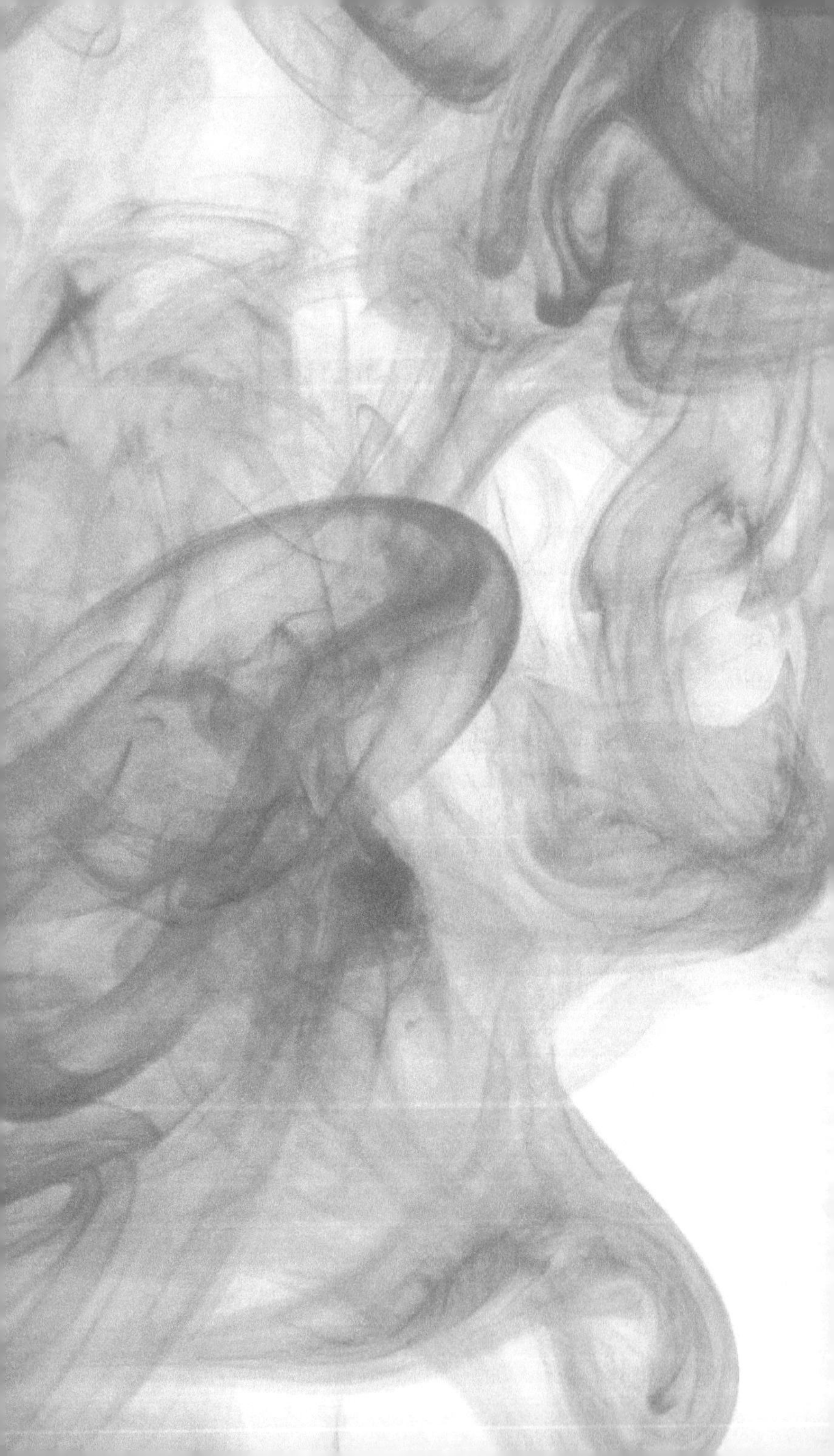

Discover more at
4HorsemenPublications.com

10% off using HORSEMEN10